HIDE 'N SEEK

Yvonne Harriott

Copyright @ 2012 Yvonne Harriott. All rights reserved. No part of this publication may be reproduced or transmitted by any means electronic, mechanical, photocopying or otherwise without prior permission by the author.
This book is a work of fiction, the names, characters, places, and incidents are products of the writer's imagination or have been used fictitiously. Any resemblance to persons living or dead is entirely coincidental.

Cover Design: www.bdsdesigns.net

ISBN: 10:1482039583
ISBN-13:978-1482039580

Romantic Suspense Series:
HIDE 'N SEEK
CAT 'N MOUSE
HIT 'N RUN

ACKNOWLEDGMENTS

I want to thank my cousin, JJ for showing me around Boston and answering all my questions. A big thank you also to my family for their continuous support. I cannot forget my beta readers, and as always, Carolyn for her marketing support.

To readers, thank you for your support! I hope you enjoy reading this as much as I loved writing it.

CHAPTER ONE

An uneasy feeling washed over Marklynn Brooks as she pushed on the door of her sister's apartment and it creaked open.

"Sydney? It's Markie. Why is your door...."

The words died in her throat as she entered the unit, stepping into the tiny foyer that led into the living room of the two-bedroom apartment unit.

Markie's gaze swept around the room and her eyes widened in horror when she saw the brown sofa. Someone had taken a knife to it, ripping out the white upholstery.

The bookshelf and the small wall unit that housed the television had been emptied of their contents. Books, music CDs and DVDs lay scattered on the floor. The glass coffee table was smashed which accounted for the broken glass strewn across the living room floor.

She closed the door, moving quietly into the living room. A scraping noise sounded from the bedroom as if someone was moving furniture and she pulled her gun from her shoulder holster and held it firm in a two-handed grip.

Sydney? Surely if she was in the apartment her sister would have answered her call. Perhaps she wasn't able to. She could be hurt.

Fear and adrenalin rolled into one as her hands gripped the nine-millimeter, semi-automatic Glock pistol. Whenever she drew her weapon the possibility was always there that someone could get hurt or killed. It could even be her, and that heightened awareness was always with her. You would think after quitting Boston PD five years ago the feeling would go away. But all she had done was trade one circumstance for another.

Markie moved around the sofa towards the bedroom. The broken glass crunched beneath her feet. She stopped and listened, ears cocked toward the bedroom. The next sound she heard was glass shattering. She ran towards the bedroom. As she rushed into the room she saw a man wearing a black ski mask crouching on the window ledge. He looked at her over his shoulder then jumped out the window.

Markie leaped over the overturned drawers that blocked the doorway and then up onto the bare mattress to get to the window. She tucked her gun in the waist of her slacks. Grabbing the down duvet dumped in a heap on the floor, she threw it over the jagged glass of the window ledge, jumped through the window and took off after him.

It should have been a smooth landing since Sydney's unit was on the ground floor, but it wasn't. Pain spiked up through her right arm when she hit the dirt on hands and knees.

Kicking off her high heels, she ignored the pain, racing after the masked man like a runner bounding out of the starting block.

Markie stuck to the grass, avoiding the hot sidewalk against her bare feet, until she stepped in something soft. She leaped onto the pavement and continued the chase, racing along River Street.

The man may have gotten a head start but she figured he would bleed out and she would catch up to him by the time he reached Central Square at the end of River Street. He had gouged himself on the jagged piece of glass on the window and left a trail of blood behind like breadcrumbs.

A bullet shot from a passing pickup whizzed by her head. She dove for cover behind a parked white van with a black cross painted on the side and looked up just in time to see a pickup race by. It could have been brown or beige. She couldn't tell. In that instant another bullet shattered the passenger window making her duck down even further. She threw her hands up just in time to shield her face from the rain of falling glass.

She heard tires screeching to a halt and when she pushed her head up over the hood of the van the man with the ski mask jumped into the pickup with no plates. Sliding down the side of the van, she waited for her breath to return to normal and her heart to stop beating like a drum.

"Are you okay?" a little old lady decked out in her Sunday best asked. She had a big old Bible in one hand. With the other she adjusted her big wide-rimmed black hat with white feather blowing in the warm breeze.

By the time Markie pushed herself up off the grass with an unladylike grunt and shook pieces of glass from her hair, a crowd had gathered. Men in suits and ladies in pretty fresh dresses with big hats and white gloves lined the sidewalk.

Markie put her gun back in the holster and buttoned her jacket. The sound of bullets flying had sent the congregation from the Baptist church nearby pouring into the street. They weren't too impressed that their church van had gotten shot up either and stood staring at her as if she was supposed to perform a miracle, to restore it back to the way it had been.

"I'm fine," she mumbled to the hat lady. As she pushed her way through the crowd, they parted like the Red Sea and she headed back to Sydney's place.

Markie pulled her cell phone from her pocket and called the police, reporting the shooting and the break in. Then she stood outside the apartment building staring at the hole where the window once was, wondering what could have happened to her sister.

Bending to pick up her shoes, she was about to step into them when she lifted her left foot to see what she'd stepped in and wrinkled her nose in disgust.

"Geez, can this day get any better?"

She cleaned up but not before practically removing a layer of skin from the sole of her foot. Then she put her feet back in her shoes…but the smell still lingered.

Markie couldn't worry about the smell. She thought about the mess in Sydney's apartment as she made her way to the building. Worry creased her brows. Sydney had just breezed into town a week ago after a month hiatus from God knows where.

How much trouble can one get into in a week? Then again, it was Sydney she was talking about. What was it last year? It was the get-rich-quick scheme that almost caused their grandmother to lose her house. Markie had to bail Syd out. How did her younger sister show her gratitude…by pulling a disappearing act. She showed up three months later as if nothing happened. It was about time Syd—

The black Navigator parked behind her green 4Runner caught Markie's attention. She crossed the street to have a better look at the vehicle, but with the tinted windows it was too dark to see inside. She wasn't sure why she was drawn to the vehicle. All she knew was that it hadn't been there when she'd parked earlier and it was parked right across from Syd's building.

It probably meant nothing, but the way the day was shaping up she made a mental note of the license plate number just in case and headed inside the apartment building.

Sydney's apartment door was open. Markie had closed it. She was sure of it. Stepping inside, she closed the door, this time locking it. Then she heard it…a muffled sound. Someone was in the bedroom, again.

What is this? Grand Central Terminal? Her heartbeat accelerated as she pulled her gun from the shoulder holster.

Was it too much to ask for hell not to break loose before noon? This was supposed to be a day of rest for crying out loud.

This time, whoever it was prowling around was not getting away. She made her way to the bedroom, avoiding the broken glass.

Markie was almost at the bedroom door when a man emerged. He brushed his hands against his black slacks as he stared at her with dark intense eyes that gave nothing away.

His blue shirt was unbuttoned at the neck and she saw the scars on his neck that almost blended into his nut-brown complexion.

His presence filled the doorway. If he was surprised to see her he didn't show it.

"Can I help you?" She asked, pointing the gun towards the center of his chest.

Dalton Beck stared at the woman he just about ran into when he exited the bedroom and at the gun pointed at him.

Her question of, *"Can I help you?"* wasn't that of someone asking if assistance was required. It was the, Can I help you, in the *'go ahead, make my day' in the Clint Eastwood kind of way*.

Beck's eyes shifted from her face to the gun aimed dead center at his chest. There was no doubt in his mind that she knew how to use the weapon. And was probably itching to with the mess the apartment was in.

"I'm looking for Victoria Kelly." He met her eyes again.

"Victoria Kelly?" Her eyes widened, but that was as far as it seemed she was going to go conversation wise.

"Yes. We had lunch plans and when she didn't show up I came here. When I arrived I saw the mess and entered to see if she was okay."

The lie tumbled out of Beck's mouth before he had given it a second thought and he knew immediately that she wasn't buying what he was peddling. He should have given it more thought before showing up at Victoria's apartment, but after she'd called him about the pictures that was it.

Giving into irrational behavior was foreign to him, but then when you're in danger of losing everything you've worked for, you do what you have to do. That was why he was there…to save his company.

The apartment looked like a tornado had ripped through it and Victoria was gone. His intention was to confront Victoria, not to play dodge the bullet with the woman looking at him as if he'd turned the place upside down.

"Who are you?" Beck asked, not feeling so comfortable under her chilling glare with the gun still aimed at his chest.

She didn't call him on the lie, just stood there staring at him as if she was trying to decide whether to put a bullet in him or not. Her heels all but put her at about eye level with him and he was six three.

Beck had to concentrate on holding her dark brown gaze as his eyes shifted from the gun to her white silk blouse. A button had escaped its hole, showing a hint of a white lace bra.

Her skin was a beautiful bronze, full lips glossed in red, and he couldn't help but stare.

"Is the black Navigator parked across the street yours?" She sounded more annoyed than anything else. Obviously assessing him as not being a threat, she pointed the gun at the floor.

"Is the green Toyota 4Runner yours?"

Answering a question with a question was not the way to go. Her eyes narrowed followed by a sharp intake of breath...clearly irritated. Was it wise to tick off a woman with a gun? Well, he figured if she was going to call the police on him she would have done so already. The question that went unasked was why hadn't she?

"Who are you?" She fired off the same question he had asked.

"Look, we can stand here all afternoon and play twenty questions if you like. As I mentioned, I had a lunch appointment with Victoria. She didn't show up at the restaurant so I came here."

The look she gave him started from his head all the way down to his wingtip shoes and back up again. Then she pinned him with a cold stare.

"Well," she tilted her head to one side. "I guess *Victoria* double booked. We had lunch plans as well. Can I tell her you dropped by, Mr.....?"

"That's not necessary," Beck said as he squeezed by her in the narrow hallway on his way to the front door. He opened the door, paused and looked over his shoulder at her. "I think you stepped in something," and he was gone.

Markie waited until his footsteps faded on the concrete floor in the hall then followed him. When she pushed open the double glass door in the lobby of the apartment building, he was gone along with the black Navigator. He moved quickly for a man of his size. He must have guessed she would follow him. She pulled out her cell phone and called her office.

"Brooks Investigations, Jamie Wright speaking. How may I help you?"

"Hey, Jamie."

"Hey, Boss Lady. How was lunch?"

Jamie was a dead ringer for Mr. T, a character from a popular eighties television show, the A-Team, Mohawk and all, minus the jewelry. They'd worked together when she'd been a cop and after she quit the force and started Brooks Investigations, Jamie had asked to join her. Maybe quit wasn't the right word. Forced out was more like it. She hadn't returned the advances of her Shift Commander and he'd taken it as a personal attack on his male pride.

He'd made it difficult for her to continue working with the other officers by spreading rumors about her. When she'd applied for a transfer out of the department he'd vetoed it and she sued him and the police department. She won her suit with a lucrative settlement and was also offered the promotion to the detective division she'd lost a year earlier. She took the money, leaving the promotion behind, and Brooks Investigations was born.

At first, clients were few and far between but Jamie stuck it out with her. When she had asked him why he'd given up his job to join her he'd said he was looking for a new challenge.

"Markie?" Concern filled Jamie's voice. "You ˙ still

there?"

"Sorry. I zoned out for a moment. What was your question?" She pulled the door open and held it to let out a freckled-faced kid pushing a mountain bike then felt the rush of the A/C when the cool air hit her face.

"I'd asked how lunch with Sydney went."

"Didn't happen. Someone trashed her place."

"What? Hold on. Carlos just walked in. I'm putting you on speaker."

Markie didn't want to be put on speaker and only wanted to talk to Jamie. He was playing mother hen again and she hated it. It didn't matter how many times she warned him about it, he still did it. And she didn't like being called Boss Lady either.

"What's going on?" Carlos asked. Markie could picture him folding his large frame into the chair in Jamie's office.

"Someone trashed Syd's place," she heard Jamie say.

"Get outta town."

"I got Markie on the phone. Close the door."

"Are you okay?" Carlos asked, sounding worried. He was the last addition rounding out her eight-man investigative team.

"Now that we've made a federal case about it, can we get on as to why I called?"

"Sure," they both said in unison, making fun of her. They were probably making faces at the phone because that was what they did when they clowned around. But they were good at their jobs.

"I need one of you to run a plate number for me. It's a black Navigator, could be '10 or '11 model."

She closed her eyes and the plate number appeared in front of her. Having a photographic memory had its advantages.

"I want *everything* on this guy, from where he went to school to the brand of cereal he eats for breakfast. If he had a dog when he was a kid, I want to know the name."

"Got it," Jamie said. "Carlos, get started on this. I'll touch base with you shortly."

"Sure thing." She heard the sliding door open and close and assumed it was Carlos leaving.

"Did the guy with the black Navigator trash Syd's place?"

"No. He was in her apartment when I got back."

Markie told Jamie about the man in the ski mask and the chase that led to her dodging bullets.

"Jesus. Why the hell didn't you leave the apartment and call for backup when you saw the door was open? One of these days you're going to get your butt shot off," Jamie barked. "What are you trying to prove?"

They'd had this conversation many times before and like all the other times it ended with her defending her decision. Not this time.

Ignoring his rant she said, "My gut feeling tells me Mr. Navigator had nothing to do with trashing the place, but he knows more than he's letting on. He was way too smooth. I think the man wearing the ski mask redecorated Syd's place."

"They could be working together."

"No," she said shaking her head. "The guy that trashed the place was a thug and Mr. Navigator was too polished. They were both looking for something and by the looks of the place, they didn't find it."

"You sure?"

"I'm almost positive. I'm waiting for the police to arrive. Once they've completed their work then I'll find the building superintendent to replace the window and front door lock. When that's done, I'll have a look around and see what I can find."

"I'll come by and help," Jamie offered.

"No. I want you working with Carlos to get everything you can on Mr. Navigator. He may be our only lead to Syd."

"So once again you're cleaning up Syd's mess." Jamie let out a disgusted sigh. "The woman is twenty-five years old and doesn't know what the word responsibility means. You should—"

"I'm not in the mood, Jamie."

She cut him off and hit the end button, shoving the

phone into her pocket. The phone started to ring and she thought it was Jamie calling back, but when she looked at the caller ID it was her grandmother.

"Hi, Nan."

Their parents had died in a car accident when she was thirteen. Sydney was three years younger. Nan had raised her and Sydney. Not wanting to worry Nan, Markie thought she would wait until Syd surfaced before getting her involved.

"Marklynn," Nan said, voice deep with worry. Her voice was strong for an eighty-year-old woman. Markie could picture Nan in her pink house frock with her gray hair in a neat bun pacing the floor as she often did when she was troubled. And Sydney was usually the cause of her worries.

Nan was the only one who was allowed to call her by her given name. To Markie, it sounded too formal and since Nan was born in England, it just made sense somehow.

"Are you okay?"

"Sydney is in trouble," she said without missing a beat.

"Did she call you?" Markie asked, as she was about to enter Syd's apartment building then stopped at the glass door and turned to look out onto the road where the Navigator had been parked.

"No. It's just a feeling," Nan said. "Have you heard from her?"

Nan was better at predicting the weather than any meteorologist around. Since Nan's premonitions were always correct, Markie paused before answering. She didn't want to upset Nan.

"I'm at her place. We were to have lunch today but she's not here."

"What has she gotten herself into? Why can't she be more like you?"

Yeah, right, Markie thought. How many times had she heard that? Sydney was Sydney. She loved adventure and didn't want the responsibility of taking care of anyone but herself. Sometimes she wished she were more like her sister instead of taking care of the whole world. But wasn't that what she did best?

"There's no need to worry. She'll show up in a day or two wondering what all the fuss is about."

"No. Something happened to her. I can feel it," Nan insisted. "She could be hurt."

"Let me look into it and get back to you."

"You need to find out what happened to her. Can I count on you to do that? She's not like you."

There it was again, the responsibility that she didn't want being shoved upon her, as it often was when they were growing up. That had created some friction between her and Syd.

"Marklynn? Are you still there?"

"Yes, Nan. I'll take care of it," she said, weary, when she saw the uniformed officer step out of the squad car. "I gotta go."

"Hi I'm Marklynn Brooks," she said as the officer approached the building and she opened the door to let him in. She dropped the phone in her jacket pocket. "I made the call."

He followed her into the building and she waited by Sydney's apartment door until he motioned for her to enter.

"Did you touch anything?"

He was a senior from the Cambridge police department. She could tell from the pins on his collars. He was tall, of athletic build, his head shaved.

Cambridge was across the river from Boston. Even though her issues were with one man, not the entire Boston PD, word still got around. The way he looked at her she knew that he recognized her after she'd shown him her ID. Maybe she was being paranoid. After all, it had been almost five years ago.

"I used to be a cop," Markie said. "I know the drill."

"I didn't ask if you knew the drill. I asked if you touched anything."

Oh yeah. He was still carrying a grudge and so were some of her former colleagues.

"No. I didn't touch anything."

Police officers were a tight-knit group. There was a

bond between them and if you went against one you suffered the wrath of all. In her case, it was a select group that worshiped the Shift Commander, Jeffery Booker.

The complaint she'd filed against him had never been forgotten. To make sure she never did, she was reminded with every speeding ticket as well as with having her vehicle towed without cause. Of course, the police officers were only doing their job.

The tickets became fewer as the years went on and they'd stopped towing her car.

She'd had her fight. It was over. Maybe not for them but it was for her. It was about Sydney and what had happened to her.

"What time did you arrive at the apartment?"

"Just before noon. I heard a noise coming from the bedroom and approached it. There was a man wearing a black ski mask. I'd say he was about five eight, one hundred and forty pounds. He could be of Asian descent."

"If you didn't see his face, how do you know he's Asian?"

She suppressed the urge to talk down to him as he was doing to her.

"I could see his eyes. He also had a tattoo on his left ankle. It was some kind of dragon symbol. I saw it when he jumped out the window. I chased after him but he escaped in a pickup."

Markie gave him a description of the pickup and what she saw of the driver. She watched as he reluctantly wrote the information down all the while giving her the *I'd rather be some place else look*.

"Anything else?"

"No."

Markie didn't tell him about Mr. Navigator. Although she didn't think he and Sydney were involved she couldn't say for sure. Until she figured out what her sister was up to, Mr. Navigator was her problem.

He was lying about something and she intended to find out what it was.

CHAPTER TWO

Sydney groaned as she opened her eyes. Her head throbbed and each time she tried to move a blinding pain shot through her skull. She tried to lift her hand and that was when she realized her hands were tied behind her back. Her feet were bound with rope and her mouth was covered with silver duct tape.

With no window and no watch she was disoriented, unable to tell where she was or even the time of day. Someone had taken her watch and now she knew why.

She worked the rope until her wrists felt raw. They were probably bleeding. Couldn't they have at least put her in a chair? Then she would have had a better chance of freeing herself.

She wiggled to the edge of the mattress that covered the cot and wrinkled her nose. What was that stench? Oh God. A cross between vomit and urine assaulted her senses and she scrambled to sit up.

Using her shoulder, Sydney pushed herself into a sitting position then lost her balance and fell over at the other end of the cot. She needed to get her hands in front of her body. All those years Nan had forced her to do gymnastics training had to be worth something.

Rolling on to her back and taking a deep breath, she widened her elbows then wiggled her buttocks between her bound hands, gritting her teeth when the pressure of the rope bit into her wrists. With her buttocks on the bed, and with careful precision so as not to dislocate any joints, she was able to put her legs through her bound hands to get them in front of her.

Smiling at her small accomplishment, she ripped the duct tape from her mouth and almost screamed with the pain. She had to check the tape to see if her skin had parted company with her face.

Now that she'd removed the duct tape from her mouth, she worked at the rope on her wrists. It loosened enough so her fingers could untie her feet then she made her way over to the steel door. It was bolted from the outside. There was no keyhole to see what was on the other side of the door. All she heard was something that sounded like a generator kicking in.

What she wouldn't give to have another round with Blondie. Although Sydney had her doubts she was a real blonde. She could have taken the woman down had she not introduced Sydney's right side to a taser gun. An introduction she would have been happy to live her life without.

There was no furniture in the room except for the cot. Given the size, Sydney concluded that it was some sort of storage room. Only a single bare light bulb hung from a white electrical cord that cast a snake-like shadow against the cement wall. The concrete floor was a dingy brown and she didn't want to think about what the brown spots were that covered it all the way to the door.

"What now?" she asked aloud. The question of the moment raced through her mind. She breathed in deep and exhaled slowly several times, trying not to give in to the fear that threatened to suffocate her.

How was she going to get out of this mess? Would anyone notice she'd gone missing? She didn't think so. Through the haze, bits and pieces of information floated into her thoughts. Lunch with Markie…pictures….men with guns.

She was supposed to meet her sister for lunch. This wasn't the first time she'd stood Markie up. Markie would think she'd brushed her off and go on about her business. The way she lived her life had finally caught up to her. Fear settled over her like a blanket.

Sydney thought about Derrick. He was tall, strong and full of life. She had wanted to be a better person because of him. He'd made her laugh and told her she was special. Then she remembered he was dead. Given her present situation, she might suffer the same fate.

It had taken the entire day but the bedroom window was boarded up to be replaced within a few days, and the front door locks changed.

At 7:00 p.m. the police finally left and the superintendent, a lanky man with sunburned face, dropped the new set of door keys in Markie's hand, leaving her to deal with the mess inside the apartment.

Since Markie's name was on Sydney's lease as an emergency contact he had no problem giving her the keys.

Before she thought about sweeping up the glass or putting the books back on the shelf, she removed her jacket and threw it on the sofa. She grabbed a white garbage bag from under the kitchen sink and proceeded to the washroom.

Kicking off her shoes, she threw them in the garbage bag and set the bathtub. She sat on the edge of the tub, rolled up her pant legs to her knees and sank her feet into the warm soapy water.

Oh, I think you stepped in something.

She thought about Mr. Navigator as she sat on the edge of the tub drying her feet with a towel. Nothing gets by him.

Then something occurred to her. The bathroom was the only room that was still intact. Everywhere else, in the apartment was in a shambles except for the bathroom. Why? It was the only place that hadn't been searched yet.

Her eyes focused on every detail in the bathroom. From the white pedestal sink, to the silver medicine cabinet with the mirrored door, to the white tiled floor covered with the red bathroom mat.

The toilet was beside the tub. Above the toilet was a framed picture of a baby sitting in the midst of mounds of toilet paper. Above the picture was a vent for the washroom fan.

Throwing the towel aside, she rose to her feet. With one foot on the toilet lid and the other balanced on the edge of the tub, Markie peered through the slits of the vent and thought she saw something inside.

Markie jumped to the floor then raced towards the kitchen. She grabbed a dinner knife from a drawer and headed back to the bathroom. Using the flat edge of the knife she pried the cover off the vent and pulled out a manila envelope folded in half with a telephone number written across the top. Sitting on the edge of the tub, she brushed off the dust from the envelope and opened it.

Inside the envelope were several pictures of a black van with the company name, Beck Security Systems, written on the side. The van was parked in front of a large white brick house with columns along the front entrance. The digital date and time stamped on the picture was four days ago at 3:30 a.m.

One picture showed people in the background. Sydney had highlighted their heads in yellow and above them were question marks in red. Markie sat staring at the pictures and wondered if they were the reason Sydney had called and invited her to lunch. She remembered asking Sydney what the occasion was but Syd had only laughed saying, "Can't I take my sister to lunch?"

Now that Markie thought about it, it had been one of Sydney's nervous laughs. That should have alerted her that something was wrong and the lunch invitation was just a cover.

Placing the pictures back in the envelope, she hurried to the living room to grab her phone. She punched in the number printed on the envelope and waited.

"Thank you for calling Beck Security Systems. Our office hours are from—"

Markie hit the end button cutting off the automated voice. Reaching for Syd's laptop that had fallen between the bookshelf and the desk, she turned it on and drummed her fingers on the desk as it booted up. She selected the Internet browser and googled Beck Security Systems.

After wading through pages of information on the website she wasn't interested in, she found the page with the management team. And there he was, staring at her from the computer screen as he had a few hours ago.

"Well hello, Mr. Navigator."

Beck stared out of the bedroom window of his twenty-fifth floor penthouse condo. With two thousand square feet of panoramic view it was a retreat at the end of a long workday, but not lately. He'd been spending all of his time at the office. Home was an extension of his office. The long grueling schedule would continue into the night and tonight was no exception.

At 4:00 a.m. while the world slept, his legs pounded on the treadmill as sweat poured from his body. He hadn't been able to sort out the latest test data he'd gotten yesterday from his partner, Malcolm. That spiked his frustration level up two more bars on the frustration meter. He had stared at the computer screen until his head started to pound and his eyes began to burn.

With a degree in computer science and an MBA, he was still stumped. The review of the program code written for the installation of the alarm system looked flawless. But looks can be deceiving because something was wrong.

Beck jumped off the treadmill and turned it off. He grabbed the towel from the handle of the treadmill, wiped the sweat from his face. Then he draped the towel around his neck thinking about Victoria Kelly and his run in with *Miss Rambo*.

Victoria Kelly had called him five days ago with damaging information she said she had on his company. When he'd told her he didn't know what she was talking about, she said she had pictures and would call him back to arrange a time and meeting location. He wasn't going to sit around and do nothing while she buried his company with false allegations.

When he had the call traced to an apartment in Cambridge, he wanted to confront Victoria Kelly, not Marklynn Brooks of Brooks Investigations. That's who the plates on the 4Runner was registered to.

Why would Victoria hire *Miss Rambo*? And what happened to Victoria Kelly?

Questions bounced around in his head as he made his way to the adjoining bathroom. After a long shower, he stepped out of the glassed-enclosed shower stall. Wrapping a towel around his waist, he left behind wet footprints on the smooth black and white tiled marble floor.

The bathroom was divided into two large sections separated by a glass-blocked wall. One side housed the shower, toilet and an oversized soaker tub that he had never used and the other side a large vanity with double glass sinks. With its black and white décor, the bathroom was all about luxury, a luxury he was too busy to enjoy.

He caught a glimpse of his reflection in the mirror over the vanity and paused, remembering the sound of crushed metal and broken glass.

It had been four years since the car accident. He stared at the scars that ran up his torso to his neck. After two surgeries, this was the best the doctors could do.

Everything happens for a reason, right? Well, he hadn't figured that one out yet.

It had taken him a while to let go of the turtleneck sweaters and graduate to shirts. He was never a tie person and at first it bothered him that people would stare when his shirt was unbuttoned at the neck. Let them look, he thought, and with that he dressed and headed out the front door.

It was 7:00 a.m. when Beck pulled into his parking spot in the underground parking of Beck Security Systems. On his fifteen-minute commute he had already done more than most people would accomplish in an entire morning. He didn't believe in wasting time. His ex would attribute it to what she would call his Type A personality. He called it being efficient.

Beck had decided that Marklynn Brooks would not derail his plan of finding Victoria Kelly. He believed she was the key. He had formulated a plan of action in his mind, step by step to catch the person sabotaging his company. A meeting with his executive team to execute the plan was on the agenda this afternoon after Malcolm's meeting with IT.

He stepped out of his SUV and saw Malcolm heading towards him. At forty, Malcolm Rivers had a full head of gray hair that one would assume came with age. But in his case he'd come by it prematurely. He also sported a natural tan as a result of being biracial.

Malcolm was smart intellectually but when it came to women, his choices weren't always the greatest. But who was he to judge? Look what happened to him and Monika. To say their divorce was bitter was an understatement. Then she died and he was accused of murder.

"Good morning," Beck said as Malcolm approached. Pushing that part of his life behind, Beck juggled the two laptops and his briefcase then closed the door with his hip. "You look like you haven't been to bed yet."

"Have you?" Malcolm raised his brows.

Beck shook his head. "I'm still trying to go through the network vulnerability assessment data. I can't figure out how our security system is being hacked into. There was nothing in the port scan. I thought for sure it would help us identify *Shadoe*."

Shadoe was the name that Malcolm had given the hacker. Beck didn't see the point in giving the hacker a name. To him it meant giving the intruder more power than he warranted. Power taken by force, power he didn't deserve.

"I've been through it; our IT people have been through it and we're still going through it. Now you have and can't find anything either."

"It's like finding a damn needle in a haystack, but I have a plan. I'm calling an executive meeting this afternoon. This has gone on three months too long. What if we…"

Malcolm adjusted his tie, but didn't say anything. Beck sensed something was wrong.

"Did we have another alarm malfunction?"

"The Lincoln Heights account. I got a call early this morning from the account manager. He said they're hearing rumors about the possible instability of Beck Security Systems and wants to discuss their contract with us."

Lincoln Heights was a new sixty-unit luxury condominium in Jamaica Plain located on the southern edge of Boston. Beck Security Systems had gotten the contract to install the security system for the project. The thought of losing the account made his stomach turn over. His mind raced. They couldn't lose the account. He was going to shut down the account manager's worries before it turned into a problem.

"I'll talk to him," Beck said abruptly.

"There's no need for you to do that. Or do you want to take over my job, too?"

Part of Malcolm's job was managing the installation process as well as working with the Account Managers on multimillion-dollar accounts such as Lincoln Heights. If Malcolm couldn't calm the client's fears then it was his job to step in.

Beck started towards the door that led upstairs to the main lobby of the building but Malcolm stood rooted to the spot waiting for an answer to his question. The underground parking was not the place to launch into a full-blown discussion as to why he should take over, but it would have to do.

"We need Lincoln Heights, Malcolm," Beck said turning to face Malcolm. "Set up a meeting with them and we can both go in. We can't afford to lose that account. We need the revenue."

"I know that."

"I don't see the problem if I —"

"We have a company with about a hundred employees," Malcolm said, lowering his voice when he heard laughter and a car door slam. "Are you going to do their jobs as well? I hear you've been showing up on the job when the guys are installing the security systems. Why?"

"Why? I need to be there until we can figure out what's going on. Doesn't it bother you that we're installing alarm systems that malfunction?" Beck bit out.

"Hell, yes it bothers me. The difference between you and me is that I'm not trying to solve the problem by myself."

Beck ignored Malcolm's comment. This wasn't the first time Malcolm had accused him of trying to manage everything himself. What was he supposed to do when he was asking questions and no one could give him the answers he needed?

They started walking towards the door and Beck said, "Our insurance carrier is breathing down my neck. They want to drop us."

I know. I've taken care of it."

"When? The last time we spoke about it—"

"…was yesterday and I told you I would take care of it. It's my job," Malcolm said in his southern drawl. Only when he got angry did his Texas roots surface. "Stop interfering and let me continue to do my job."

They headed up the stairs from the underground parking to the main floor in silence and crossed the lobby to the bank of elevators before Beck spoke again.

"I'll back off, but —"

Beck lost his train of thought when he saw her leaning both elbows on the security desk smiling at the security guard, Adam, who managed security for the day shift. Adam was a middle-aged man with blond hair who wasn't easily swayed by a pretty face.

At two hundred pounds, he held a black belt in karate and could easily snap her in half, yet he seemed captivated by her. And why not? Beck had felt the same way as Adam when he'd met her at Victoria's apartment yesterday.

"Adam seems smitten," Malcolm said when he'd seen where Beck's gaze had landed. "By the look on your face, I'd say you are too. She's heading in our direction. Who is she?"

Beck watched her as she walked towards him in her black power suit with that same determined look on her face he'd seen yesterday.

The black pencil skirt sat just above the knees with a red blouse tucked in. The outfit was completed with a form-fitted jacket and red heels. He figured the gun was probably in the handbag she had slung over her shoulder.

She was the kind of woman who walked into a room and commanded attention without even trying. Malcolm was right. He was smitten.

"Shall we dance again, Mr. Dalton Beck?" she asked when she stopped in front of him. Her red lips turned up in a smile, but her eyes were forty degrees below zero. "You must be Malcolm Rivers." She turned to Malcolm and flashed that smile again. A smile that was a whole lot warmer than the chilling one she had sent his way.

She seemed to have caught Malcolm off-guard. Malcolm, who Beck believed had written the book on pickup lines for women, was at a loss for words. If he wasn't a bit irritated by the way she was fawning over Malcolm, albeit orchestrated, he would have been amused.

"Malcolm, meet Marklynn Brooks," Beck said with some reluctance.

"You've been holding out on me," Malcolm said, looking at Beck with a sly smile. He took Markie's hand and held on to it a little too long for his liking. Why that bothered him he couldn't say. "You'll have to tell me about it later. I'm late for a meeting with IT. We'll definitely meet again, Marklynn."

"It's Markie and I'm sure we will." She smiled again, another breathtaking smile.

"Until then, Markie. Hold the elevator," and with that Malcolm was gone, leaving them in the atrium staring at each other.

"What can I do for you, Marklynn?"

"It's Markie. To begin with, you can tell me what happened to Sydney Brooks."

"Sydney Brooks? I'm afraid I don't know what you're talking about."

"Your first phone contact was five days ago. Phone records don't lie. I think she had *information* you needed."

With her emphasis on the word *information*, he made the connection. Was Sydney Brooks and Victoria Kelly the same person? If not, what happened to Victoria Kelly and why was Marklynn involved?

"Let's go to my office."

Markie let out a sigh of silent relief and followed Dalton Beck to the four sets of elevators that serviced the building from the main floor. At first she wasn't sure how her plan was going to unfold.

After she'd found the pictures yesterday, she stopped by her office, had them scanned and put on a CD, then left Sydney's computer for Jamie to see if he could get into her email account.

She had also spent the better part of the night, at home, online going through Beck Security Systems' website. By the end of the night she was familiar with every page on the site and the executive team. Then she went through the file on Dalton Beck Jamie had left on her desk.

The only connection she could find between Sydney and Dalton Beck were the pictures. Armed with them this morning, she wanted answers and was determined she would not leave Beck Security Systems without them.

Her plan to show up unexpected and throw him off guard somehow wasn't working. His body language was all about control. Confidence.

She glanced sideways at the man beside her as they stepped into the elevator when the doors opened. Even though the elevator was glass enclosed, his presence seemed to dominate the small space as he had at Sydney's apartment.

The elevator stopped on the fourteenth floor and the doors opened with a swish. Markie followed Dalton down the hall past an office with Malcolm's embossed nameplate affixed to the door, as well as a room which appeared to be a lounge area. They walked towards a corner office with Beck's name on the door.

When she entered the office it wasn't what she expected at all. There were two steps leading up to a raised seating area by the window where two black leather sofas faced each other. A chrome and glass coffee table was nestled on a white shag rug between the sofas.

"Have a seat," he said without looking at her.

The rest of the office consisted of a long table that spanned one wall. There were several computers on the table that hummed to life when he powered them on. There were stacks of what looked like data printouts placed neatly on the floor and some on several metal shelves.

She watched him as he removed the two computer carrying cases from his shoulders and placed them and his briefcase on the table. There were no personal photos on his desk. The only pictures on the walls were that of security units and the company's head office.

He wasn't the typical executive she was used to, nor was he a suit person. She could tell. Dressed in navy slacks, his white shirt was unbuttoned at the neck. His brown complexion coupled with strong features gave him an almost warrior quality.

The scars on his neck only added to it and she found herself wondering if the scars were the result of the car accident. Jamie had briefly mentioned the accident in the file he'd prepared for her.

"Coffee?"

"No," she said shaking her head. "Mr. Beck—"

"Just Beck."

"You already know who I am so I'll get to the reason I'm here. I'm looking into the disappearance of Sydney Brooks."

"I need some coffee. Be right back."

"You don't have an assistant?"

"I get my own coffee," he said and shot her one of those you-should-have-known better-than-to-ask-that-question look.

She watched Mr. *I-get-my-own-coffee* leave the room and return a few minutes later with a cup that said, "I'm the boss." There was no doubt in her mind he was the boss. It was probably his way or not at all.

Beck placed the cup on the coffee table and sat on the sofa across from her. The aroma of coffee filled the air. It seemed he didn't believe in small talk when he returned to their conversation.

"As I told you downstairs, I've never heard of Sydney Brooks."

"She called you."

"I can assure you, Ms. Brooks, I never heard of Sydney Brooks until you mentioned her name."

"Then you know her as Victoria Kelly."

"You're here because you have something or you think you know something. Get to the point."

Markie could always tell when someone was lying, usually by their body language or their response to questions, but not with Dalton Beck. It bothered her that she couldn't read him. She reached into her purse for the envelope she had found in Sydney's bathroom vent, removed the pictures and dropped them on the coffee table in front of him. They scattered across the table. Beck's expression didn't change but there was a new tone in his voice when he spoke.

"Where...did you get these?" Beck leaned forward picking up the pictures. He looked at each picture then placed them back on the table and sat back into the sofa. "Let me guess, you want money?"

"I'm not in the habit of blackmailing people. All I want to know is where my sister is."

"I can't tell you what I don't know."

He divided his attention between her and the pictures on the coffee table. The stone-like expression settled on his face again.

Markie watched him closely, but he wasn't revealing anything he didn't want her to know. She thought she saw him react to one of the pictures but wasn't sure which one. Sydney had disappeared because of the pictures. She was sure of it and decided to run with the idea brewing in her mind to see if he would let anything slip.

"You want to know what I think."

"No, but since you're going to tell me anyway, go ahead. I wouldn't want to deprive you of the pleasure."

"I think you knew about the pictures. Sydney called you about them and that's why you went to her apartment." He didn't even so much as bat an eye as she laid out her conclusion. He just sat there and stared at her as if she was speaking in a foreign tongue. Tough. She had a lot more to say. "The thug you sent to trash the place didn't find them so you went back to see if you could. Is that it?"

"You have a very active imagination. I'll tell you again I've never met or spoken to Sydney Brooks."

"What were you doing at her apartment?" Markie pressed. "And don't give me that lunch date crap because you're not her type."

That brought his eyebrows up but that was it.

"I've no interest in whatever type or category you've decided to slot me into. I've a full day. If you'll excuse me…"

He stood up. Conversation was over, but she wasn't finished.

"I could've gone to the police with the pictures," Markie said deciding to play one more card. The police card. That usually got people talking, but not him.

Beck looked down at the pictures but didn't respond right away. Dark eyes with a flicker of curiosity bored into hers. "Why didn't you?"

"Because I don't want them interfering with my investigation. It's none of my business what you or your company is up to. All I care about is my sister. You know where to find me if you want to come clean."

"Don't forget your pictures," Beck said when she got

up and walked towards the door.

"You can keep them. I have copies. Call it insurance just in case I disappear."

She felt his gaze on her back as she left his office. When she got into the elevator and the doors closed, she slumped against the wall and closed her eyes. She was glad she didn't get the glass elevator.

Markie was shaking. What had she done? What if Beck knew where Sydney was and … She hadn't slept in almost twenty-four hours and was making mistakes. Second-guessing herself was something she tried not to do because in her line of work it could mean the difference between life or death, hers or her clients', and in this case, Sydney's life.

She pushed death from her mind as she left Beck Security Systems. Sydney was still alive, she told herself, and she was going to find her.

"Malcolm, get in here," Beck yelled into the phone then slammed it down on the desk and sank into the leather chair.

He looked at the pictures Marklynn had left behind again. The one with the woman leaning against the van caught his attention. The moon shining through the trees cast a shadow across her face. There was something familiar about her… the way she stood with her head cocked to the right. Maybe he was just grasping at straws. People didn't come back from the dead.

"What happened that has gotten you so riled up?" Malcolm asked when he entered Beck's office. "If this is about Lincoln Heights, I took care of it."

"It's not about Lincoln Heights."

Malcolm's eyes drifted to the pictures on Beck's desk.

"Marklynn left these behind." Beck handed the pictures to Malcolm.

His eyes widened as he looked at the pictures then back at Beck. "Where did she get these? Is she trying to blackmail you?"

"I don't think so. She said she's trying to find her sister,

Sydney Brooks."

"Sydney Brooks? Why would she think you have anything to do with her sister's disappearance?"

"Because I think Victoria Kelly and Sydney Brooks is the same person."

"I don't get it. Why would Victoria lie about her name?"

"I don't know, but I want you to find out everything you can about Sydney Brooks/Victoria Kelly. I want to find her before Marklynn does."

"She may not find her," Malcolm said with doubt in his voice. "You said the woman vanished."

"Oh, I wouldn't bet on it. She found me. Marklynn appears to be very good at what she does. She's a private investigator."

"Private investigator?"

"Yes. Maybe she's working for her sister. Although, I don't know…Sydney's place was trashed when I got there."

"Beck—"

"I want to know who took the pictures and why. If Sydney is involved with what's going on here, which I believe she is, why my company?"

"Don't you think you're going a little overboard?" Malcolm said, looking at him as if he'd lost his mind.

"No." He thought about the other accounts that they were barely holding on to. How many accounts would they lose before they caught *Shadoe*?

"You know at some point you're going to have to admit we need outside help," Malcolm said. "We can't run the company by ourselves and you can't go around playing detective. Why would you even go to Victoria's, or whatever her name is, apartment? You're lucky Markie didn't call the police on you yesterday and have you charged with breaking and entering."

Beck knew Malcolm was right, but he wanted to get the person responsible for sabotaging his company. He wasn't going to stand by and have it all taken away from him.

He'd grown up with nothing because his mother's

illness had bankrupted his father. His divorce from Monika had almost cost him everything, but he'd managed to hold on to his company. He was not going to start over again. Not this time.

"What about the pictures?" Malcolm asked, looking at the pictures again before handing them back to Beck.

"Leave that to me."

"I can look into it," Malcolm offered. "One less thing for you to worry about."

"No. You have enough on your plate." Beck started going through the pictures again, then fanned them out on his desk. "Do you recognize anyone?" He didn't point to any particular picture and was hoping Malcolm would put his fears to rest. "Have a look again."

"No. What is it? What are you seeing?"

"I'm not sure."

CHAPTER THREE

It was hot.

Markie didn't mind the tropical heat as she stretched out on the beach towel. She could feel the hot sun against her skin as she listened to the waves crashing against the shore and the palm trees swaying in the gentle breeze.

Moments ago she'd emerged from the turquoise water in her Itsy Bitsy Teeny Weeny Yellow Polka Dot Bikini. There was nothing shy about her and she certainly wasn't afraid to come out of the water. She began humming the popular song from the sixties then started to laugh.

She should reapply the sunblock. After all, that was what one did after a swim. Sitting up she poured a generous amount of lotion in her hands and rubbed them together. She started with her arms, first the right then the left, and proceeded to her legs. After she was satisfied that her front was covered, she started on her back. Stretching her arm over her shoulder to reach her back wasn't getting the job done.

"Allow me," someone said.

The voice was soft, smooth and sexy. She recognized the voice but couldn't remember his name. Why worry about a name anyway? She had no responsibilities. No responsibilities meant freedom. She had all the time in the world.

Markie didn't turn around. Just handed him the lotion over her shoulder and waited. He moved his hand in a circular motion starting from the nape of her neck, each shoulder getting equal attention, and then he moved towards the center of her lower back ... The lotion was cold when it hit her skin but heated up within seconds.

She was mesmerized by his touch and she closed her eyes,

allowing him to take her on an erotic journey of exploration where his hand moved across her skin leaving a trail of heat. When his lips replaced his hand, they mimicked what his hand had done a few minutes ago. He kissed her neck and shoulder, moving around to her face. She felt as though she was on fire but it wasn't from the heat of the sun.

His lips found hers. Soft and sensual. She opened her eyes and dark intense eyes locked with hers.

Beck.

Markie bolted straight up in bed, her heart hammering in her chest. For a moment she was confused and then she realized where she was – in her house, not on a tropical island.

Alone in bed.

Sitting up against the headboard, she pushed her fingers through her hair then pulled at the neck of her damp nightshirt. The dream was still vivid in her mind. It felt so real. She didn't think of Beck that way so why was she dreaming about him? She had never had a dream like that before. It left her tingling on the inside, and hot, very hot.

Darkness had settled over the room. As she reached over to turn on the bedside lamp her cell phone started to vibrate, skidding around on the nightstand. Reaching for the phone she hit the talk button.

"Marklynn Brooks."

"Tell me you're not going to do what you're thinking of doing."

"What am I thinking of doing, Jamie?" Markie yawned glancing at the clock. She'd left a message earlier that afternoon for Jamie to call her at 6:00 p.m. after he had finished the report on the missing person's case.

It was after six. She'd slept most of the afternoon away. If she hadn't jumped out of her sleep, she and Beck…it was a dream she told herself…a dream…not real.

Focus.

Think.

"Are you okay?"

"I just woke up a few minutes ago," Markie said jumping right into conversation with Jamie. She didn't want him to pick up on the nonsense that was going on in her head. And it was nonsense. Pure and simple.

Her and Beck? Please.

"You needed it since you've been running on chocolate since you woke up yesterday morning. Maybe you should just have your teeth extracted instead of waiting for them to fall out."

"Aren't you the comedian?"

"I aim to please," Jamie chuckled. "How did it go with Dalton Beck this morning?"

With the dream locked away in the back of her mind, Markie was in work mode once again. "It didn't. I couldn't get a straight answer out of him regarding Sydney. When I showed him the pictures I thought I saw a flicker in his eyes but I couldn't be sure."

"Perhaps you should have used your feminine charm. Cate said he's easy on the eyes, and I quote, her words not mine, 'He's someone I could dream about.'"

"Cate is a great office manager. But, come on, she's a fifty-two-year old grandmother who is living the second half of her life after her husband dumped her. I think she should stop dreaming, don't you?"

"She should leave the dreaming to you."

"Can we get on to business?" Markie snapped and immediately wanted to take it back but it was too late. Jamie was only being Jamie.

"Lighten up. I was kidding."

"Sorry. Sydney's disappearance has got me on edge."

"I know." Jamie's voice took on a serious tone. "Was the information I gathered for you on Dalton Beck helpful?"

She closed her eyes for a moment, allowing the information she'd read earlier to come to mind.

"Dalton Beck, thirty-five, university grad with honors, MBA. He started Beck Security Systems after his studies. Got into a horrific car accident four years ago. Hit and run.

Never found the driver. Divorced shortly after that. Ex-wife's name was Monika. She died in a boating accident."

She recited seven of the ten-page document word for word from the file, listing everything about Beck including all the awards he achieved along his career path.

"I bet you don't even have the file in front of you."

"Not yet."

"You're starting to scare me."

"Only starting to?" She smiled.

Markie swung her legs off the bed, pushing her feet into her slippers. The hum of the window unit air conditioner worked overtime to cool down the bedroom. With the queen-sized bed pushed up against the wall, there was room enough for a nightstand and a mirrored bureau.

She crossed the hall to her closet-sized office, flipping on the light switch, flooding the room with light. The desk and chair were the only pieces of furniture in the room.

The file on Beck was where she'd dropped it when she'd arrived home earlier, on top of the black wooden desk with her car keys and handbag.

"I now have the file in front of me. Does that make you feel better?"

"Only because you didn't read the entire report."

"I didn't get to the police report on Monika's death. It said they never found her body," Markie said sitting in front of the desk, staring at the report.

"Given the explosion there wasn't much left but debris."

"I see Malcolm Rivers joined the company after Beck's car accident. That's convenient," Markie said, flipping through the file. She didn't see a picture of Monika Beck.

"Could be a coincidence."

"Umm."

"You have a suspicious mind," Jamie said with a yawn.

"Occupational hazard. I don't see a picture of Monika Beck in the file."

"We just got it. I left it on your desk."

"I'll get it tomorrow." She leaned back into the chair.

"Something is going on at Beck Security Systems. His office is littered with computer printouts. It's as if they're looking for something. Malcolm was off to meet with their information technology group after I showed up. I know people have meetings with IT all the time, but something is up. I can feel it."

"Your feeling is dead on."

"How so?"

"The company had been doing very well financially up until about three months ago. Something about the malfunctioning of newly installed systems. It's all hush hush. I'll ask around and see what else I can come up with. When I get all the information together we can figure out how Sydney fits into all of this."

Markie didn't want to get Jamie involved in this. Eight months ago, News Television International hired Brooks Investigations. They'd worked with Michael Blake, an investigative reporter from Atlanta to locate a missing woman, Wendy Lawson. Michael was helping out a lawyer, Angela Douglas. The missing woman was Angela's client.

They found the woman in Maine and so did her husband, Jim Lawson. He wanted her dead and Jamie had gotten caught in the middle. One of Jim's goons had kicked Jamie in the face several times, resulting in the loss of his left eye.

That did not sit well with Markie. Getting hurt was a given in their line of work yet she had felt responsible somehow for Jamie's injury.

Well, Sydney was her responsibility. Her disappearance was personal and not related to the agency. The investigators on staff were busy with full workloads, including Jamie. She didn't want to order him to stay on his current projects so she opted for another approach.

"To respond to your earlier question of, 'Am I going to do what you think I'm going to do?' The answer is yes. I'm going to follow Beck and see where it leads. I need you in the office while I focus on Sydney."

Markie thought he would argue with her and braced

herself for it. He didn't.

"Be careful," was all he said and hung up. He didn't sound happy but he hadn't challenged her, yet.

She hit the end button, dropped the cell phone in her bag and got up from the desk.

He is the kind you dream about. That sounded like Cate all right, Markie thought and buried the dream further in the back of her mind. Yet, she couldn't shake how it made her feel.

"Malcolm Rivers speaking."

"Hello, Malcolm Rivers," Phoenix said, letting out a purring sound she knew he would appreciate. She figured she would call him and stroke his ego.

Men liked that. But after, she had to see what Beck Security Systems was up to through the backdoor access in the network she'd created.

Fools.

Did they think they could stop her by changing passwords and installing additional security restrictions?

Her former employer, Next Generation Computers, could attest to her skills when she shut down the company by locking everyone out of their computers. Giving all the employees a fifty percent raise, except upper management of course, was also something she was proud of.

Phoenix designed and built computers, designed tools that converted programs into language that computers could understand.

Did they really think they could keep her out? She knew the monitoring software used by Beck Security Systems and was able to upload her little surprise.

Even if she didn't know the software she would have been able to hack in anyway and would have just for fun. But she didn't want to waste time. She had a plan. Destroy Dalton Beck, and she was right on schedule. Well…almost.

"Where have you been? I've been trying to reach you all day."

Malcolm was pouting like a little schoolboy, she could tell. If he wasn't vital to her plan she would have cut him loose a long time ago. He was her eyes and ears at Beck Security Systems.

Phoenix found him on the company's website and then followed him for about a month to pick up on his habits. He liked blondes and sushi. She became a blonde as her complexion was fair enough to pull it off but passed on the raw fish, finding more pleasurable ways to hold his attention.

"I had to take care of some personal business. I do have a life besides you, darling."

He didn't take kindly to her comment, she could tell. He was quiet and sulking like he always did when he didn't get his way. Wanting to soothe his ego she said, "Why don't you come by tonight and I'll make it up to you? I bought a new bottle of honey. I know how you like honey."

There was a pregnant pause on the other end of the line and she put the phone on speaker. Phoenix picked up the nail file from the end table and stretched out on the green chaise. Soon she would be able to afford more than this cramped one-bedroom apartment and would have the rich lifestyle she deserved.

Dragging the nail file across the tip of the long red fingernail of her thumb, she blew away the white dust that landed on her lap, waiting for Malcolm to respond. She knew what his answer would be but would allow him to play his little game.

Men and their games. But not all men played games. Dalton Beck didn't play games.

Pity.

Whether he wanted to play her game or not, he didn't have a choice. He would play her game of hide and seek and when the game was over, he would be dead. An eye for an eye.

"I'll see you tomorrow night," Malcolm said after a while. "I have to work tonight. You know Beck."

She gave a low throaty chuckle. "Only from what you've told me, sweetheart. Is he cracking the whip again?"

"We're all busy working to figure out who has been trying to destroy the company."

Phoenix smiled. A knowing smile. She could see the deep frown on his face. If he was sitting in front of his desk, he would be twirling his pen and biting his bottom lip.

"What's the crisis this week?" she asked, sounding bored but far from it. She stared at the bubbles the filter in the fish tank blew to the top of the water.

"I know you find my job as much fun as watching paint dry but do show some interest."

"I'm sorry, sweetheart. I'm all ears," she purred. The nail file chipped the nail polish on her thumbnail. Reaching for the small bottle of red nail polish on the end table, she opened it and touched up the nail. She blew on the nail until it dried and then continued filing.

"Marklynn Brooks showed up in Beck's office this morning with pictures."

"Who is Marklynn Brooks and what pictures does she have?"

Phoenix listened as Malcolm filled her in on the private detective trying to find her sister. She already knew about Marklynn and *if* she didn't work with inferior people, the private detective would not have found Beck. *If* she was in the pickup and had the gun, she wouldn't have missed. Marklynn would have been dead outside of Sydney's apartment. Oh well, just another wrinkle in the plan she needed to iron out.

"Marklynn Brooks thinks Beck has something to do with Sydney's disappearance."

"Really? Why?" Phoenix said keeping her voice level, trying not to tip her hand. All Malcolm needed was a little coaxing and he usually told her everything without realizing it. She wanted to know about the pictures.

"Anyway, I've bored you long enough."

"No, no sweetheart. You've got me hooked. Tell me about the pictures. Please." Another purr escaped her lips.

He paused and she could see Malcolm smiling to himself. He thought he had her begging.

37

"They're pictures of what looks like our employees breaking into one of our clients' home. We didn't recognize anyone in the pictures."

"That's too bad," Phoenix said out of relief more than anything else but she wouldn't mind seeing the pictures for herself.

"The pictures were taken by Sydney," Malcolm continued. "When she contacted Beck she used the name Victoria Kelly. Beck wants to find her."

"Your job is exciting after all, darling. I guess Beck is not too fond of Marklynn then."

"I wouldn't say that. I think Beck has developed an interest in her."

At the sound of Beck's name linked with Marklynn's, she stopped filing her nails and stiffened. "What kind of interest?" She asked offhand.

"Why would you care?"

Laughing to cover her blunder she said, "Really, Malcolm. I do believe you're jealous. I'll see you tomorrow," she said and hung up the phone.

Malcolm wasn't the only one who was jealous.

At 7:00 p.m., Markie was parked across from Beck Security Systems on Devonshire Street, downtown Boston. If Beck's company was having software troubles as Jamie had mentioned then he would be working late trying to solve the problem. She would be doing the same thing.

Markie was banking on the element of surprise that Beck wouldn't expect her back and hoped he would lead her to Sydney, if not tonight then tomorrow. She popped a couple of chocolate almonds in her mouth and waited. It had been a while since she'd been on a stake out and had forgotten how boring it could get.

She pulled out her Blackberry to check her email. There was still no word from Sydney. Markie left several messages on Syd's cell phone and even sent her several emails just in case she could access her email. Still no response. She had also called Sydney's building superintendent before she'd left her house and Syd still hadn't showed up at her apartment.

Until Markie located the pictures in the vent, she didn't believe that anything had happened to Sydney. Nothing held her attention for long. At one point she had expressed an interest in photography and as far as Markie knew nothing had become of that. It was a fleeting thought like everything else.

Sydney was always searching for something and that something changed on a regular basis. Markie had settled into a career as a private investigator. After she left the police department it just seemed logical. Helping people solve their problems was what she was good at, along with being responsible and level headed.

Two hours later, Markie spotted Beck's SUV emerging from the underground parking and slid further down in her seat as he drove by. He was talking on his cell phone. She waited until there were three cars ahead of her before pulling out to follow.

Beck headed south on Devonshire past Franklin Street. She stopped at Milk Street and Devonshire, pulling to the curb to allow another car to cut in front of her. Something didn't feel right. What that something was, she didn't know.

Beck stopped at the traffic light but didn't proceed when the light changed to green. She couldn't see into the SUV because of the tinted windows.

"What are you up to?" Markie pulled out to follow when he crossed the intersection. That was when she heard the siren and looked up in the rearview mirror and saw the flashing blue and white lights.

"Great. Just Great."

Turning back towards the curb, she shifted the gear into park and turned off the engine. Markie watched in the side mirror as two officers got out of the car and walked towards her vehicle. One stopped at the rear passenger side as the other approached her at the driver's side with a flashlight.

"Get out of the car and put your hands where I can see them," the one that approached from the driver side said. He looked like the character McGarrett from the old television show, *Hawaii Five-O*.

She pulled her ID from her wallet and left it on the seat before she opened the door.

"Is there a problem?" she asked, stepping out of the car, holding up her hands so they could see.

A minivan rolled by, its occupants staring at her and the driver almost ran into the back of the car in front of him. What was it with people? Why couldn't they mind their own business and keep driving? Did they have to slow down and look?

"The vehicle was reported stolen. Spread 'em," McGarrett said.

Spread 'em? She assumed the position as he searched her. Then the full impact of his words sunk in.

"Stolen? You can't be serious? It's my—"

Beck drove past while she was being interrogated and slowed down so she could see him, then he disappeared behind tinted windows as he drove away.

"He didn't," she said as her eyes followed him.

"Excuse me?" asked the other officer who was searching through her SUV. He reminded her of the lead character from the television detective show, Kojak. All that was missing was the lollipop. She made a mental note to stop watching late night reruns of cop shows when she couldn't sleep.

"My ID is on the seat."

"She's a P.I.," Kojak said laughing. "Go figure."

This garnered a chuckle from McGarrett and she waited patiently until they were through.

"Rookies," she grumbled under her breath.

She was detained for about half an hour while they ran the plates and took their sweet time doing it. By the time they had determined that she'd not stolen the vehicle and it was indeed hers, Beck was long gone and she was fit to be tied. The fact that she'd underestimated Beck didn't sit well with her. How did Beck know she was following him? He must have guessed she would come back.

"Here's your ID back."

"Thank you." She snatched it from Kojak, throwing it on the passenger seat. He was having way too much fun at her expense.

Deciding to call it a night, she was pulling away from the curb when her phone rang.

"Hello?"

"We need to talk," Beck said tersely. "There's a restaurant with an outside patio a block from where you are. Turn right at the second set of lights."

"Why—"

He hung up.

Beck watched as Marklynn parked, got out of the 4Runner and crossed the street. Dressed in a white shirt and jeans that clad long legs that went on forever and high-heeled red boots. He couldn't help but stare. And he wasn't the only one. He was never one for fetishes, but with legs like hers he was getting pretty close.

He had chosen a trendy little restaurant he had passed a million times on his way to work, but had never given it a second glance until tonight.

The tables were covered with white linen cloths. The center pieces – tea lights floating in wide glass vases – provided the perfect romantic setting while the soft music of *Kenny G* floated in the background.

In a perfect world he would be meeting her for a drink, a romantic encounter. This was not a perfect world and she would rather put a bullet in his chest than have a drink with him.

The slight breeze in the air had vanished and all that was left was, hot muggy, stagnant air.

Markie reached the arched wrought iron trellis that marked the entrance then swept her eyes slowly around the patio. He knew what she was thinking when she'd taken in the ambience. The same thing he had a few moments ago. Her eyes settled on him and shot him a look that said, not in this lifetime. She pointed to him, bypassed the waiter, and headed over to his table.

"The police were a nice touch," she said, eyes dancing with anger as she pulled out the chair and sat down. For a moment he thought she would reach across the table and strangle him by the way she was clenching and unclenching her fists.

"You're starting to annoy me," he said, finishing the iced tea and placing the empty glass back on the table.

The cool drink did nothing to reduce his rising body temperature and that had nothing to do with the weather. From the moment he'd met her there was an instant attraction.

"That makes two of us." The waiter approached with a menu and she waved him away with an impatient gesture. "Well?"

They sat staring at each other in silence.

A faceoff.

Tension crackled in the air as Etta James' hypnotic voice floated from the speakers in her rendition of *At Last*. If it were left up to him, they would be swaying together on the dance floor like the other couples anticipating the outcome of the evening. Instead, her arms were folded across her chest and she appeared unaffected by the song. If anything, she seemed annoyed.

Who did she think she was? Barging her way into his company and accusing him not only of sabotage but kidnapping her sister as well. It shouldn't bother him what she thought of him, but it did. Why? Because he wanted her.

Beck didn't know what was going on with his company or if Marklynn was correct in implying that the disappearance of her sister was connected. If it was, then whoever was behind it could hurt her if she continued to get in the way and he didn't want that. He felt the need to protect her.

"...for you are mine at last," Etta finished on a soulful

note.

"You called the meeting," she said seeming almost relieved when the song ended, which led him to believe he wasn't the only one affected by the ambience. "You have the floor or are you going to sit there and stare at me?"

"You don't listen very well so I feel compelled to repeat myself," Beck's voice was hard, Etta James forgotten. "I don't know where your sister is. Yes, she called me but we *never* connected."

"I don't believe you because I have a set of pictures that says otherwise."

"The pictures you have are just that, pictures. You don't know what they mean," he said, downplaying the fact that she could cause a whole lot of trouble for him. He wanted time to find out what the pictures meant and who had taken them. "Furthermore, whether you believe me or not is irrelevant. I want you to *back off*."

She didn't respond and Beck let out an inaudible sigh.

"Fine. Stay out of my way or next time you'll be permanently detained."

"Is that a threat?" She sat up straight in the chair staring at him, eyes burning with anger.

The waiter appeared again and this time it was Beck that waved him away.

"Call it whatever you like. We're done here."

Beck left her sitting at the table fuming. If he thought she was mad before when they first met, she was ticked royally now. He wasn't sure what to expect when he'd called to set up the meeting, but it wasn't the woman sitting in front of him unmoved by his words.

There was no way she was backing away and his little, 'Call it whatever you like' may have added fuel to the fire. A fire that he might just get caught in.

Marklynn Brooks wasn't going anywhere. That was evident in the way she glared at him. If he had a sister and she was in trouble, he would have done the same thing, moved heaven and earth to find her.

He would have to be content with her following him

until he could figure out a way to get her off his back. Beck got into his vehicle and slammed the door with more force than intended, cursing under his breath.

The woman was infuriating. He watched as she started across the street to get to her 4Runner, ready to follow him, a defiant stare stamped on her face. With the taunting look of "what are you going to do now?"

The squealing of tires burning against the asphalt dragged his attention away from her towards the speeding pickup rounding the corner. It barreled down the middle of the street right at her

He shoved opened the door and yelled, "Watch out!"

CHAPTER FOUR

Markie turned her head when she heard the screeching tires and saw the pickup barreling towards her. Whoever was behind the wheel wanted to kill her. She raced towards the patio restaurant. People scattered in all directions screaming as the pickup jumped the curb.

She made it to the brick partition that separated the sidewalk from the restaurant and sailed over it just before the pickup slammed into the wall with a loud bang. It was like being caught in an avalanche as she fought to keep from being buried under tables, chairs, bricks and whatever else that landed on her.

Something hit her in the eye as she went down and got pinned under the debris. She couldn't breathe and forced herself to remain calm, not giving in to the darkness that wanted to claim her.

There were voices. People yelling and cursing. Someone was screaming. Someone was crying. It wasn't long before she felt debris being lifted off her and a hand reached out and pulled her to her feet.

Beck.

"Are you alright?"

She saw sheer terror in his eyes. It made her forget for a moment that he may have been the one responsible for destroying a city block. And then she got mad because if he was responsible for...

"I had nothing to do with this, Marklynn."

"I bet."

Pushing a table out of her path with his foot, he practically lifted her out of the debris onto the sidewalk and set her down but didn't let her go.

"Are you okay?"

If the throbbing around her right eye was anything to go by, she'd say she would have one mother of a shiner tomorrow.

Beck was getting all touchy feely and it was affecting her thinking. Like how warm his hands felt as he encircled her waist. Like how she wanted to just rest her head on his shoulder…to let him take care of her. But she would not give in to any of the haphazard thoughts racing through her mind. He tried to kill her and he was also responsible for Sydney's disappearance. Or, had he? What about Sydney? He said he didn't know anything about her disappearance yet there were the pictures to tie him to her sister.

"Don't waste your breath."

Markie pushed out of his arms, her palms on his chest to shove him away. It was bad enough someone tried to run her over. Now she was giving in to an emotional meltdown. She used to be a cop, for heaven's sake. Where was this erratic behavior coming from? This wasn't like her at all.

"I don't know who did this, but I can assure you it was not me or anyone working on my behalf." His thumb smoothed away some of the dirt from her face. "If you still want to talk about Sydney, I'm ready to do that."

"Talk," she said, pushing trembling hands through her hair, and hoped he didn't pick up on the tremor in her voice. Her eye began to throb causing her whole face to ache.

"You're in no shape to do anything but go home. On second thought, forget home. You need to go to the hospital."

"I'm fine."

"No you're not."

She looked into his eyes and saw confusion…warmth…need. Like a coward, she didn't want to even go there because she was feeling the same way. She didn't want to need him.

"Come by my office tomorrow at 10:00 a.m.," she said and hobbled towards her 4Runner already missing the warmth of his touch. She could feel Beck staring at her, but didn't turn around.

"Just a minute. Where are you going?"

She remembered that voice. It was Kojak and she was not in the mood to talk to him. She had heard the sirens but paid no attention to them.

"Home," was her response and she kept on hobbling.

"What are the odds that we pulled you over an hour ago for driving a stolen vehicle and you end up in the middle of a crime scene investigation? From what everyone tells me, you were the intended target."

She shrugged. Yes, the meltdown was coming. She could feel it and wrapped her arms around her body to keep from trembling.

Sydney was missing and could very well be hurt. Nothing she'd uncovered so far had helped to locate her. Now this. Someone wanted her dead and they were willing to destroy a city block, leaving behind a trail of damaged cars and properties along the street to do it.

Maybe she was entitled to a meltdown, but not in front of Kojak or Beck, for that matter. She wanted to go home where it was safe.

"Why would someone want to kill you?"

Kojak stood there hovering over her. He wasn't laughing, as he had earlier, when he'd pulled her over. He was getting set to interrogate her and she wasn't sure if she could stand up to it. Her legs felt like they were about to buckle under her from fatigue and her eye started to water from the constant throbbing.

Beck came to her rescue and stood behind her. She felt the warmth of his hand on her back and leaned back into him, thankful for the strength he provided.

"And you," Kojak pushed out his chin towards Beck, "the waiter said he overheard the two of you in a heated conversation at the table when she arrived. What was that all about?"

"I didn't like the wine," Markie said with a dry smile.

"You think this is funny?"

"Hey, Montana," his partner called out. Montana, who Markie had been referring to as Kojak, turned away to respond to his partner.

Montana turned his attention back to her and said, "I could bring you in, you know. You were reported driving a stolen car earlier."

"Which was deemed to be false. You can arrest me if you like and I'd tell you the same thing at the station that I'm telling you now. You'll just be wasting your time and mine."

They had a staring contest to see which one would back down first and she probably would have fallen over if Beck wasn't behind her holding her up.

"Better put some ice on that eye," Montana said and marched off to talk to his partner.

The pickup may have missed her, but she felt like something had run over her. She pulled away from Beck and headed toward her SUV. She was about to cross the street when he called after her.

Markie stopped and hung her head, not trusting herself to turn around. She swallowed hard and waited for Beck to catch up to her. She slowly turned around to face him.

"Are you sure you're going to be okay?"

He was all touchy feely again. The back of his hand swept along her jaw slowly and instead of pulling away as she should have, she stood there under the streetlight and laid her head on his shoulder. Just this once she thought…just this once. She allowed him to hold her as she listened to the soothing rhythm of his heartbeat while his hand gently caressed her back.

Just this once, she would give in and lean on someone and not be afraid that they would walk away. And she did. Forgetting about the chaos around her, she slipped her arms around his waist and held on. He was warm, strong and just what she needed.

"Do you want me to take you home?"

His voice shattered the delicate balance of peace she found in his arms and she stiffened. The world around her was once again alive with the reality of what had just happened and the destruction it had caused. Smoke from a damaged car curled into the air, a woman crying pinned under debris, blue and white lights flashing...chaos. And she was at the center of it.

"No. I'll see you tomorrow," she said when his hand tilted her chin upwards and she met his eyes.

When Markie got home half an hour later, she was still hurting. Every muscle in her body ached. After a long hot shower, she took two ibuprofens and climbed into bed.

For the first time in a long while she wished she had someone lying next to her, holding her, telling her everything would be okay and that Sydney was all right. Beck came to mind and she closed her eyes, remembering how it felt when he held her. With that thought, she fell asleep.

Exhausted and wired, Beck punched in the security code to enter his condo. All he could think about was Marklynn as he entered the kitchen, opened the refrigerator and grabbed a bottle of water.

Beck wondered if she'd gotten home okay. He actually entertained the idea of calling her but decided against it. It didn't seem like she relied on anyone and would probably interpret his concern as an intrusion.

She could have been killed and that didn't sit well with him at all. There were many unanswered questions regarding the security breach that plagued him at his company. His team was working around the clock to find answers.

Tonight more questions surfaced. Like, did the attempt on Marklynn's life have anything to do with what was going on at his company? And if it did, why was she targeted? How was Sydney involved? Was she working with the hackers?

Opening the water bottle, he looked beyond the stone countertop towards the living room. The large white sectional sofa spanned two walls. Behind the sofa were wall-to-wall arched windows with a view that stretched across the city.

Two Greek columns marked the entrance of the dining area and stood proud from floor to ceiling. A large glass table with eight white leather high back chairs sat beneath a two-tier white chandelier. And strand-woven bamboo in a deep brown, almost chocolate, covered the floor.

If it weren't for his stepmother the condo would still be void of furniture and accessories. After the divorce he had rented for a few years then finally bought the condo last year. The only piece of furniture he had invested in was a bed. His stepmother had taken charge and decorated, footing the bill for everything. He had been too busy working at the time to notice that her decorating style was not necessarily his but it grew on him, even the Greek columns.

The flashing red light on the phone caught his attention and he remembered he hadn't called Malcolm back. Malcolm had called while he was at the restaurant. He'd been about to return the call when he'd seen the pickup racing towards Marklynn.

Leaving the water behind and picking up the cordless off the kitchen counter, he dialed Malcolm's number on the way to his office. The office, which also doubled as a den, was huge and uncluttered. A large mahogany desk sat in front of the floor-to-ceiling window, an oversized leather chair in front of it. There were a couple of lounge chairs and a painting that hung on the wall over the fireplace.

The painting, the only picture in the room, looked like someone had taken a brush and flashed the paint off of it onto the canvas in a rainbow of colors. It was a gift from his stepmother on his last birthday. It was entitled, *"Confusion,"* and he had to agree with the artist there.

"Hello?"

It was a woman's voice aroused from sleep that answered the phone. He apologized for waking her, hung up and dialed Malcolm's again paying careful attention to the number. It was Malcolm who answered then.

"It's Beck."

"Did you call before and hang up?"

"Yes. I thought I had the wrong number. Tell your lady I'm sorry."

"Don't worry about it. Give me a minute," Malcolm said. Beck heard a female voice in the background and what sounded like a door closing.

"It happened again," Malcolm sighed into the phone. "The fire alarm malfunctioned or something. I don't know the full details yet."

"When?" Beck's pulse raced.

"A little after nine. I tried calling you."

Beck dropped into the leather chair beside the fireplace and ran his hand roughly over his face. "Which house?"

"The Franklin's."

Beck remembered them well. The husband was an investment banker and the wife was a plastic surgeon. They owned an estate in Jamaica Plains. The eight-bedroom house overlooked the Jamaica Pond, a circular pond surrounded by a beautiful path.

Beck was there for the installation of the security system two months ago. He tested the system the day it was installed. A month later another series of testing was completed and the security system was fine. The fire alarm worked.

"There's nothing left of the house," Malcolm said.

"Was anyone hurt?" Beck asked and was silently praying that there would be no fatalities. He couldn't live with that.

"No, they were on vacation. This is not like the others, Beck. We were dealing with breaks-in before. Now this. Whoever is responsible is stepping up the game."

Beck was thinking the same thing but he refrained from voicing it. This was a personal attack. What if the Franklin's had been home? Whoever was sabotaging his company wasn't going to stop until someone got killed.

"There's speculation it could be faulty wiring as a result of the alarm system," Malcolm said with hesitation in his voice.

"By whom? That's not possible."

"You and I know that, but we'll have to wait until the investigation is completed. If they're correct this may lead to charges."

"If they're correct? Who are they?"

"The fire marshal's office."

This can't be happening. Beck didn't realize he was pacing the floor or had gotten up out of the chair until he was in front of the sliding door.

Charges? What would happen to Beck Security Systems? Would he lose everything? He had made it back financially from his divorce and liked where he lived. His company had recovered and —

"I've scheduled a meeting with Peta Ann and Mona," Malcolm said cutting into his thoughts.

Peta Ann was the Director of Communications, and Mona was the company lawyer Beck hired last year.

"Mona feels we should discuss how we're going to address the fall out from this. Peta Ann is worried about the financial impact. How are we going to get out from under this?"

"I don't know." Beck wasn't thinking about damage control. All he could think of was why? Why was this happening? Who would do this? "I'll talk to you tomorrow."

"One more thing, I emailed you a file on Sydney Brooks. That's her real name by the way. Victoria Kelly is her grandmother's name."

Once he ended the call with Malcolm, he reared back and hurled the phone at the stone fireplace. It shattered into little black pieces that littered the bamboo floor. What was he going to do now?

He thought of Marklynn, the only person he believed could help him but may not because she thought he had something to do with Sydney's disappearance. He needed help. The question on the table now was would she help him?

Markie laid in bed staring at the ceiling. Day three of Sydney's disappearance and the responsibility of finding Sydney rested heavily upon her. She turned her head towards the digital clock when it alarmed again for the third time at 9:45.

She would not make it into the office for her meeting with Beck. What had she told Beck 10:00 a.m.? The alarm had gone off two hours ago and she'd hit the snooze button repeatedly trying to buy some more time. Hitting the snooze button was not something she routinely did, but this morning she couldn't get out of bed.

With two attempts on her life, it was nothing short of a miracle that she had walked away from both incidents without being seriously hurt. This morning she was sore from head to toe. She felt as though someone had used her body as a punching bag.

Last night Beck had said he would talk to her about Sydney and what he knew. Being sore wasn't going to stop her. Slow her down yes, but certainly not stop her from meeting with Beck.

First, she needed to call Cate to tell her she'd be late. After that was done, she called Nan to let her know she hadn't found Sydney yet, but she had a lead. Big mistake.

"It's bad, isn't it?" That's how Nan answered the phone.

"We don't know that," Markie said watching the ceiling fan's circular motion. Sometime between when she'd gotten home last night and an early morning trip to the bathroom, the air conditioner had stopped working.

"Well, I do."

"Nan, it's too —

"You're hurt."

"I'm fine."

"No, you're not."

Before Nan started up, Markie said, "I have a meeting with someone this morning that may know something about Sydney's disappearance. Once I know more, I'll call you."

"Who?"

Markie pushed herself up in the bed, ignoring the pain shooting through her body and switched the phone to her other ear. She was going to get up then changed her mind wanting to finish the call with her grandmother.

"You don't know him."

There was a dead silence on the other end of the line. Markie knew what was coming next and braced herself for it.

"I had a dream last night that you were hurt," Nan said. "In it I saw a man but I couldn't see his face. You're not to fear him. He'll help you but not in the way you think."

Childhood memories flooded back, of Nan walking over to the phone and waiting. Then a few moments later it would ring.

Nan would tell the neighbors things. Sometimes it brought her praises like when she'd found Ms. Fisher's missing six-year old daughter. Or disappointment, when she'd told Mrs. James her missing husband was dead. Mrs. James hadn't believed her until the body had been found.

Markie didn't want to believe that Nan had gifts as her grandmother called them. She accepted these *gifts* as luck. Plain and simple luck.

"Why is your dream relevant and how is this going to help me find Sydney?"

She wasn't in the mood to hear about Nan's dreams, the man in it or her premonitions this morning.

"It breaks my heart to see how far the two of you have drifted apart." Sadness marred her voice.

"That's Sydney's doing," Markie said not liking the path the conversation was heading down. It was the 'defend Sydney path.'

"Maybe, but you're sisters. Sydney is not as strong as you. She never recovered from your parent's death."

She'd heard that argument more times than she cared for and had always kept quiet. It was one excuse after another with Sydney. She couldn't go to school because she was sick. Real reason – She hadn't studied for her chemistry test. When she'd gotten arrested for fraud, it was her boyfriend's fault. It was always someone else's fault. This morning she couldn't hold her tongue. All the years of resentment bubbled to the surface. It was time Sydney grew up and Nan to stop making excuses for her.

"I survived, Nan. When Jared called off our wedding I got through it. I walked away from my job as a cop and I got through that, too."

"By throwing yourself into your work and shutting people out," Nan said. "When I die it'll just be you and Syd left. If we have to carry her until she finds her footing then so be it. She's your sister."

Silence.

"Now, about this man…"

Markie didn't want to hear about the mysterious man because she knew it was Beck. The fact that she kept dreaming about him was starting to get on her nerves.

That can be easily explained, she told herself simply. It was because of his connection to Sydney why she kept thinking about him. Nothing else. Once she found Sydney then she would no longer dream about him. He would no longer be a presence in her life.

"I don't have time to hear about your dream, Nan," she snapped.

"Why are you angry with me?"

"I'm not. I get uncomfortable when you talk about that hocus pocus stuff."

"Hocus pocus stuff? I can't help what I see or feel and will not repress it because it makes people uncomfortable. What about you? Do you think it's normal to glance at a five-page document and repeat it word for word?"

With the sequence of events that had happened in the last couple of days she could do without Nan's predictions or being called abnormal. Then she thought, why should she be the only one feeling lousy and carrying the burden.

"Fine. Why don't you save me the trouble and look into your crystal ball and tell me where to find Sydney?"

There was silence on the other end of the phone and she heard a sniffle. Markie felt like an eel. Nan didn't deserve that. She was trying to help the only way she knew how.

She'd given up her life when her son and daughter-in-law died to raise their children. Not once did she complain.

"I'm sorry, Nan."

"I know. I'll talk to you later."

"Wait. Why don't you drop by the office today? You can see that I'm okay and you don't have to spend the day worrying."

"I will," Nan said and Markie could almost hear the smile in her voice.

Placing the phone back on the cradle, she slipped out of bed and headed to the small adjoining bathroom. She turned on the light and wanted to turn it back off. It wasn't the avocado green walls, sink or tub that had her wanting to run. It was her reflection in the mirror.

Last night her right eye had been slightly swollen, with mild discoloration. This morning the skin around the eye was almost black, the sclera red. No amount of makeup in the world could hide her black eye and she didn't even want to try.

Instead, she opted for the bag of frozen peas in the freezer and held it against her eye for twenty minutes. Then she showered, dressed, and left for the office.

Would Marklynn help him?

The question still remained in the forefront of Beck's mind as he parked at the corner of East Berkeley not far from Washington Street. He grabbed his laptop and made his way to Brooks Investigations.

That question had kept him up after he'd read the information Malcolm had sent on Sydney Brooks. She had a juvenile record that was sealed. She'd also been arrested a couple of times for fraud. In both cases the charges were dropped, resulting in no jail time. He figured Marklynn had something to do with it.

It was clear to Beck that, however Sydney got her hands on the pictures, she wanted money for them. It had to be, with her history. What else could it be? If that were the case, then criminal charges would be laid. Would Marklynn help him knowing that it would land her sister in jail? He didn't think so.

"Good morning. I'm Dalton Beck. I've an appointment with Marklynn Brooks," Beck said to the woman seated behind a glass wall. The nameplate on the glass said Cate Jackson. She got up and came around the glass partition to greet him as he entered the foyer of the office.

She was a short round woman about fifty-five years old, wearing a white summer sweater and black slacks. Her short fiery red hair didn't seem to complement her dark skin tone.

"Good morning, Mr. Beck. Ms. Brooks will join you shortly. I'll show you to the conference room. Did you find the office okay?"

Beck followed her as they made their way up the metal staircase with the glass railing to the second floor. They passed a series of empty offices with glass walls separating each office. Glass walls also lined the hallway. Only frosting along the walls and glass doors provided some privacy.

The woman was looking at him as they approached the conference room and he realized she was waiting for a response from her earlier question.

"I'm familiar with the area," he said.

The conference room was different from the offices. It was enclosed with real walls and entry was accessed only by a key code pad. There was a sign on the door that said the door must be kept locked at all times. She punched in the code and the door buzzed open.

An oval black lacquer table sat in the centre of the room. Floor to ceiling silver cabinets were mounted on the back wall with a desk between the cabinets. It wasn't the furnishings they'd spent money on. It was the technology equipment. And there was something, a spy gadget he would guess, displayed on a wall of shelves above the desk.

"I'll leave you in Jamie's capable hands," Cate said when they entered the room. "And yes, he looks like the guy from The A-Team. Our clients get a kick out of it."

Jamie stood up from the head of the oval table and walked around to greet Beck. He extended his hand to Beck, scowling at Cate's comment.

"It's Mr. T. that looks like me. Jamie Wright."

"Dalton Beck."

The man was built like a linebacker. He wore a black patch over his left eye and his Mohawk and beard could do with a serious trim. Wearing a black T-shirt that stretched across massive chest, with Brooks Investigations written on the front in white, black pants and black boots, Jamie could pass for a soldier of fortune like the television character B.A. Baracus.

"Have a seat."

Jamie went back to his seat staring at Beck from the head of the table. There were juices and bottled water with fresh pastries on the table along with a projector. Paper and pens were placed in front of five of the six chairs in the room and Beck wondered about the other two people that would be joining the meeting.

"Markie said you're going to help us find Sydney."

Beck took his laptop from the carrying case, placed it on the table, lifted up the screen and turned it on.

"I'm not sure how much help I can be with that, but it appears our problem might be connected somehow."

"Somehow?" Jamie grunted his eyes hard as steel. "We have pictures that link your company to fraud or theft and that's just for starters. What would the police think if they received an eight by ten glossy of *your* company van parked in your client's driveway moments before they were robbed?"

"That van was stolen. We had—"

"How convenient. I'm sure they would take that into consideration when they throw your butt in jail after what happened to your client's house in Jamaica Plains last night. Didn't think we knew about that, did you?"

"I found out about that early this morning and planned to mention it in our meeting."

Jamie leaned back in his chair, lacing his fingers behind

his neck, his eyes still on Beck. He looked as if he'd already made up his mind that he was guilty of something and Beck had to wonder how productive their meeting would be.

"What I can't figure out is, why? It doesn't make sense."

"If I were you, I'd be thinking the same thing. But you're wrong," Beck said. He was in defensive mode now and didn't like it one bit.

"I don't believe you."

"Why would I try to kill Marklynn last night and then show up here today?"

"What do you mean *try to kill* Markie?" Jamie sat up like a cobra about to strike.

"She didn't tell you?" Beck's eyes widened in surprise.

"Tell me what?" Jamie placed his palms on the desk and pushed himself up to his full height leaning forward.

"Someone tried to run her over last night," Beck said, knowing exactly what was on Jamie's mind. "Before you start swinging," he held up both hands, "I had nothing to do with it."

The woman whose very name had changed the conversation from unfriendly to hostile walked into the room, sporting a gray power suit. The skirt flirted above her knees. With legs like hers, clad in sheer silk stockings wearing high-heeled black leather pumps, she was definitely a candidate for some type of leg commercial.

Her hand went to her hip to secure the gun into the hip holster as she moved effortlessly towards the front of the room. After the attempt on her life it was a wonder she wasn't walking around with the gun in her hand.

"Good morning," Markie said and dropped the file folder on the table. "Sorry I'm late."

She pushed the wraparound sunglasses from her face to the top of her head and Jamie exploded, "Sweet mother of God!"

CHAPTER FIVE

Sydney sat up on the cot when she heard keys jingling on the other side of the door. She scrambled to her feet just as the door opened and a woman, tall, with skin the color of honey strolled in. The black bodysuit she wore looked like it was painted on showing off her well-defined muscles. A body suit in the middle of summer makes perfect sense for a lunatic.

Sydney had named her Blondie. She'd gotten a glimpse of her before she'd passed out earlier. The woman's left hand was behind her back. In her right hand she had water, a small bottle. Sydney took her eyes off the water when Blondie moved slowly into the room staring at her like an animal stalking its prey.

"Aren't you a clever girl?" The woman's eyes fell on the tape Sydney had ripped from her mouth.

Sydney worked at the ropes to free her hands as the woman neared her. She wasn't going to —

"Sit down." A taser appeared from behind Blondie's back. "Do I need to remind you what I'm capable of?" She smiled a cold smile that made Sydney shiver.

Blondie set the bottle of water down on the floor by her feet. She looked down at the water then at Sydney with that cold smile again.

"Thirsty? You can have a mouth full if you tell me what I want to know. Sit down and let's have a chat. Shall we?"

"What do you want?" Sydney sat down on the cot

eyeing the taser gun, not wanting to push her luck with Blondie. Her side was still sore from the introduction and she didn't want a repeat performance. What she did want was a taste of the water. Her throat was parched. She eyed the water.

"Who do you work for?" Somewhere out in the hall a vent came on and Sydney could feel cold air circulating into the room. The woman looked over her shoulder into the hall then closed the door. "You were going to tell me your employer's name."

"I don't work for anyone," Sydney said and swallowed as she watched the woman and the taser gun.

"Wrong answer." Blondie turned on the taser gun and stroked it as if it were a pet. It was as though she had some sort of connection with the device. "Why did you take the pictures?"

"I don't know what you're talking about."

"Your sister is very pretty. Quick on her feet, too." She stopped stroking the taser, but kept looking at it. Maybe it was talking to her. "You're not like that, are you? Quick on your feet, I mean. I guess if you were, you wouldn't be here."

"Put that taser down and I'll show you."

Blondie paused as if considering what Sydney had said then laughed. "She's much prettier than you. I bet she was the favorite. You know, always had her life in order." Her mouth twisted in a bitter smile. "She probably did everything right. And you were a royal screw up."

Whatever issues she had with Markie she wasn't going to discuss them with the mad woman standing in front of her having a séance with the taser. "Why did you bring me here?"

"Your sister survived the accident last night, but I'm not sure she'll be so lucky the next time around."

"What accident?" Sydney froze. Cold sweat washed over her body. "Is she okay?"

"She's still standing. Whether she remains that way is up to you."

What has she done? A tear slid down Sydney's cheek.

After her phone call to Dalton Beck, she had decided to hide the pictures until she'd spoken to Markie. She didn't think anyone would find them. Markie's life was in danger because she had been impulsive. Impulsive was her middle name Nan had told her once. Why couldn't she be more like Markie.

"Tears. How touching. I'm still waiting for an answer. Who do you work for and why were you taking pictures in Jamaica Plains?"

"I'm a photographer for *Upscale Design Magazine*."

It was a one-off assignment. A friend had gotten her the job. She probably wouldn't get another chance with the magazine again because she wasn't going to make the deadline. Right now making the deadline was the least of her worries.

"Why don't I believe you?"

"I'm telling you the truth. I was taking pictures for a layout in the magazine. After that, I decided to go for a walk. I didn't see anything or take any other pictures."

"Then what's your sister doing with the pictures?"

Either way, she was going to be tasered again. Blondie was moving a little too close for comfort. Sydney pushed herself up from the cot and balled her fist the best she could with her hands bounded together, ready to swing.

"I don't—"

The shock from the taser gun cut off her reply. She lost her balance and hit the floor.

Pain.

Darkness.

All eyes focused on Markie when she removed the sunglasses. She wanted the meeting to be about Sydney, not her eye. Jamie looked like he was about to burst a blood vessel. She didn't call him last night because she didn't want to worry him. Now she wished she had because she was going to hear about it after the meeting.

"Gentlemen," she said to Carlos and Karter who strolled into the conference room a few minutes later, "I'd like you to meet Dalton Beck. Beck, meet two of our other investigators, Carlos and Karter whom I've asked to join us."

Carlos was built like a refrigerator with short black spiked hair, olive complexion dressed in Brooks Investigations shirt and jeans. Since he and Jamie were allergic to suits, Markie had no objections to them wearing promotional gear.

Karter, on the other hand, was a reed-like man with thick black glasses who always had a handful of tissues. His thin body was lost in the brown suit that was at least two sizes too big.

Both men shook hands with Beck after the introduction and took their seats at the table.

Markie shrugged out of her jacket and hung it over the back of her chair. She wasn't one for fuss and frill when it came to fashion, but today she'd pulled out the long sleeved green silk blouse with the white pearl buttons to hide the bruises on her arms. Then she had spent the extra time it took to put a few curls in her hair and apply a plum shade lipstick. The goal: draw attention away from the black eye. The finishing touch was the wraparound sunglasses. But she couldn't very well hide behind them all day. Could she?

Markie sat down next to Jamie and grit her teeth when every muscle in her body screamed at her in pain. Her eye began to throb. The throbbing was accompanied by an annoying twitch that began on her drive in when the sun penetrated the dark lenses of the glasses. The florescent overhead lighting didn't help. It made her injured eye hurt even more.

"At first, I thought Sydney's disappearance was something I could handle alone," she began, "but the two attempts on my life have made me see the light…even if it's out of one eye."

The last part of her comment had gotten a chuckle out of everyone except Beck. Jamie picked up on it and stared at her. His eyes were asking what was up between her and Beck. She ignored him.

"Here is what we know." Markie used the remote she

picked up from the table to lower a screen from the ceiling in front of the room. "Sydney called me four days ago to meet for lunch and said she wanted to run something by me. The "something" I'm assuming is," Markie nodded to Jamie to turn on the projector on the table, "these pictures. Why she took them, and I'm assuming at this point she did, I don't have an answer yet."

The room was quiet as everyone's attention focused on the screen. Markie waited until all twenty pictures were shown one after the other.

"Jamie, bring up the picture of the woman. Yes, that's the one. Thanks." Markie got up and stood facing the screen staring at the picture. The woman in the picture had on white capris and a white tank top. Turning to Karter, Markie asked, "Can you remove the shadows from her face so we can get an ID? Don't worry about the other two men. She's running the show. Find her and we'll find the men."

"It's going to take some time." Karter blew his nose in the wad of tissues in his hands and sniffled.

"You've got twenty-four hours. Cate has all the pictures."

"I'd better get started." Karter stuffed the tissues in his pocket then grabbed the notepad containing his notes and left the room.

"Go back to the picture of the house, Jamie. Yes that's the one. You can pretty much see the entire house."

"Carlos, I want to know where this house is. If we can figure out where the pictures were taken then we'll have a starting point in our search for Sydney. Beck can help. It's their client."

Beck met her gaze and nodded. "I know where it is. I'll get you the address."

"Anything from Sydney's computer, Jamie?"

"Someone deleted a bunch of files. It could be Syd. I'm working on getting them back. Still working on trying to get into her email account."

The phone on the desk in the back corner of the conference room buzzed and Carlos wheeled back in his chair and grabbed it. "Hello? Thanks, Cate. I'll be right out." He hung up the phone and Markie looked up at him. "My 11:00 a.m. appointment is here," he said.

"Go. You and Beck can talk later," Markie told Carlos as he made his exit.

"Okay Beck, you know what we know. What can you tell us about Sydney and what's going on at Beck Security Systems? And the million-dollar question…who is the woman in the picture? Any ideas?"

"No."

Jamie brought up the picture of the woman on the screen again.

Beck tried not to react to the picture. Could that really be Monika? Telling Marklynn his thoughts would be premature. He had to find out first.

He shifted his gaze from the screen to Marklynn. She kept squinting at the screen and he knew her eye was bothering her. She sat down gritting her teeth then let out a slow breath. The woman belonged in a hospital and by the look on everyone's face he wasn't alone in his assessment. She was there because he had agreed to help. He wanted to but not just because he wanted to save his company. Something was happening between him and Marklynn. Something he didn't want to walk away from. Not yet.

"Sydney called me," Beck said. "Must have been right before she called you. She said she had pictures. But the name she used was Victoria Kelly which I'm told is your grandmother's name."

He waited for an explanation of some sort from Marklynn. Perhaps even a hint at Sydney's past or why she thought she'd taken the picture. She offered none and sat in silence waiting for him to continue.

"I agreed to meet with her as she requested," Beck continued. "She said she would call me back with a time and location. She never did. I traced the telephone call to her apartment. When I arrived the place was ransacked."

"I'm guessing whoever it was knew she had taken the pictures. Perhaps they thought she called you and didn't want the two of you connecting?" Markie said.

"I don't know." Beck leaned back in his chair and rubbed his hands over his eyes. Tired. "Three months ago seven homes that we've installed security systems in were broken into. In every case, the security system failed even though the system was activated. Each system was fully inspected before and after they were installed. They were tested after each incident and we're at a loss as to why each one of them failed."

Beck remembered when the first break in occurred and he'd gotten the call. They thought it was a glitch. The security system was replaced and tested. Only jewelry was stolen. No fire. The next house, it was the paintings that went missing, no jewelry. Since the homeowners were art dealers, the police believed they were involved because of a bogus insurance filed. The two incidents were enough for him to be concerned. He had everyone on high alert checking and rechecking every installation projects.

"That can't be good for business," Jamie said. He had been taking notes, but paused for a moment staring at Beck.

"Tell me about it. They are some of Boston's wealthiest citizens."

"I can see that. Your company is not exactly the most well known alarm company on the market. Yet, you've garnered some very influential clients."

Beck knew what Jamie was doing. He was trying to goad him and Marklynn looked on, saying nothing. Well, he wasn't going to be bullied.

"How did you get a copy of my client list?" He asked with a sharp edge in his voice.

"Why are you sabotaging your company?"

That question brought Beck's back straight up in his chair and he leveled Jamie with a cold stare. Marklynn intervened.

"What Jamie is trying to ask in his own unique way is how you've acquired such an affluent client base. I think that's a fair question in light of what's happening at your company."

He looked from Jamie to Markie before he answered. "My stepmother's name is Anika Taylor."

"Oh," Marklynn said.

Beck assumed she had a file on him but they must have missed that. It was Jamie's eyes widening in surprise and Marklynn's "oh" that said it all.

His stepmother was the interior designer to the very rich and the very famous. Most people thought that she was the reason for his success. With that assumption came the thought that he didn't have to work for anything and Marklynn was probably thinking the same thing.

"I wasn't born with a silver spoon in my mouth," Beck said, anger creeping into his voice. "Beck Security Systems was built on my sweat. My stepmother may have referred some of her clients to us, but we did okay on our own acquiring other high-profile clients."

"Beck—" Markie started but he held up his hand to silence her.

"We may not be as well known as the other security companies," he looked at Jamie, "but we have a solid reputation in this industry. Well ... at least we used to."

"How did your clients handle the break-ins?" Markie asked.

"We weren't able to save all seven of the accounts. Four of the seven home owners went with different security companies and we picked up the tab."

They were lucky that three accounts stayed. The clients were good friends of his stepmother and they decided to stay with him pending no further incident. So far there had been none.

"Your insurance company would have taken care of it," Jamie said, looking at him with raised brows. "Why pay if it wasn't your fault?"

"It was our responsibility," he said with force. "Our clients trusted us with the safety of their families and their possessions. We failed them. It shouldn't have happened.

The systems shouldn't have failed."

"How is it possible that a working system malfunctions for no reason? Is it possible, Jamie?" Markie asked.

"Anything is possible, Markie, and any system can be hacked into."

"I want to know how it's being done. This isn't making any sense to me at all," Beck said in frustration. "I have a team of people scrambling to find answers but they keep coming up with nothing. I want answers."

Markie should have known better than to leap to conclusions. She had enough of that in her life with people who she thought were her friends when she left the police department. People, who didn't know the entire story as to why she left, yet formed their own opinion of her. She had no right to judge Beck.

Markie glanced at Jamie who, in turn was staring at Beck as if he'd just appeared out of nowhere. He had missed that information about Beck's stepmother. He rarely missed anything. And if he did, it wasn't worth mentioning. She also knew Jamie. How he thought. He was assessing Beck and was caught off guard when Beck had taken responsibility for the failed security systems.

However, being caught off guard was no reason to commit to helping Beck. That was what Jamie had written across his face, flashing like a neon sign. And if he felt that Brooks Investigations should not get involved then he would insist they back off and let Beck fend for himself.

The only thing was, Markie wanted to help Beck and would, regardless of what Jamie thought. It wasn't just because of Sydney. It was something else and she wasn't ready to admit to what that was at the moment.

Beck sat at the table rubbing his forehead with the heels of his palms as if his head suddenly hurt. On impulse, she wanted to comfort him, to smooth the tired lines from his face and probably would have if Jamie weren't in the room. Why? Because he had done that for her last night after the pickup had tried to make her a part of the pavement.

As much as she fought against her reaction to him last night, she came to the conclusion that she wouldn't have gotten through it without him. Being in his arms had made her feel safe if only for a moment and she liked it.

Markie understood Beck's frustration and wanted to give him answers or at least try. "Any thoughts, Jamie?"

"What we're looking at is some sort of custom software, malware to subvert the monitoring software," Jamie replied.

"Yes, but how is—?"

"Malware?" Markie interrupted Beck not wanting to be left in the dark. Although, the topic was familiar territory to Beck and Jamie, it was foreign to her. "I've never heard of that word."

Jamie's hostility towards Beck had turned into intrigue. When it came to computers he was in his element. He'd been on the Cybercrime Unit when he worked for the police department before he partnered with her.

"Malware is formed from two words. Malicious and software," Beck explained. "Take the first three letters from **mal**icious and the last four letters of soft**ware**. It's a software designed to infiltrate and damage a computer system."

"You're talking about a computer virus," Markie said simply. "That's Jamie's stomping ground."

"How so?" Beck asked.

"Before I joined the police department I was an independent information consultant with experience in performing security assessment for fortune 500 companies. I've held various information and technology roles over the years. Education: Bachelor's degree in Computer Engineering Technology and PHD in Management Technology. Bottom line…I can pretty much hack into anything."

"Trust me, he's telling the truth," Markie said with a grin, "and he's being modest."

"Can he find the trail of an invisible hacker?" Beck

laughed, a weary laugh. "The tech guys named him *Shadoe*."

It was Jamie's turn to laugh. "The name fits."

"I know computers and software and how they work," Beck said. "I've looked at the software data every which way possible and I still can't figure how the system is being accessed. The alarm systems are installed and tested. The Jamaica Plains property that went up in flames last night that system was tested. I did it myself. There was nothing wrong with the system."

"Nothing that you could find," Jamie said staring at Beck. The intimidation factor once again present and Beck rose to meet the challenge.

"You're saying that *we*, my entire team and I, will never find it."

Jamie shrugged.

"Who designed the monitoring software?" Markie asked, already knowing Beck's answer.

"Malcolm led the design team at the time and he still works closely with them."

"How does the system work?" Jamie asked, as he scribbled across the pad of paper in front of him.

Beck looked at him as if to suggest with his credentials Jamie should already know the answer.

"He's asking for my benefit," Markie assured Beck. "Since I would probably ask him about it later anyway."

"There are two components to the security system— the hardware and the software. The hardware is the unit that's installed in the house. The software side of it is the code that tells the system what to do," Beck explained.

"Software meaning if someone breaks into the house, it tells the system to call the police or if there is a fire, to call the fire department?" Markie asked as she got up to grab a bottle of water from the table. It was still cool and she resisted the urge to roll the bottle across her eye.

"That's correct." Jamie glanced up from his writing pad. "*Shadoe*, has infiltrated the monitoring software at Beck Security Systems, uploaded a computer virus and I'm assuming that same virus after it's completed its task destroys itself."

Markie started twisting the lid off the bottled water and stopped her hand still on the cap.

"You're saying that *Shadoe* is hacking into Beck Security Systems, uploading a virus that tells the system if there is a break-in, fire, or whatever, in any of the houses they've installed alarm systems in not to call the appropriate response unit. And then this *virus* destroys itself?"

"Yep," Jamie replied.

"Is that even remotely possible?" Markie asked, wondering who would go through all that trouble and why. She sat down again, taking a long drink from the water bottle.

"Think about it," Jamie said pushing his chair back from the table and stretching his arms above his head. "All a computer does is follow orders. It doesn't know right from wrong and it doesn't question what you tell it to do. It does it."

"I understand that," Beck said impatience creeping into his voice. "What I don't understand is why we can't find a trace of this," he finished, rubbing the back of his neck.

"You can't because you don't know what you're looking for," Jamie said simply. "And therefore you'll never find it."

"And you could?" Beck asked staring at Jamie with skepticism.

"I'd have to see the monitoring software program, but more than likely yes. It takes a hacker to catch a hacker."

"Malcolm would have access to do that," Markie said eyeing Beck, voicing her thought out loud gauging his reaction. "He would know how to create a virus like that. He has the educational background for it."

Beck shook his head. "Malcolm wouldn't do that. I was struggling with the company after the car accident. With the divorce following that, I was a financial train wreck. Malcolm came in with the capital we needed to turn the company around. Why would he sabotage the company after all that?"

Because he didn't get the recognition he deserved. He wanted a bigger chunk of the pie. All those reasons and more came to mind, but Markie kept them to herself. Beck wasn't ready to hear that his right hand man could be involved in the sabotage.

"You said you started having problems three months ago. Why? What's so special about three months ago? Did you fire someone at the company who you think could be holding a grudge? Jealous girlfriend wanting to get even...any ideas?"

"We fired no one three months ago, we checked. We went as far back as to when we started the company and no red flags. As for the jealous girlfriend theory about holding a grudge...there is no one."

"What about employee background security checks?" Jamie asked.

"It's mandatory for all employees. We found nothing." He was silent for a moment looking at Markie. "I've been told the same thing Jamie said about the malware. What we need is someone that specializes in this sort of thing. Perhaps Jamie can work with our team at Beck Security Systems to get to the bottom of this, if that's okay with you. Sydney is tied up in this somehow."

Markie hadn't responded right away. She didn't really know why she hesitated because she had decided to help him. Perhaps it was that look in his eyes that she couldn't quite read. Perhaps he thought she wouldn't help him because of Sydney. His next words confirmed it.

"I didn't try to hurt you last night, Marklynn and I had nothing to do with Sydney's disappearance. You have to believe that. Do you believe me?"

His eyes met hers, searching. It was as if his eyes were pleading for her to believe him and she was lost in the heat they generated as her dream floated into mind. She was vaguely aware of Jamie leaving the room, something about making a call.

Beck got up and moved over to her chair. He turned her swivel chair to face him and pulled her gently to her feet to meet his searching gaze.

He smelled of soap, a spicy woody scent. She was aware

of his masculine strength, the feel of his hands as he touched her. Again she wanted to offer comfort. She wanted to reach up to smooth the tired lines from his forehead. Her heartbeat sped up as she felt his warm breath on her cheek.

"Marklynn? You do believe me, don't you?"

She nodded her head not trusting herself to speak at that moment. A smile lit up his face and she found she liked his five o'clock shadow more than the clean-shaven face he had when they first met.

Beck was gearing up to be all touchy feely again and she welcomed it. He ran the back of his hand along her cheek and a kiss as light as a feather touched her bruised eye. Their lips were a whisper apart and she waited in anticipation for the kiss that she knew would follow. He dropped his hand from her cheek when he heard Jamie's loud voice outside the conference room door announcing his presence.

"You owe me a rain check," Beck whispered. "And I fully intend to collect," he added with a teasing grin.

Her heart was beating so loud she was sure Jamie heard it when he came into the room.

"What now?" Jamie asked. He grabbed a Danish and bit into it wiping his mouth with the back of his hand.

Beck moved over to his computer and started to pack up. "I've a meeting with our company's lawyer this afternoon. We could meet later and talk."

His comment was meant for both her and Jamie, but Beck's eyes never left hers when he said it.

Jamie who wouldn't know the meaning of the word tactful even if it hit him over the head said, "Two's company and three's a crowd."

"Call me later," she said ignoring Jamie's comment. What did she expect after he'd given them a moment together? And he wasn't going to let her forget it either.

"I'll see you out," Jamie said to Beck winking at Markie as they left the conference room. Oh yeah, he wasn't going to let her forget it.

Beck was having a hard time reading Jamie as they exited the conference room into the hall. The row of offices that were empty when he'd passed earlier was now occupied except for the one with the pile of tissues on the desk. Perhaps the man went out to buy more, he mused. No sooner had the thought crossed his mind Karter came up the stairs carrying a box of Kleenex.

Two's company and three's a crowd.

Beck thought about Jamie's comment and glanced over at the man walking beside him in silence. It was clear they both had an interest in Marklynn and he figured Jamie was using the excuse of walking him out to set the record straight. But then, why had he given them a moment alone in the conference room?

"What makes you think you have a chance in hell with Markie?" Jamie asked and continued walking without breaking his stride as they came to the stairs.

Beck stopped at the top of the stairs but Jamie jogged down. "Are we going outside to the parking lot to settle this with a fist fight?"

"You think you'd win?" Jamie waited until Beck joined him at the foot of the stairs. "I think you like her. A whole lot, I reckon. Want some free advice?"

Beck was annoyed. His likes and dislikes were none of Jamie's business. It didn't matter if Jamie was right.

"I don't see why it's any of your business how I feel about Marklynn."

If he was offended by Beck's response he didn't show it.

"Markie takes care of everyone and sticks her neck out for everyone. Sydney is the worst. She's a spoiled brat who doesn't give a damn about anyone but herself. Syd calls and Markie gets shot at and mowed down. And that crackpot grandmother of hers who thinks she's some kind of voodoo priestess with her visions…"

"I'm still waiting for the free advice."

A scowl appeared on Jamie's face. "It's about time someone takes care of her for a change instead of her taking care of everyone else."

"And you've appointed yourself that *someone*." He was jealous and if need be would throw a punch or two if it meant landing Marklynn.

Jamie broke into laugher that ended in a cough. Beck was not amused. To add insult to injury the man grabbed on to the railing and bellowed out another roar of laughter.

Cate looked up at them, a stern expression on her face. Her office was across from the stairs and she had someone with her. Jamie mouthed the word "sorry" and they moved towards the door stepping outside into the warm sun.

"If you knew Markie then you'd know why I'm laughing. All the woman does is work. Besides, if I ever, and I mean *ever*, think I'm man enough to go there I would have to give my *wife* my head on a stick. It would be less painful. Then she would kick the rest of me from here to Canada."

Beck smiled at the thought and he saw the features in Jamie's face softened when he mentioned his wife. Jamie was a no-nonsense kind of person. He said what was on his mind and Beck couldn't help but like the man. Jamie also had a genuine affection for Marklynn.

Genuine affection he could handle. Jamie being married he could handle that too.

"You forgot I was coming, didn't you?"

Markie was sitting at her desk thinking about her meeting with Beck and what had happened between them in the boardroom not more than fifteen minutes ago, when her grandmother appeared at her door. Cate always send her up if she didn't have a client with her. Nan must have passed Beck in the hall Markie thought and stifled a groan. If that was the case, then she was about to hear the rest of her grandmother's dream.

"Sorry. I just got out of a meeting." She got up and hugged her grandmother then closed the door. A scent that was distinctly hers, gardenias, filled the office. "Come in and have a seat."

Nan gently touched her face. "Does it hurt?"

"Only when the light hits it. The sunglasses work outside, but I can't see a thing when I wear them in the office," she smiled.

"It looks painful," Nan said and began taking off her lace gloves as she sat in the chair smoothing down the front of her red floral summer dress. She took off her matching hat and set it on the edge of the desk.

"I'll live," Markie said as she sat down behind her desk. "Where are you off to all dressed up?"

"There is more to life than just surviving, Marklynn."

Deep worry lines were etched in her strong face. She didn't want her grandmother fussing over her. Markie leaned back in her chair and watched her.

"Maybe," she said choosing her words carefully. "But it's all I can do right now with everything that's happening."

Nan settled back comfortably in the chair. She was ready for one of her long drawn out talks. Markie could tell by the way she clasped her hands together in her lap. Trying to hurry her along would only make it longer so Markie just sat back and waited. She was probably just as scared about Sydney's disappearance if not more so and wanted someone to talk to.

"Life doesn't have to be only about surviving. I'm here for you. I guess it doesn't seem that way sometimes. I'm always bailing out Sydney or fussing over her then running to you."

"I'm sorry about what I said this morning. I didn't mean to hurt you."

"What you said made sense. It got me thinking about your father. Do you remember him?"

It was the first time in a long while she'd mentioned dad and she dabbed at the corner of her eyes with a white-laced handkerchief then drew in a deep breath. Markie hadn't seen her cry in a long time either. Chalk it up to Sydney's disappearance, and her black eye didn't help either.

"Yes. I remember him."

"You're a lot like him in many ways. Strong, stubborn

and you don't easily forgive," she said, wagging a finger at Markie. "He would have been proud of you with all that you've accomplished."

"You think? He would've wanted me to be a doctor just like him."

"No. He would have wanted you to be happy. Being a police officer made you happy," Nan said getting all misty eyed again.

"That's ancient history."

"Maybe. Do you remember why you became a police officer?"

"Yes."

Markie didn't know where Nan was going with her line of questions, but it was easier to respond than to put her off with the mood she was in.

Answering, however, meant digging up the past. She had gotten shot at nineteen, when she attended a birthday party. It had taken a long time for her to feel safe enough to leave her house back then. That was one of the reasons why she became a police officer. She wanted people to be safe, to feel safe.

"When you walked away from your job it broke my heart. I think a piece of you died that day also," Nan said, pulling at a thread on the laced handkerchief in her lap.

"I suppose," she hesitated.

Nan's eyes focused on the stack of file folders on the credenza before she turned her gaze back to Markie. "I confronted Jared a few days after you broke up. He told me why he'd called off the wedding."

"Oh, Nan," Markie groaned. Where was this coming from? And why was she dredging up the past?

"I never told you I knew because I wanted you to tell me, to trust me. You never did." She sounded hurt. It was as if she wanted some kind of explanation.

"You had your hands full with Sydney."

"That may be. I just wish you had told me. That's all."

"It doesn't matter now. Does it?"

Markie didn't want to talk about it then and she didn't

want to talk about it now. Nan wanted it out in the open and Markie didn't know what she hoped to accomplish with dredging up the past. She didn't have to wait long for an answer.

"I think it does. Jared wasn't the right man for you. You need to be open when *he* does come along."

Markie braced herself ready to hear her grandmother's declaration about who "*he*" was. She was sure Beck's name was going to come up, but it never did.

Instead Nan said, "I know you're scared, but you're not alone, Marklynn. Remember that." Nan stood up. "I've taken up enough of your time. Call me later."

"Sure." She didn't know what to say after all that. Nan had opened old wounds…wounds she had not allowed to heal. Unresolved issues she had buried rather than confront were right in front of her again. But she would not tackle them today or tomorrow.

"I love you," Nan said. A quick peck on Markie's cheek and she was gone.

CHAPTER SIX

Phoenix watched Beck and the man with the Mohawk emerge from Brooks Investigations, laughing as if they were old friends instead of meeting for the first time. She had been keeping an eye on him from a distance over the last three months. He was more focused than Malcolm and she didn't want to be careless and get caught.

Beck was the taller of the two, more refined, looking handsome in his tailored suit. He was wearing a suit. He didn't like suits. Monika said so. The only time he wore them was for business meetings and that depended on the client. He wore one to his wedding…the wedding that…

Phoenix shook her head and blinked. It didn't matter anymore. That was in the past. There were more important things to worry about. With Sydney's pictures now in circulation, she had to assume that Beck and Marklynn would meet to discuss them in an effort to find Sydney and she was right.

Phoenix thought about the woman she'd left unconscious on the floor. She couldn't get a straight answer out of Sydney about the pictures or why she'd taken them. A call to the magazine she claimed to work for was unreturned.

The woman loved her sister and wanted to protect her. She would rather die than tell the truth about the pictures. Isn't that what sisters were supposed to do? Protect each other with their lives.

Monika wouldn't risk her life for her. She was the perfect one and Phoenix was born with problems. Her mother said so. That didn't matter, for Monika had promised to take care of her, to protect her. Dalton Beck had made her break that promise. Now he'd moved on with his life and she was all alone, left with nothing.

She would not allow him to live happily ever after. Not with Marklynn Brooks. The way he held her last night after the accident that should have been her. He had never held her that way. Never cared about her that way. No need to be jealous she consoled herself. It was time to move on with the next phase of her plan.

"Go home," Jamie said as he knocked on Markie's door. He invited himself in and took the guest chair in front of the desk "Your grandmother said if you weren't gone by early afternoon to send you home."

"I thought as much."

"But you're still here."

"I wanted to get some work done."

Since everything possible was being done to find Syd, instead of worrying she thought her time would be better spent catching up on paper work. She'd just signed off on the expenses for the Miller file.

Child abduction cases she took once in a while. She hated handling them when they had to find the spouse who abducted the child. The Miller case did not have a happy ending.

"I'll be packing up soon. I thought you were going to see Sara?"

Sara Miller was a lovely petite Asian woman who'd come to Brooks Investigations a few months ago when the police couldn't find her ex-husband. He'd decided not to return their son after a weekend visit.

"I spoke to her sister a few minutes ago. Sara is still in the hospital under a suicide watch," Jamie replied with a grim look on his face. "The police should've told Sara about her ex-husband killing the boy then turning the gun on himself, not you."

The Miller case had rattled Jamie. He'd found both bodies in a roadside motel after tracing Mr. Miller's credit card usage. A four-year-old child with a bullet in the head does something to you.

Markie had driven up the coast of Maine that weekend to get away. Jamie had disappeared for a week. It was his wife who had called to say he was fine. Markie never heard from him. Then he returned to work the following week and they never spoke about it.

Leaning her head back on the headrest of the chair she closed her eyes for a moment. She could still hear Sara's wail of anguish when she'd told the woman about her son.

"Sara was our client. I couldn't let the news of her son's death come from strangers. The suicide note, I couldn't handle. That's why I had the police tell her about the note."

"Bastard," Jamie spat. "Just because he wasn't given full custody of his son, he would rather kill the boy than have him live with his ex-wife."

"The file is closed. Let's not dwell on it. We can't save everyone."

Jamie grunted. "If only you believed that. Now you've taken on another cause."

"What cause are you referring to, my sister or Beck? Either way I think you're out of line."

"I don't think Beck is a *cause*. We had a nice chat when I walked him to the door," Jamie smiled. A genuine smile she hadn't seen since the Sara Miller case.

"If you said anything to embarrass me, I'll fire —"

"Right." He waved away her threat. "The man likes you. You should've seen the look of relief on his face when I told him you were free as a bird."

"One of these days—" Her warning was cut off.

"Please. I see the way you look at him."

"That doesn't mean I —"

"What were the two of you doing when I left the boardroom? Shaking hands?"

That silenced any further protest from her. She didn't have a leg to stand on. She knew it and he was just stating the obvious.

"Why did you leave the room?" She asked suddenly wanting to know. It was totally out of character even for him.

"Because you look like a train wreck and you needed someone. No need to thank me," he said with a smug look on his face. "Anyway, I'm on board with helping Beck. What do you want me to do?"

Markie stared at him, shaking her head. There was no point. He had a thick skull and no amount of threats would get anywhere with him. The one thing she knew for sure was that he always had her back and for that she was grateful.

When Jamie had asked to join Brooks Investigations, Markie was concerned that he would be bored. She didn't have the clients with computer security issues he was used to working with. He'd told her that it didn't matter and took whatever cases were assigned to him. When the case with Beck was over, she would look into expanding that side of the business and have him manage it.

"Work with Beck and his team to see what you can come up with. The more I think about it, the more I'm convinced it has to be someone on the inside of his company. Get Carlos to run a full security check on all the employees."

"Beck did that already," Jamie said.

"I know, but maybe we'll find something they missed. In the meantime, I want to give Sam O'Malley a call."

"The detective assigned to Monika Beck's accident four years ago?" His brows were drawn together. "Why? What are you looking for?"

"I don't know yet."

"I reckon when you know you'll tell me. Not." Jamie pushed himself up from the chair. "Go home. You're no good to yourself or to Sydney if you don't take care of yourself. You look like you're about to drop."

"I'm fine."

"No, you're not." Jamie frowned. "Why didn't you tell me about last night? Beck said you were almost killed."

"You're right. I'm not fine, but I also don't want to talk about it. Okay?"

"You're not alone, Markie. Remember that. You have a team of highly skilled investigators who would do anything you ask. We all care about you."

"I know." It was the second time today she was reminded of that. "Do you think Syd's okay? I mean if we lost her…"

A picture of her, Nan and Syd in a black wooden frame sat on her desk next to her laptop. Up until a few days ago, it was on the far corner of her desk behind a stack of file folders. Now it was within reach, clear from all obstacles.

The picture was taken when Sydney returned from one of her trips. Nan had insisted they all meet for dinner. They all had a good time and Syd had seemed happy. She had even talked about settling down.

Markie lifted her gaze from the picture to Jamie's face, waiting for his answer. His eye was clear. Sharp. Sometimes she didn't even notice the black patch over his left eye.

Jamie knew what she was asking. He knew what she wanted from him at that moment. It was assurance. He had never lied to her or kept anything from her. If he said Sydney was fine then she would believe him. Jamie moved beside her chair, laying a hand on her shoulder.

"If anything had happened to her I think your grandmother would've said something."

"You believe in the supernatural?" She was surprised that he would bring up her grandmother. He always said her basket was a couple of eggs short of a dozen.

"I don't disbelieve it. Right now it's all we have."

Jamie wasn't one for showing affection so she was surprised when he leaned over and gave her a quick hug. It didn't matter that her nose smashed into his broad shoulder. The fact that he'd done it made her feel better.

"Go home and get some rest. If we hear anything, we'll let you know."

"I'm heading out soon."

Looking at a box of papers and files she'd taken from Sydney's apartment beside her desk Jamie said, "Why don't I believe you?"

When it rained it poured. It wasn't just pouring. It was a monsoon. It hit Beck as soon as he'd stepped into his office. His assistant had been taking calls all morning and what she couldn't handle was transferred to his voicemail. The result: Nineteen messages and counting.

He didn't get the chance to take off his jacket before his phone started to ring. If it wasn't his cell phone, it was the phone on his desk.

As soon as he ended one call he was pulled into another. Clients were concerned with their security system. These were people he knew. Shook hands with. They all wanted reassurance from him, no one else, that when it came down to it their alarm system would not fail. All he could promise was a reassessment and even that wasn't good enough. There were also a handful of messages on his desk that he didn't even attempt to look at. He would respond to those after his meeting.

He'd left Marklynn's office just after the lunch hour with renewed hope about two things. One, he wanted to get to know her; the real Marklynn Brooks not the tough front she showed the world. Two, with Jamie on his team they would find *Shadoe* a lot faster and he could focus on business again.

Progress.

That was what he would call today. For the first time in three months he was seeing a light at the end of the tunnel. That put a smile on his face as he left his office for his second meeting of the day in the executive boardroom with his team.

From the sleek custom-made wooden cabinets and oval mahogany table, the boardroom was all about luxury that catered to their clients. Swivel comfortable brown leather chairs could be turned in any direction to enjoy a wall of windows showing off a spectacular view across the downtown core.

As he entered the boardroom and sat down across from Malcolm, Mona Rogers and Peta Ann Taylor, the progress he thought he'd made seemed insignificant. All conversation ceased and all eyes focused on him. It was the dark cloud before the storm.

"How are we going to spin this?" Mona sprang on him. A thin blonde with a pageboy haircut, dressed in a white Ralph Lauren suit and Jimmy Choo shoes, she was all business. A moment ago when he'd entered the boardroom she was in the middle of telling Peta Ann about how her shoe had cost her a mint.

"I understand that a communication message needs to be considered, but we need to look at the legal implication before trying to spin anything," Peta Ann said, tapping her pen upside down on the legal pad in front of her. She was a petite dark-skinned woman with short reddish brown curls dressed in a simple gray suit.

"Don't you think that's a little premature," Malcolm said looking down at his Blackberry when it vibrated then pushed it to one side on the table.

"The Franklin's are not going to go quietly into the night," Peta Ann replied. "Their lawyer contacted me this morning to set up a meeting. I'll put off the meeting until we receive the official report as to the cause of the fire."

"That's why we need to put messaging together for our customer service reps. "This should have been done from the first incident in anticipation of this, but you wanted to wait. Now the cat is out of the bag. We need to move now," Mona said waiting for direction from Beck.

Some progress…One step forward, three steps back. What was there to tell the clients? 'Your house burned down, sorry.' Or, 'Your installed system may or may not work, but trust us? We'll keep you safe.'

Beck didn't know how the communication team was going to do it, but Mona was right. Something had to be done.

"Okay," Beck said exhausted. His sleepless night had caught up to him. "Since I've been told that I'm a one-man show…"

"I told him that," Malcolm said with a laugh.

"Here is what I propose. Mona, craft your wording and run it by Peta Ann. If you are both in agreement proceed."

"I can live with that," Peta Ann said looking at Mona who nodded her head in agreement. "Our stance on this should be clear with the Franklin's. We're not responsible for what happened to their house."

"I'm with you," Malcolm agreed. "The security system was in perfect working order."

"I'm sure they're going to want to talk settlement," Peta Ann said. "We have to at least—"

"If you're talking settlement then we're admitting fault and that's not good for business," Malcolm said. "If we are going to take the company public then we need to be careful in our wording. Never assume blame. We're not responsible."

"We're not responsible?" Beck asked.

He listened to them arguing about blame, taking the company public. What about the clients? The company had a responsibility to the people who trusted them with their personal possessions. As hard as that pill was to swallow, they needed to see that. And because they couldn't see beyond the almighty dollar it made him angry.

"The damn house burnt down!"

The room fell quiet. Mona's mouth dropped open. Her eyes widened as she sunk back in her chair. Peta Ann straightened in her chair looking at Malcolm.

Voices from outside the hall filtered into the quite conference room. Beck rubbed his forehead taking a deep steadying breath trying to calm himself before he spoke again.

"Let's be rational for a moment. How can the alarm systems be in perfect working order? Our clients are being robbed and their house up in flames."

"You ran the test yourself and everything was fine," Malcolm reminded him.

"Yes, but it wasn't. I don't understand it," Beck said shaking his head. "The house in Jamaica Plains is a pile of ashes. What if they were home?"

Malcolm stared at Beck for a long while before he spoke again. "Don't put this on us. My guys haven't seen their families since this whole thing started. We're all working 24/7 to find *Shadoe*. It's not enough. I've told you that. If you let us get outside help as I've requested maybe we can alleviate some of the stress we're all putting ourselves under."

The room fell quiet once again. This wasn't Malcolm's fault and there was no point in taking out his frustration on the people who were trying to help him. Having his employees working to the point of exhaustion wasn't good for business either.

"I'm sorry," Beck said looking at Peta Ann and Mona. "You're right, Malcolm, about the outside help. I had a meeting with Marklynn Brooks, from Brooks Investigations this morning."

"You'd mentioned you were going to see them, but weren't sure if they would help," Malcolm said relaxing back into his chair.

"They've agreed to help us. Jamie Wright, Marklynn's associate, is an expert when it comes to hackers. He's coming on board. I need to finalize the details, but it could be as early as tomorrow."

"He's an ethical hacker then?" Peta Ann asked, brows raised in concern.

"Is there such a thing?" Mona asked.

"You'll have to ask him that," Beck replied, picked up the leather folder and stood up. "Are we done?"

Everyone around the table nodded in agreement. In his present mood they were probably all glad he was leaving.

When Beck returned to his office it was after five. After an afternoon of meetings, he was tired and on edge and needed to unwind. He picked up the phone to call the only woman that had been on his mind since the day began.

Wouldn't it be nice to end the day with her in his arms?

Markie gathered the papers she'd taken from Sydney's apartment and put them back in the box. She hadn't intended to go through the entire box, but once she'd gotten started the time just slipped away. All she wanted to do now was to go home and crawl into bed. She was about to step out of her office when the phone started to ring. Any other time she would have let the call go to voice mail, but she couldn't take the chance with Sydney missing.

She hurried back to the desk and picked up the phone. "Brooks Investigations."

"You sound exhausted."

Markie sat on the edge of the desk, smiling. "So do you. How did it go today?"

"Long. We can talk over dinner."

She'd forgotten they were supposed to meet. As much as she wanted to see him, she had to wonder how productive their meeting would be if she were falling asleep on her feet. But to see his smiling face…

"I was on my way home but I could detour."

"But you would rather go home and kick your feet up."

"Yes, to tell you the truth. The eye looks bad. I'm starting to scare children," she said remembering the little boy that pointed and gasped when she'd popped across the street for a deli sandwich earlier.

Beck chuckled. "How about this? I can come by your place and bring food. Then we can both kick our feet up. Should you fall asleep you're already home."

His argument was sound and well thought out and too good to pass up. And, she wanted to see him. What if he fell asleep? She wanted to ask, but shied away from the question.

Beck exuded a certain strength that drew her to him and she found that she wanted to be with him. Then she remembered what happened in her office that morning and made up her mind.

"Come by around seven," Markie said and gave him her address.

Markie glanced at her watch as she hurried out of the office. Two hours. If she timed it right she would get home before Beck's arrival with enough time for a quick nap. Wishful thinking she thought as she hit I-93. It was stop and go traffic all the way home to Quincy thanks to lane restrictions due to road construction.

When she pushed the key into the front door of her house an hour and half later, she felt drained. Everywhere hurt. Her back and her neck. Even her eye started to twitch again.

With Beck coming over, she should remove the newspapers from the sofa, straighten up the small living room, and maybe run the vacuum over the area rug. That was as far as that fleeting thought went as she entered the house.

Kicking off her shoes, she struggled out of her jacket and headed for the bathroom. Shedding her clothes, she pushed back the shower curtain, turned on the shower and stepped into the tub. The hot spray felt so good. It soothed her aching muscles sending steam curling up to the ceiling.

Shutting off the water, she grabbed the towel, dried off and put on her robe then headed for the bedroom. She sat down on the bed, resting her head on the pillow and felt herself drifting off.

It was the vibration of her cell phone that pulled her from sleep. She jumped up and grabbed the phone. She cleared her throat. "Hello?"

"I've been knocking and ringing the doorbell for the last ten minutes. I think your next door neighbor is gearing up to call the police. She's standing at the window glaring at me."

"Beck?"

"Yes."

"Hold on."

Markie looked at the clock. It was after seven. Groaning, she raced out of the bedroom to open the door.

"Hi, I was about to…"

Beck lost his train of thought when Marklynn answered the door in a short black silk robe, tied at the waist. The robe stopped at mid calf showing off long shapely legs. Her hair fell in ringlets around her face. She looked soft, sleepy and sexy all rolled into one. And he stood there, like a kid with his first crush staring at her. He didn't think she was wearing anything underneath the way the thin fabric clung to her body outlining her tall slender frame leaving nothing to his imagination.

"I…ahh…I fell asleep."

She ran her hands through her hair then pulled the belt on the robe tighter around her waist. What he should do, is roll his tongue back up in his head and quit making her uncomfortable, he scolded himself.

"I can see that," he said staring at her. This was not one of his finer moments.

"Come in," she stepped back from the door. "You can put the food in the kitchen. Plates and glasses are in the cupboard above the sink. Utensils are in the drawer to the left of the stove." She started towards the bedroom. "Give me a minute to change."

"I brought chicken and pasta salad, mango cheese cake, a bottle of wine and …chocolate covered almonds," he said not wanting her to leave.

Marklynn stopped, turning around slowly at the bedroom door. "I don't think I like you and Jamie talking about me behind my back."

He smiled as his gaze traveled the length of her body then settled on her face and he felt warm all over.

"The only thing he told me was your food preference. He said anything else would have to come from you."

"Right."

She didn't believe him for a minute. She just shook her head and entered the bedroom closing the door.

By the time she'd emerged from the bedroom dressed in a pair of black leggings and a long white T-shirt, he had all the food laid out on the table and was leaning against the arch at the entrance to the kitchen door.

He missed the black robe.

At seven hundred and fifty square feet, the two-bedroom house was the perfect size for Markie. With Beck standing there it appeared tiny all of a sudden.

He'd shown up for their meeting that morning in a navy suit, white shirt and a navy tie. The jacket and tie were gone and the shirt unbuttoned, with the sleeves rolled up to his elbows showing off strong arms.

There was something about the way his gaze ran over her body that made her feel like she wanted to jump out of her skin. It also made her forget the pain in her body and her throbbing eye.

When she tried to pass him at the kitchen door, his body pressed hers against the doorframe and a slow lazy smile settled on his lips. He wanted to play and was looking for a playmate.

His lips touched hers. Gentle at first, as if he was testing to see what her reaction would be. Then he started out with a slow long kiss that made her legs turn to jelly and she returned with a kiss that told him without a doubt he'd found his playmate.

Her arms circled his waist, pulling him closer still. It has been a long time since she'd allowed anyone to get this close to her, to touch her this way and she didn't want him to stop.

She needed it. Needed him in ways she hadn't wanted anyone before. She came to the conclusion that she could get use to the warmth of his kiss and his caress.

Leaving the world behind and allowing him to set the pace, she was lost in a wave of passion she didn't want to end.

Nothing mattered but the feel of him and she wanted more. She pulled his shirt out of his pants, sliding her hands up his back under the shirt. His skin felt hot against her palms.

Nothing mattered but the taste of him and she opened her mouth accepting his tongue. His response was a groan of pure satisfaction as their tongues danced together. Then his stomach rumbled and she laughed against his lips pulling away.

"No," he groaned out capturing her lips again, but it was her stomach that interrupted this time. "Let's satisfy the food hunger first." He touched his forehead to hers.

His eyes settled on her lips and with one final kiss, he took her hand and led her to the table pulling out her chair.

"Everything looks good," Markie said, trying not to react to his blatant stare as she spooned the chicken and pasta salad onto her plate. She took up his plate. "What do you want?"

"You." His gaze was bold. Hot.

The enamel plate slipped from her hand and hit the table landing on the silverware. "Oh, you meant the food," he chuckled. "I can take what I want. Haven't eaten since breakfast."

She picked up the plate and handed it to him. He proceeded to fill it up with the chicken and pasta salad. Then he opened the napkin, placing it across his lap. She watched him put a fork full of chicken salad into his mouth and licked his lips.

"This is good. I can see why you like it."

His eyes settled on her mouth again as he picked up the wine bottle and she realized he was a lefty. And a sexy one too. Everything about the man was sexy. And the kiss? Lord have mercy…She was still reeling from that.

"Wine?"

"Not yet."

Markie looked down at the food she spooned on her plate. It wasn't the wine she wanted or the food. It was Beck and he knew it too. His leg brushed against hers under the table and he smiled. He did it on purpose. Not once but twice.

She felt like she was on fire…a wild fire burning out of control. Reaching for the pitcher of water, she poured herself a glass. She finished it and poured another, but it didn't put out the fire.

Sydney opened her eyes to a brown blur and realized she was face down on the floor. She couldn't remember how she'd gotten there. When she tried to get up a sharp pain shot through her right side. Blondie must have zapped her again. Her knuckles felt sore and she worked her fingers to ease the pain. Perhaps her fist did connect to Blondie's jaw after all before her lights went out.

She pushed herself up from the floor. That was when she saw the bottle of water under the cot. It must have rolled under during her scuffle with Blondie. She sat staring at the water, almost afraid to grab it. Wanting it yet thinking it was an illusion like her life.

As hard as she tried not to disappoint Nan and Markie it never seemed to work. She didn't set out to disappoint them. It just happened. Like when she used Nan's house as collateral against a loan. Nan said it was okay. When she couldn't pay back the loan the bank came for Nan's house. Markie stepped in and saved Nan's house. She and Markie had never gotten past that.

How did her life get so out of control? How did she end up so afraid and alone?

It started because she was an insomniac, had been since Derrick's death in Afghanistan. Don't think about Derrick.

Focus.

Think. She forced herself to remember how she ended up in a storage room struggling to reach a bottle of water under a smelly cot.

Her assignment was to photograph the interior of Macy Henning's newly decorated six-bedroom, three bathroom house for *Upscale Design Magazine*. It had a master bath the size of Sydney's entire apartment. The designer – Anika Taylor, interior designer to the stars.

It was coming back to her now. She thought it would be better to photograph the house while Macy was on vacation. Macy was not only the homeowner, but also Derrick's sister.

Arriving mid-afternoon that day…Friday, Sydney had taken most of the pictures required. When she'd lost the natural lighting needed, she'd decided to spend the night at Macy's and finish up in the morning.

That night she couldn't sleep and decided to explore the historic neighborhood of Jamaica Plains.

Derrick said she was good at photography and she loved him for saying it. It gave her the encouragement she needed. After he said that, she never went anywhere without her camera and that included strolling down a quiet tree-lined street.

Sydney wasn't sure what was going on, but when she'd seen the two men loading what looked like paintings in the Beck Security Systems van she knew something didn't feel right. The more pictures she took, the more the idea formed in her mind that she could make a career out of taking pictures and everyone would be proud of her, even Markie. Markie wouldn't have to bail her out anymore.

Sydney didn't think anyone had seen her behind the oak tree just four doors down from Macy's house. When she'd taken enough pictures she ran back to Macy's house, grabbed her car and hightailed it home. She'd downloaded the pictures from her camera to her computer that night printed a set and hid them. The following day she called Markie.

In retrospect, calling Beck about the pictures as well wasn't a smart move. She didn't even think he would be in the office on a Saturday and was surprised when he'd picked up his line. The day after she'd called him she was picked up by Blondie and her thugs. That would put her abduction on Sunday.

The throbbing in her head was getting worse. Then she remembered she'd banged her head when she hit the floor.

Water. She reached under the cot and for the bottle of water, opened the bottle and drank too quickly causing her to choke.

She put the lid back on the water bottle leaving some for later and pushed herself up off the floor. With some effort she took her time and flipped the mattress on the cot before sitting down. At least the other side of the mattress didn't smell as revolting.

Closing her eyes, she lay on her left side with her hands under her jaw, pulling her knees up to her chest, willing herself to keep calm.

Markie would find her just like she found the pictures.

CHAPTER SEVEN

The kitchen was full of raw sexual energy. Beck made sure Markie knew what he was thinking and what he wanted when the meal was over as he watched her while she ate. Markie didn't think she could deny him what he wanted. She wanted the same thing.

The corner of his mouth turned up into a seductive smile and she remembered the kiss they'd shared. How his mouth felt against hers…how his hand felt against her skin and she pulled on the neck of her T-shirt.

All she could think about was her dream. The clear blue water…the hot sun…the way he smelled… a spicy woody scent.

He put his fork down and asked out of the blue. "Ever been married?"

She half laughed. "Where did that come from?"

He shrugged. "Just curious. You're beautiful, smart and very talented. Beautiful."

"You said beautiful already."

"I know. It's worth repeating. Even the black eye looks sexy."

"I think you're good for my ego."

"I was hoping to be more than just good for your ego, sweetheart."

"That's not a bad place to start."

She didn't want to talk about marriage and wanted to keep the mood light between them.

"I'm all for stroking the ego among other things," he said with a smile taking flirting one step further. Are you going to answer my question or side step it all together?"

Beck was persistent. He wanted an answer and wasn't going to be happy until he got one. She wasn't prepared to give him one.

"Is marriage all it's cracked up to be? You were married and it ended in a bitter divorce."

Beck poured wine in his glass before he answered. "We both started out wanting the same things and then we didn't."

He became serious. Like a shift of the wind his playful mood changed and he had a faraway look in his eyes. It made her wonder if he still carried a torch for his dead wife.

"That simple." Her gaze narrowed on his face. "You've summed up the dissolution of your marriage into one sentence."

"There was nothing simple about it. It tore me apart. I had to put it into perspective to move on. I thought I'd found the woman I wanted to spend the rest of my life with, to share my dreams. In the end, we didn't want the same things. Then when I got into the car accident, I emerged less than perfect and I think my shortcomings were too much for her to handle."

"What do you mean?"

Beck sipped his wine then placed the glass back on the table. "I was damaged goods." He pointed to the scars at the base his neck. "It goes to about mid waist."

He avoided her glance, staring at the red liquid in the glass. It was clear he wasn't as comfortable with his scars as he appeared to be. At the meeting that morning he'd said after his divorce he was broke. Monika had taken a lot more from him than just his money.

"That's my story. What about you? Ever been asked to take the plunge?"

The marriage question again and she couldn't side step the question. Not after what he had just shared with her.

"I've never been married, but I've been asked." Markie

didn't want to talk about her relationship with Jared and changed the subject. "What did the company lawyer have to say this afternoon?"

She picked up her half empty plate and got up to go to the sink. He caught her hand and took the plate from her setting it back on the table. His thumb began stoking the back of her hand and she sat down again pulling her hand away.

"No running away, sweetheart. I told you about my divorce. It's your turn to share. Why didn't you say yes?" His eyes held hers and a smile played at his lips.

"I said yes. But he decided I wasn't what he wanted anymore."

"Why?" His smile disappeared.

Markie didn't respond. She didn't want to talk about it. Why did he have to pry?

"Why?" He asked again reaching across the table lacing his fingers through hers. "Why did he change his mind?"

"Damaged goods."

"I don't understand?" Sheer confusion settled on his face and she knew she had to explain.

"Most men have aspirations as far as children are concerned." She pulled her hands away. "They want a son to carry on the family name or maybe a little girl to walk down the aisle one day. Since I was told I couldn't have any, it was a moot point." She raised her wine glass. "I think I'll have that wine after all. Then you can tell me about your meeting."

"Whoa. You can't say something like that and change the subject."

"Why not?"

Beck made no move to fill her wine glass. He sat there staring at her. Was it pity or shock? She couldn't tell and didn't want to know.

Her hand shook as she picked up the bottle of wine. She thought she'd gotten over the hurt Jared had caused when he'd told her he couldn't go through with the wedding but she was wrong.

The invitations were sent, the church was booked, the caterer was hired and a month before the wedding the groom-to-be couldn't go through with it. He could live with anything else…the deal breaker was children. He wanted his own and she couldn't have any.

The odds they'd given her on getting pregnant were not worth dwelling on. What were the words the doctor had used? *More than likely*. More than likely she would not conceive.

Jared didn't like the odds. What he wanted was assurance not 'more than likely' and that she couldn't give him.

Markie had decided not to open herself up to that hurt again, but had taken the chance and told the man who had made her want to think about marriage again. The look in his eyes was the same one Jared had.

Pity. It had to be.

She couldn't stand it and pushed him away before she got pushed away. What was she thinking?

They were together to have a business meeting and nothing more she told herself pushing the kiss they'd just shared out of her mind. He was a client. The number one rule you don't break in business – Never get involved with a client and she was beyond involved.

"The purpose of the dinner is for you to fill me in on your meeting earlier and also discuss how Jamie can assist you."

"Marklynn?"

She didn't want him to feel sorry for her. She couldn't take it and pushed him further away.

"May I remind you that the reason we're together is to find my sister and —"

"This isn't about Sydney or Beck Security Systems. It's about you."

"It's all about Sydney and what happened to her and *your* connection to her disappearance."

The accusation that he might have something to do with Sydney's disappearance had reared its ugly head once again. It was her anger talking and she said the one thing she knew would hurt him.

"Just to be clear," his eyes burned with anger. "What's happening between us means nothing because it's all about finding Sydney."

"Yes." She lied. Lying was easier than facing the truth. Lying was easier because she could keep him at arms length.

"Have you given any thought as to why Sydney took those pictures in the first place, given her history? Yes, I know about her colorful background."

Marklynn had given a lot of thought as to why Sydney took the pictures. She didn't like the conclusion she arrived at. She didn't want to believe her sister was capable of blackmail or involved with what was going on at Beck's company. There had to be another explanation. Yet, she couldn't come up with one given Sydney's past.

"God forbid if you should care about anyone else but Sydney."

Beck threw his napkin down on the table and got up. She turned away from his probing gaze. The concern that was reflected in his intense dark eyes turned to anger. Anger she could deal with, not pity.

"I have to focus on finding her."

"She calls, you jump. Is that it?"

"My sister is missing! She's my responsibility." Her parents said so and Nan said so she wanted to shout at him.

"Twenty-four hours ago a pick up truck just about ran you over." He frowned. "Finding her doesn't have to be your responsibility alone. You've an office full of investigators. Let them help you. Jamie could've handled the meeting this morning. God," he raked his hand through his hair, "you could've been killed last night!"

"I can take care of myself." First Nan, then Jamie now Beck…all of a sudden everyone was jumping on the "you're not alone train." She could take care of herself and had been doing it far too long to depend on anyone now, let alone Beck.

"Look at you…if you're not careful you'll fall flat on

your face."

"I don't intend to fall flat on my face. I can do what needs to get done which is to find Sydney."

Not liking the way he was glaring down at her, she got up from the table and left the kitchen. He followed behind her when she entered the living room and moved over to the window, her back to him.

"Sydney is a big girl and I'm sure she can take care of herself *if* given the chance."

"What is that supposed to mean?" She whirled around feeling a sharp pain in her back. Her eye throbbed.

"Sydney is not a child and her problems are not yours to shoulder. Help her, yes, but trying to fix her problems or her is not your job. She calls and you get shot at and—"

"You sound like Jamie. I'm not having this conversation with you."

He went on without even acknowledging the fact that she'd spoken. "If you allow Sydney to take responsibility for her life, then you would be free to live yours. Or maybe you're afraid." Dark eyes locked with hers.

"My relationship with my sister is none of your business, Beck."

"Maybe you need to —"

"I think you should leave."

She didn't think he was going anywhere until he turned on his heel and headed for the front door.

"Get some rest," he said closing the door quietly behind him.

Appetite gone, Markie returned to the kitchen and dumped the food in the garbage. Then she crawled into bed. Her conversation with Beck had taken center stage in her mind.

Was it possible that Beck was right about Sydney? He couldn't be. She wasn't responsible for Sydney's behavior. The phone rang and she hesitated before she reached over to the night table to pick it up.

"Hello?"

"Hey it's Jamie. Good news. I got into Syd's email. I

pulled off a couple I think you should have a look at."

"Okay."

"Are you alright, Markie?"

"Yes. Why?"

"You sound funny."

"I'm fine."

"No you're not. What's wrong?" Alarm registered in his voice.

"Beck and I just had an argument" she said after a while because Jamie would needle her until he got it out of her.

"What was the argument about?"

"Does it really matter?" She didn't want to get into it with him. A tear slid down her cheek and she wiped it away with her shoulder.

"Yes, if it's about Sydney."

"Between the two of you, you would think I'm obsessed with Sydney," she snapped. "She's missing and could be hurt. I didn't ask for this."

"I know."

"No you don't know. What you need to understand is that she's my responsibility and I have to find her."

"Markie, I—"

"Good night, Jamie."

Beck sped along the 1-93 North towards Boston. He had a plan when he left his office earlier and it didn't involve him leaving Marklynn's house until morning. He wanted a quiet evening. Ah hell, who was he kidding he wanted more than that. He had a seduction scene laid out in his mind.

Everything should have been perfect. Nothing was left to chance. He'd called Jamie to find out what food Marklynn liked to surprise her. The chocolate covered almonds were at the top of the list. Even the wine was carefully selected.

The evening started out promising. The kiss was incredible, intense. It had been a long time since he felt such passion for someone. And what did he do? Messed it up.

Rule number one: Never talk about your ex, dead or

alive, in a conversation when you're trying to impress. The evening moved from seductive to serious in a flash and he had no one to blame but himself.

Marklynn couldn't have children. He had to let himself digest that information. Once that conversation started the mood changed. She had changed and wouldn't discuss it. Beck wanted to talk about it, but she had shut down the topic before it got off the ground. By her reaction, he knew that topic was off limits. Period.

Damaged goods.

Beck had thrown the term out in conversation in reference to himself. When Marklynn latched on to it to describe how she felt about not being able to have children he didn't like the term anymore.

They were both wounded from past relationships. Would they be able to see their way clear to trust each other? He wanted to.

He had always wanted a large family being an only child. Would he be willing to give up children to be with Marklynn? There were options available to childless couples. It was a discussion he was willing to have, but he wasn't sure about Marklynn. Then again it was a little premature to entertain that kind of thought since he wasn't sure whether or not she would want to have anything to do with him again other than a business relationship.

A part of him had died when his marriage ended to Monika. To him it signified failure and he never thought he would meet anyone again that would make him feel alive, until Marklynn.

Marklynn had not only made him feel alive…she made him want things he hadn't thought about in a long time. It wasn't about sex, but that would be incredible if their kiss was anything to go by. He wanted more, a relationship.

Marriage.

Marriage? Whoa. He hadn't thought about marriage since Monika. Then his hand went to his chest absently stroking the scars beneath the shirt. How would Marklynn react when she saw him without his shirt? Would she even consider marriage to him? He was more damaged than her in more ways than one. There had been other women since his divorce but he was always careful, hiding behind the cloak of darkness.

Beck thought about Sydney and could've kicked himself. When the topic of conversation shifted to Sydney, he didn't want to talk about her. That was the last thing he wanted to talk about.

What did he do? Throw a tantrum like a child that had his toy taken away and picked on the very subject he knew was a sore spot for her, her relationship with Sydney. She had every right to throw him out of her house.

His cell phone rang. He reached across to the passenger seat and grabbed it. "Beck."

"It's Detective Samuel O'Malley returning your call."

Beck had forgotten he had called the man after Marklynn had shown up in his office with the pictures.

"Thanks for calling me back."

Heavy bass played in the background as O'Malley yelled into phone. "I was surprised to hear from you."

Beck had to pull the phone away from his ear. "I need to see you. It's important." He hit the breaks when a car cut in front of him and he laid on the horn.

"I've had one helleva a day and—"

"It's about Monika Beck."

After a long pause O'Malley said, "I'm at an Irish Pub off Union Street. "If you show up before the band starts the second set at 10:00 p.m. we don't have to yell at each other."

"I'm just getting into Boston. I should be there in about fifteen minutes," Beck said and tossed the phone back on the passenger seat.

Beck made the drive in ten minutes and found parking on the street. When he got to the door of the pub, he turned pointing the keypad towards the Navigator locking the doors, setting the alarm.

He opened the door and paused at the entrance searching for O'Malley. A thin layer of smoke from the open kitchen hovered around the ceiling at the back of the pub.

Wood and lots of it seemed to be the decorator's choice. From the tables to the chairs and booths against the wall, everything was crafted out of rich mahogany and it made the pub appear dark. Not even the cone shaped lighting that hung above the tables could brighten up the place.

The Tuesday night crowd ranged in age from the thirty something's to the fifty plus. The thirty something's huddled around the bar in groups talking and laughing. Others leaned against the wall with beers in hand.

"Beck, over here," O'Malley yelled waving at him.

Beck made his way over to the booth and narrowly missed the waitress, a brunette with an attitude, almost spilling her tray of drinks.

"Sorry." He apologized to the palm of her tattooed hand when she held it up to his face and kept on walking.

O'Malley hadn't changed Beck thought as he slid into the raised booth. He had to be about mid or late thirties. With black wavy hair cut close to his temples, he was still the same clean-cut-neat-suit-and-tie-wearing man who'd showed up at his door to tell him about Monika's death.

Beck had thought he was Irish when he'd first heard the man's name. With no accent to go with the name, he assumed the man was Caucasian. He wasn't expecting a dark-skinned man whose father was from Trinidad and his mother from Ireland. A rare combination, O'Malley had called himself during one of their conversations.

"Beer?" O'Malley asked and lifted his hand to call the waiter, a punk rocker with a bull ring through the cartilage dividing his nostrils.

"What can I get for you guys?"

"I'll have whatever is on tap," Beck said trying not to stare at the waiter.

"Make that two," O'Malley told the waiter and he disappeared into the thick of the crowd towards the bar leaving O'Malley shaking his head. "Kids today. I thought only cows had rings through the nose."

Beck smiled.

"The suspense is killing me." O'Malley grabbed a handful of peanuts from a bowl on the table and tossed them into his mouth then dusted the salt from his hands. "What's this about your late ex-wife?"

Beck pulled the picture from his jacket pocket, laid it on the table and pushed it towards O'Malley. He picked up the picture squinting at it while working his mouth then brought the picture closer to the light above the table.

"You think it's Monika," O'Malley stated. Another handful of nuts went into his mouth. "Though, you can't really be sure with her face in the shadows. Where did you get this?"

"You never believed Monika died in that boating accident. Why?"

The ink hadn't dried on the divorce papers before the boating accident had happened.

Monika had felt she was entitled to everything. To some degree maybe she was. He didn't have a nine-to-five job. The company had taken up all of his time and a lot of things were put on hold. He didn't want to start a family until they were financially ready because he wanted to give his kids all the things he didn't have growing up. She didn't understand that because she grew up with money.

When he'd achieved the success he was striving for with the company their marriage had fallen apart. She had wanted him to sell Beck Security Systems, but after months of bitter negotiations she'd accepted a cash buy out of her share. Their boat, a twenty-eight foot cruiser and the four-bedroom colonial was also a part of the deal she received.

"Here you go, two beers," the waiter said placing the drinks on the table pulling him back to the present. "Anything else I can get you?"

Beck shook his head. "Nothing for me. Thanks."

"I'm good." O'Malley waited until the waiter left then took a long drink of his beer before he spoke. "Monika's death was too neat. Nothing was found. According to her dentist, she had extensive dental work done the previous year. If she was on board when the explosion occurred we should have found something to match up with her dental records."

"You said yourself she was seen getting on board," Beck said wanting to believe even though the evidence wasn't supporting the facts.

"People lie." O'Malley paused for a moment, twisting his mouth. "There was something I never told you since you'd made it clear back then you didn't want to lay eyes on me again."

"You thought I killed her."

"Until your alibi checked out," O'Malley said simply.

O'Malley didn't apologize back then and Beck knew he wasn't about to get an apology now. Because of the divorce settlement, O'Malley felt Beck had something to do with the explosion and set out to prove it. O'Malley was wrong, but according to him he was just doing his job.

O'Malley looked at the picture again. "I take it you no longer believe she's dead."

"With the picture I don't know."

The band started up. Heavy bass from the electric guitar filled the air drowning out their conversation. There was a stampede to the dance floor and O'Malley shook his head jerking his thumb towards the door.

"Not quite the sounds of Ireland."

"It draws the younger crowd," O'Malley said.

"I got it," Beck said when O'Malley reached for his wallet to pay the bill.

After Beck paid the tab, they maneuvered their way through the crowd on the dance floor towards the door. They stepped out onto the sidewalk and were greeted by a warm gentle breeze and a clear sky. Even with the pub door closed, they could still hear the beat of the music outside.

"There's something you should know," O'Malley said fishing through his pocket and pulled out his car keys. "I got a voicemail from Marklynn Brooks right after you called. She was a cop, now a P.I. I think."

Beck followed O'Malley as he walked towards a black vinyl top red corvette parked at the curb. If he had to guess would say a '72.

"Nice."

"It's a hobby," O'Malley shrugged. "I've a lot more work to do both on the inside and out."

"Did you call back Marklynn?" Beck asked still looking at the car. The driver side door had rusted along the trim. The car distraction bit didn't fool O'Malley. Trying to downplay the fact that Marklynn wasn't important didn't wash. The man saw right through him.

"By the look on your face, I take it you know her."

"Yes." Beck didn't want to elaborate.

"I didn't call her back, yet. I wanted to talk to you first. She said something about a picture she wanted to show me." O'Malley glanced at Beck when he stopped beside the car and opened the door. "The picture she wants to show me, I'm assuming, it's the same picture you gave me."

"Yes. I think her sister, Sydney took the picture and now she's missing."

"And you both believe there is a connection."

"Yes."

Beck heard a low whistle from O'Malley.

"Brooks is probably trying to track the sister down on her own. She has the manpower for it. Well, I can't blame her. What she went through when she filed the lawsuit against the department. Most of the guys treated her like she had the plague or something."

"You didn't," Beck guessed. From what he could remember of the man, he was tough but fair.

"She was a good cop. Sometimes things just happen," O'Malley said and Beck thought he detected a note of regret in the man's voice, but he wasn't sure for what.

"What was the suit about?"

"You'll have to ask her that yourself. From what I remember some hotshot investigative reporter named Michael Blake did a story about her fight that nearly brought down the department. Heard she walked away with a truck load of money."

"Maybe she deserved it."

"Maybe." All of a sudden O'Malley turned his head towards the parked cars that lined the street.

Beck followed his gaze. "Something wrong?"

"Nah. Look, I can't officially reopen the investigation again on Monika Beck. The picture is not enough to go by." After Beck filled him in on what was going on at Beck Security Systems O'Malley said, "Okay, there is enough to pique my curiosity. I'm not making any promises. Let me look into it and get back to you."

"That's all I ask."

"What about Marklynn Brooks?"

"Leave her to me."

"Whatever you say."

O'Malley's gaze slowly swept the parked cars that lined the street once again as if he was looking for something.

"What's wrong?" Beck asked following O'Malley's wandering gaze. "Don't give me that nothing answer."

"We're being watched."

Phoenix ducked down into the seat of her white Volvo when Sam O'Malley's gaze swept up and down the street. She knew she couldn't be seen, but didn't want to take the chance. It didn't matter that she was parked in the shadows between the two light posts. She had to be careful.

It was only a matter of time before Sam O'Malley was contacted. She thought for sure it would have been Markie she would see with Sam, not Beck parking outside the pub an hour ago.

A hunch. She played it and it paid off. Since she didn't know for sure if she was in any of the pictures Sydney had taken, she'd err on the side of caution and assumed she could be recognized.

It would have been nice to see the pictures. Malcolm said Beck had a set Markie had given him. Asking Malcolm to show the pictures to her would throw suspicion in her direction. She had already tipped her hand when she'd expressed her jealousy over Markie.

It didn't matter that Malcolm had said Beck didn't recognize anyone in the picture. Beck must have suspected something or he wouldn't have connected with O'Malley.

With Markie and Beck meeting already, she figured she would track down O'Malley just in case. He seemed to like the Irish Pub. Why was beyond her. The place was a dump. One beer was his limit and he drank alone.

Phoenix had assumed the next meeting would've been between Markie and O'Malley. Beck was the surprise. She hadn't expected to see him. It shouldn't have been a surprise to her. Beck was smart. He always seemed to land on his feet. Look what he'd accomplished after the divorce. His company was a success, not to mention the penthouse condo where he lived. That should have been her address, not his.

Well she would take it all away from him just like he'd taken everything from her.

Phoenix watched as Beck and Sam shook hands and parted company. They were getting too close.

Marklynn woke up the following morning a force to be reckoned with. Mad at the world would be an accurate description. Beck was a part of the world and he was at the top of the list.

"How dare he tell me I'm afraid to live my life?" She mumbled in front of the bathroom mirror while curling her hair. After she finished, she combed her fingers through the curls allowing her hair to fall just below her ears.

Her eye didn't hurt as bad as the day before, but it didn't look all that great either. The black coloring around the eye had turned a nice shade of purple and once again she stayed away from makeup. Staring at her reflection in the mirror, she applied a plum shade of lipstick and then dropped the tube in her purse.

She didn't feel like dressing up today. With no scheduled meetings for the day, her choice of attire was the Brooks Investigations white shirt, a pair of jeans and the red stiletto boots. Sydney's boots. They were the only footwear in her closet that fit. When she'd taken them from her sister's closet after the break-in, it was only to wear home. She hadn't intended on wearing them again. Yet, she reached for them and pulled them on.

They were not only different in personality, but in fashion style as well. Where Markie was conservative, Sydney was all about the latest trends and hot colors. The red stiletto boots was not something Markie would purchase. It wasn't practical. Yet, when she looked down at her feet, she didn't mind them. They made her feel close to her sister quashing the dreaded fear pooling in her stomach that she may never see Sydney again.

She had never shared anything with Sydney. They never had that typical sister relationship. Perhaps that would change once they were reunited. She would make more of an effort.

Today she would focus on Sydney. Jamie had said he'd found a couple of emails he wanted her to have a look at.

Forget Beck she told herself as she left the house, but it was kind of hard since she had dreamt about him last night again. They were on the beach. She'd jumped up out of her sleep drenched in sweat. After she'd showered and changed, she laid awake for the better part of the night thinking about Beck and the fight they had. Thinking about the kiss they had shared. Wanting…

"Wanting what?"

She wasn't going to answer that question. Not today she told herself as she headed out the door.

Marklynn arrived at the office just after eight, told Cate she didn't want to be disturbed unless it was an emergency, and closed her door.

The only thing she couldn't lock out of her mind was Beck and that stupid dream. She couldn't forget about her conversation with him. Sydney was missing and yet he made her feel as though she was responsible for Sydney's behavior.

Well, she didn't ask to be her sister's keeper. Her mother had decided that Sydney couldn't take care of herself on her deathbed and made Markie promise she would. Nan had also told her it was her job to look after Sydney.

Markie leaned back in her chair remembering the fight they'd had after Nan's stroke.

"I'm going away for a few days," Sydney said looking at Markie over the rim of her mug while she drank her coffee. Since she arrived at Nan's that morning, she hadn't said much but paced the floor so Markie knew it was coming.

Sydney had only been home a week. Nan was released from the hospital two days ago after suffering a mild heart attack and she was leaving, again.

Yes Nan was fine, but Markie was afraid. She couldn't lose Nan. It was obvious Sydney didn't care. Her place was at home with her family not jet setting around the world doing God knows what.

Turning off the tap, Markie yanked a sheet of paper towel from the fixture mounted to the wall and the silver holder crashed on the counter. Sydney jumped.

"Nan just got out of the hospital," Markie said glaring at her sister. "She needs you here."

"Nan doesn't need me. She has you. You've moved in," Sydney said looking at the blanket and pillows on the pullout sofa bed. "The place is clean and her refrigerator is stocked. You take care of her better than I ever could. You don't need me here either."

"This is not a competition, Sydney. Beside, I can't do it all by myself.

"Really? You're doing just fine by yourself."

Sydney emptied the coffee in the sink and rinsed the cup before turning it down in the dish drainer. Grabbing her purse from the counter, she headed towards the door.

"What do you mean by that?"

Sydney turned around, biting her bottom lip. "Nothing."

"No. If you've something to say, say it. Don't go crying to Nan. She needs her rest."

"I guess we can't all be the pillar of strength you are."

"As usual, I've no idea what you're talking about." Markie focused on trying to mount the paper towel fixture back on the wall.

"Nan told me about your settlement regarding your sexual

harassment suit. I didn't even know you were unhappy at work. She said you quit your job."

Markie paused for a brief moment to glance at Sydney then back to her task. She would need a screwdriver to mount back the fixture and Nan didn't have one.

"I can't talk about it. Besides, there's nothing to tell."

"Just like there is nothing to tell about Jared," Sydney said. "I heard the wedding is off."

She put down the paper holder. Nan would be up soon from her rest and she needed to prepare her lunch, not talk about Jared.

"That's what I thought."

"You can think what you like. You're never around anyway. You breeze in to say hello and you're gone. We're not a family just a pit stop for you when you need something."

"Why should I hang around? You're just fine on your own. I don't know why I came home."

"You came because of Nan, remember?"

"Nan is fine and you're fine. I don't see the need to be here." Sydney slammed the door and left.

"Sydney!"

CHAPTER EIGHT

"Markie? You okay?"

The voice pulled her back to the present away from the painful memory. She opened her eyes and saw a very polished Jamie standing at the door in a suit and tie. Did he own a suit? She never thought so. Brooks Investigations promotional gear was all he ever wore.

His hair was cut low making the Mohawk almost non-existent. Who knew? And the beard was also trimmed and lined.

"I'm...aah fine," she said looking at him with raised brows from his head to his polished-shine shoes. She had to rub her eyes to ensure she was indeed seeing clearly. He was also wearing dress shoes, not the black boots laced up to mid-calf.

"Yeah, I know I clean up nicely," he grunted. "Go ahead and get it out of your system. Cate just took a picture with her phone. She said I should get out of the office more instead of hiding behind a computer all day."

As much as she wanted to tease him about his attire she couldn't muster up the energy. The memory of the fight with Sydney was too fresh in her mind, and that was one of many over the years. She and Sydney weren't sisters. They were strangers.

Jamie entered her office with a copy of the two emails in hand he'd retrieved from Syd's computer. One was from Macy Henning confirming an appointment for a photo shoot with Syd and the other from the editor of an interior design magazine. He had said he would drop them off before heading to Beck's office.

She should apologize for snapping at him last night after that disaster with Beck. The truth was she didn't want to bring it up. And if she didn't bring it up then he wouldn't. Solution – leave it alone.

"Thanks." Markie took the emails from him glancing at two sheets of paper. "Have you gotten in touch with Macy or the editor?"

"Macy is on vacation, as you can see in her email to Sydney. Her assistant said she'll be back tomorrow morning and has scheduled a meeting for us to meet with Macy then. As for the magazine, Cate called the editor. He's out of country returning tomorrow as well. She left a message for him to call us."

"Is there someone else at the magazine who can talk to us today?" Markie asked annoyed. That feeling of helplessness was starting to get to her. She was tired of waiting and wanted to do something. Anything.

"No one at the magazine wants to talk to us and there is no point in wasting our time by forcing our way in. The email came from the editor. We'll talk to him together. Okay?"

There was an underlying edge to Jamie's voice that he tampered with a gentleness that he didn't often show. He was being what she wanted right now…a friend.

"You're right. I'm sorry."

Jamie sat back in the chair studying her, elbows resting on the chair arm, his fingers steepled together, ready to spout some words of wisdom she didn't want to here.

"Just had a telephone conversation with Beck." He watched her as he spoke as if waiting for a reaction. When he didn't get one, he said, "I'm heading over this afternoon to meet with him and his team."

"Good," she said shifting her eyes to her laptop. When the mail icon popped up, she opened the new mail. It was from Cate wanting to schedule a lunch meeting with a potential client. New business.

"He asked if you were in today. Said he has been trying to reach you."

Until she found Sydney her schedule was put on hold. "I've been busy."

"Busy brooding."

She shot him a look that told him if he valued his life he should back off. He ignored the warning. Typical Jamie style. He would say what he had to say and then shut up. She didn't want to hear what was on his mind because most of the time he was right.

"I've never seen you this worked up about someone in a long time. Not since that idiot, Jared. Mind you I'm not sure what happened with him and I don't really care."

"Is there a point to this?" She looked up from the computer, eyes blazing.

"Yes. My point is I think Beck is good for you, Markie. Okay, okay you don't have to give me the death stare."

"Thanks for the emails. Is there anything else?"

"I'm going." Jamie pushed himself up from the chair. "Beck wants you to call him," he said, on his way out the door grinning.

Markie pushed Beck and Jamie to the back of her mind and went to work trying to find out all she could about the magazine Sydney was on assignment for and Macy Henning, the journalist.

In the email from the editor there were specific instructions about a photo shoot. Sydney was taking pictures of Macy's house? That had to be a mistake. She had to reread the email again to ensure she hadn't misinterpreted the content. But there it was in black and white.

As far as she knew, Sydney didn't have a job. She lived for the next get-rich-quick scheme. What else was she hiding? Markie reached for the box she'd taken from her sister's apartment and removed the lid.

By the time Markie had finally lifted her head out of the box, it was well past eight that evening. This was the second time she'd gone through the box, and like the first time, she found nothing, only more unanswered questions.

And if she thought working straight through the day would help her frame of mind, she was wrong. Coming up empty handed further soured her mood.

She was still upset, but it wasn't with Beck. It was with herself. Her thoughts were all muddled. The fear that Sydney was hurt haunted her. Losing her parents was bad enough. She couldn't live with the thought of not having Sydney at all in her life even if it was only once a month. Beck needed to understand that. She didn't know why but he just did.

Markie was packing up her desk when Carlos passed by her office and stopped to pop his head in. Picking up the gun off her desk, she placed it in her hand bag.

"Heading out?" he asked looking at her brief case.

"Yes." She figured Jamie put him up to it.

"I'll walk you out."

She was going to say no but why not. If someone was watching her and decided to attack, she would gladly unleash Carlos on them even if his bark was bigger than his bite.

"Thanks. Give me a minute."

She said her goodbye to Carlos in the parking lot a few minutes later and instead of driving home she found herself in Back Bay. Beck's neighborhood. It was ritzy and upscale. Newbury Street to be exact.

Jamie had included Beck's address in the file he'd prepared for her and she'd committed it to memory. Who knew she would be driving past his high-rise condo complex, making a u-turn and parking across the street from the glass tower?

What she was doing in front of Beck's condo she wasn't entirely sure.

Beck stood leaning against the balcony railing staring across the city. He'd called Marklynn at least six times throughout the day. All his calls went to her voice mail and not one was returned. At one point, he'd connected to Cate and was told Marklynn was unavailable.

"She was just being stubborn," he muttered to himself.

It was hard keeping his mind on work as the day went on. Once he'd met with Jamie and introduced him to his team it was all work until he'd left the office an hour ago. He thought about his conversation with O'Malley about being watched. He wanted to know she was being careful, to tell her to be careful.

The first thing he did when he stepped in the door was to check his voice mail but she hadn't called. He thought he would give her more time. So, he'd showered, then grabbed a beer from the fridge and headed out onto the balcony to wait.

Picking up the cordless from the patio table, he decided to call her again. Sitting around waiting for things to happen was not in his character. He was all about being proactive. If he wanted something he went after it. And he wanted Marklynn.

She should be on her way home. If he didn't get her, he would go to her house. His cell phone rang and he grabbed it.

"Dalton Beck."

"You're a jerk."

He smiled in relief not caring that she was still mad at him. The only thing that mattered was that she'd called.

"I know and I'm sorry."

Silence.

"I'd a perfect evening planned yesterday," Beck explained as he sat down on the lounge chair propping his feet up on the railing. "I wanted to make love to you. The evening didn't go as planned and I turned on you. I'm sorry about what I said. It wasn't my place to judge you."

Silence stretched on…one…two…three minutes. He waited.

"You don't understand about Sydney." Her was voice heavy with sadness.

"No I don't. Tell me about her."

Beck heard the wailing siren and the horn of a fire truck over the phone and stood up looking over the balcony. He saw the flashing red lights of the truck as it raced passed the building.

"Marklynn, where are you?" he asked as he entered the condo.

Silence.

"Jamie said you've a lead on Sydney through a couple of emails he found." He grabbed the security card for the underground parking lot and exited the condo wanting to see if his instinct was correct.

He reached the elevator and jabbed at the button and kept at it until the door opened. The elevator had only taken a few minutes to arrive on the floor, but it was too long for him.

"Yes," she said after a while. "We won't know until tomorrow if they'll pan out."

More silence.

"That's positive."

When the elevator hit the ground floor, Beck sprinted past Ray, the security guard in the lobby. His nose was buried in the paper and he lowered the paper raising his large frame out of the chair from behind the security desk to see where Beck was headed.

Beck saw Marklynn's SUV as he approached the front door and exited the building. He jogged across the street and she turned towards him just as he reached the driver's side then dropped the phone in his pocket.

"You're supposed to be up in your *Trump Tower*," she said when he opened the door.

"Move over."

"Why?" She had a stubborn look on her face.

"You're not going anywhere tonight. Not until we talk."

"I don't want to talk."

"Then you'll listen."

She picked up her handbag off the passenger seat and dropped it on the floor then slid over the gearshift into the passenger seat. He jumped into the driver's seat. Turning into the driveway of the building, he proceeded to the underground parking lot.

After he parked, he came around to the passenger side to open the door for her and held out his hand. She stared at his hand before taking it and they walked in silence from the underground parking garage to the elevators.

Inside the elevator, she leaned against him, her head rested against his shoulder. Beck slid his arm around her waist pulling her close. She was tired. He could feel it in the way she clung to him.

"It's going to be okay. We'll find her." He kissed the top of her head. "I promise."

She looked up at him and he saw doubt in her eyes. Whether it was from the promise he'd just made he wasn't sure, but he didn't want her second-guessing her decision about coming to see him.

Tonight he wanted her to lean on him forgetting about the outside world if only for a few hours.

"Did I ever tell you how sexy you look with that black eye," he said kissing her eye.

"You got a fetish for black eyes?"

"Sweetheart, since meeting you I've got all kinds of fetishes I never knew I had."

"What…"

"Shhh." He pressed his forefinger against her lips. "Tonight, I want to take care of you."

Somewhere between exiting the elevator and Beck's front door Markie had decided to let him take care of her. No sooner had he closed the front door, her shirt came off and she stood there in her lacey white bra and jeans under his hot gaze. He had a way of looking at her that made her feel like he wanted to devour her and she had to admit it turned her on.

"I always wondered what that bra looked like. Pretty," he said with a kiss. A long drugging, slow kiss that made her legs weak and her head spin. "Is it the same one you were wearing that day we met at Sydney's?"

"Mmm…" She blinked looking at him. Not sure what

he was talking about but it seemed important.

"That day I met you at Sydney's apartment, you were wearing a white blouse with pearl buttons. The top button came undone and I saw the lace of your white bra." He fingered the bra gently pulling at the strap.

"You were looking at my bra. I knew it. You know there are names for men like you."

"Yeah," he smiled, a smile borrowed from the devil himself. Another kiss followed then he picked her up as if she was a featherweight, carried her to the bedroom and sat her on the edge of the bed. He outlined the edge of the bra cup with his forefinger. "It's sexy. You're sexy."

Her eyes wandered around the large room that contained a king size bed. The bedding was black and white and was complimented by the soft gray walls. No other furniture existed except for two nightstands that matched the bed frame and a treadmill by the floor to ceiling window that wrapped half way around the room.

Feeling as though she was floating above the clouds, her eyes settled back on his face, his strong gentle face. She laid back on the bed and he pulled off her boots. They landed with a thud on the floor. Her jeans and bra followed.

The seduction began with his hands, and whatever his hands did, was mimicked by his lips. His forefinger traced the outline of her lips, moving to her chin down to her neck. Then his lips repeated the sensual movement and she shivered with each butterfly kiss. Where he touched, he kissed and when he touched her breasts she waited in anticipation for him to fulfill the promise of his mouth.

As her dreams unfolded, she could have sworn she heard the ocean and felt the tropical heat. But it wasn't the tropical heat. It was Beck's heat. The same heat that had set her dreams on fire was setting her body ablaze.

She was lost in a whirlpool of desire and want. Not want…it was need. A need which, turned into a craving as his tongue dipped into her navel and drew circles around her belly button. She opened herself to him and he smiled at the bold invitation. A smile that made promises she couldn't wait for him to fulfill. And when he did, she thought for sure the windows would shatter around her when a scream on a note she never thought she could hit tore from her lips leaving her throat dry.

In the distance she heard Beck's laughter as he rose up from the bed to discard his jeans. The boxers followed adding to the pile on the floor, but he kept on his tank top then settled on top of her again.

"Take it off," she said breathless, pushing the top up over his chest. He rose up and knelt on the bed, his weight sinking into the mattress. She pushed at the top again and saw the scars on his stomach. He grabbed her hands and held them together, but she pulled her hands from his grip.

"No. The scars—"

"Yes," she said licking her lips. "I want to see you."

He shook his head. "I had to be cut out of the car. It was—"

"I want to see all of you," she whispered, touching his face. His jaw tensed. His eyes burned into hers. She saw uncertainty.

Beck pulled the tank top over his head and kept it clenched in his fist close to his leg. He didn't touch her…just knelt there watching her face as she stared at him. The scars started at mid waist then up to his collarbone and ended at the base of his neck.

He looked like a warrior, strong and masculine and she wanted him to touch her. Yet, he made no move to do so. Then it occurred to her that whatever words she uttered next would decide how the night would turn out. But there was only one thing to say.

"You're beautiful." Running her hands up his chest, she felt the texture of his scars beneath her fingers and pulled him towards her.

The uncertainty vanished from his eyes as a million dollar smiled spread across his face. There was something primal about him. He was all male. Hot and sexy. She loved everything about him. The way he kissed her as if he couldn't get enough of her. The way he touched her with such care as though she was fragile.

He was strong and beautiful and tonight he was hers. She would enjoy him. She started with his nipples as she teased, caressed and tasted.

"No," she cried when Beck pulled away.

"Shh." He silenced her cry with a kiss then reached over to the drawer of the nightstand for a condom keeping his promise to take care of her in every way.

They came together in an explosion of need meeting need. Both clinging to each other and riding the wave to a climax that had her once again singing a high-pitched note that left him laughing.

Beck rolled over on his back taking her with him nestled in his arms. She kissed his chest sliding her arm across his waist. He lifted his head turning towards the wall of windows his eyes filled with concern. The windows were bare. They were high enough that she didn't have to worry about the rest of the world.

"What's wrong?"

"I thought you may have shattered the glass," he said with a lazy chuckle.

She pinched him playfully on the arm and he caught her hand kissing her open palm.

"She's not only a screamer, she pinches too. Sexy."

He pulled her closer and she felt his warm breath on her cheek. Moments later he drifted off into sleep.

Markie watched Beck as he slept looking peaceful. Sleep was the furthest thing from her mind. She shouldn't have come. Sleeping with Beck would only complicate things between them. Her focus should be on Sydney.

Guilt ate at her.

She felt Beck's hand tightened around her waist. His breathing soft and low as his hand caressed her stomach in his sleep.

Fear consumed her. Sydney could be hurt. She should be doing more to find her sister.

Beck knew before he opened his eyes Marklynn had left the bed. Turning his head towards the dent in the empty pillow, memories of last night played out in his mind as he looked down at the scars on his chest that had haunted him since the accident.

Monika wouldn't touch him after the car accident and he assumed it was because of the scars. Their marriage was already in trouble before the accident, but he had wanted to make it work. After the accident, they both stopped trying.

Marklynn told him he was beautiful. She'd kissed every scar chasing away all the insecurities about his body he had kept buried since the accident.

Marklynn Brooks was a special lady and he was falling in love with her. He didn't think she was ready to hear his declaration of love just yet.

Her focus was on Sydney. If he wanted her undivided attention, Sydney had to be found. Until then, he would be there for her to love her and care for her.

Beck tossed back the covers and got up. Their clothes were neatly folded at the end of the bed. Reaching for his boxers, he stepped into them and out of an old habit grabbed the tank top. Then he left it where it was on the bed and went in search of the woman that turned his world upside down last night.

He found her on the balcony dressed in her white shirt, her legs bare, the wind blowing her hair across her face. Her arms were wrapped around her body as if she was holding herself together. He stood at the door watching her. She was a million miles away.

Last night she came to him, but this morning she was probably wondering what she'd done. By the stiffness in her body it looked as though she was ready to bolt. He could sense it, but he was having none of that. He stepped out onto the balcony.

"Good morning." Slipping his hands around her waist holding her from behind, he kissed the back of her neck.

She jumped.

"Sorry. I didn't mean to startle you."

"It's okay. I was lost in thought."

"Mmm you smell nice."

"You have quite the selection of Victoria's Secret body washes in the guest washroom," she said in a nonchalant way.

Was it jealousy he detected in her voice, he wasn't quite sure. He didn't want her thinking there was anyone else. Their relationship was still new and he wanted to explore it and every inch of her body.

"You can thank my stepmother for that along with my interior design," he said nodding towards the living room.

"That explains the Greek columns."

"She missed the mark with the Greek columns, but she was right about Victoria's Secret. Which one did you use? I want to stock up for you."

"The one in the purple bottle," she replied and pulled out of his arms moving closer to the railing.

Beck moved next to Marklynn with his back against the railing, but he didn't touch her even though he wanted to. His eyes settled on the throbbing pulse at the base of her neck.

"You're not having second thoughts about last night, are you?"

"No. I'm just a little preoccupied this morning that's all. Given the circumstances anyone would be. I've a meeting in a couple of hours. I need to go home and change to meet Jamie in Jamaica Plains."

She turned away from the railing and he grasped her arm then loosened his grip. The wind blew her hair across her face and he swept his hand gently across her face tucking the wayward strand behind her ear. "Don't push me away."

"You're not going to get all touchy feely on me are you?" She attempted a smile that landed somewhere between scared and terrified.

"I'm a touchy feely kind of guy. I thought I showed you that last night, sweetheart." Then she smiled. A smile that did things to him. He wanted to drag her back off to bed. "If you want another demonstration, I'll be happy to oblige."

Leaning her forehead on his chest, she breathed in through her nose and let the air out slowly through her mouth. She was trembling and it was the middle of summer.

"What is it? Talk to me."

"There's a lot going on right now. Sydney…I can't…Can we take this slow?"

Holding on to her he thanked the heavens for this gift that was in his arms. He would give her all the time she needed.

"You set the pace and I'll follow." He kissed her forehead. "I make a mean omelet. I call it the Beck's Special."

"Should I ask what you put in it?"

"Nope."

Beck's kitchen was no ordinary kitchen. It was straight out of an interior design magazine. There was an island in the middle of the kitchen with a deep sink surrounded by a dark stone counter top. A gas stove was centered against one wall. Over the stove a large hood fan hung from the ceiling.

On either side of the stove there were stainless steel and walnut cabinets mounted on the walls. Double ovens were mounted on the wall and the refrigerator, also stainless steel, completed the dream kitchen.

From where Markie sat on a stainless steel stool at the island, she had a perfect view into the living room. It wasn't the view into the living room that caught her attention. It was the man himself. She wondered what would happen if she allowed herself to take a chance on him and let what was happening between them unfold.

When she'd dressed and returned from the bedroom, he was in blue jeans and a black T-shirt whistling while cooking up a storm. The Beck's Special, his signature dish, had everything. It included all the leftovers in the fridge tossed into the omelet. For someone who worked 24/7 he sure had a lot of food in his fridge. It made her wonder who was stocking his refrigerator then came to the conclusion it was his stepmother as she was responsible for stocking the guest bathroom.

Marklynn wasn't big on breakfast. To her it wasn't the most important meal of the day. But the aroma from the eggs with all the ingredients added made her mouth water. When he placed a plate piled high in front of her with the eggs, chunks of red pepper and meat, she ate as if she hadn't been fed in years.

"Mmm," she said when she placed a fork full into her mouth savoring every delicious bite. The man can cook in the bedroom and the kitchen. "I had my doubts when I saw you putting all that stuff into the omelet including the Italian sausage, but it's rather good."

"Thank you." Beck sat down beside her and started eating. "If you're impressed with my breakfast culinary skills, you'll be blown away with what I can do for dinner. You can come right after work."

"No." Marklynn shook her head and she saw disappointment reflected in his eyes.

She should be out trying to find her sister. It had been five days since her sister's disappearance and not a word. Sydney was out there alone, afraid or even hurt. How could she push Sydney from her mind again?

"You're doing all you can, Marklynn," he said reassuring her. His hand covered hers. "Just because you've taken some time to regroup doesn't mean you don't care about your sister."

"Is that what last night was? Regrouping?" The guilt she'd felt earlier rose up in her and made her angry. She was itching for a fight to create distance between them. He knew it too and didn't rise to the bait.

"If you change your mind about dinner, let me know." He took up their empty plates and placed them in the sink. "I'll take you downstairs when you're ready to go."

That was her way out and she took it. She'd been ready to go since she'd gotten up out of his bed. For some reason her heart and her feet weren't on the same page. Beck's condo was comfortable and she felt right at home. She could get used to it and him. Yet, she didn't want to get use to it or him. She was afraid to.

"Let me brush my teeth and we can go."

"There are several packages of toothbrushes in a small basket on the sink," he said watching her as she slid off the stool making her way to the bathroom.

"I know. I opened one. I'll be right back."

Marklynn thought he would bring up dinner again when she returned a few minutes later, but he didn't. He slipped his hand in hers. They left his condo and rode down to the under parking garage in silence. When they reached her 4Runner, he opened the door for her then his lips brushed the palm of her hand just before she slid into the driver's seat and he waited until she drove away.

He was giving her the space she needed. So, why wasn't she jumping for joy she asked herself as she exited the underground parking lot? Because she had no intention of going down the aisle with Beck. He wanted that. She could sense it and it was far more than she was willing to give.

Could she walk away from Beck when it was all over? That was the question she had on her mind when she arrived at her house, changed and headed out to meet Jamie in Jamaica Plains.

Beck pulled into the parking lot of the café located a block from his company. He was late for his meeting with O'Malley. When he returned to the condo after Marklynn left, all he could think about was last night. He couldn't get her out of his mind or the look in her eyes when she'd driven off.

She was afraid. Yes, Sydney was still missing and that was weighing on her mind but he had to wonder where her ex fit in. Did he have something to do with the distance she had put between them after breakfast?

He was so wrapped up in trying to figure out Marklynn that he'd almost missed the voice message from O'Malley. The message was very short and abrupt ordering him to meet O'Malley at 9:00 a.m. sharp.

The smell of coffee and cinnamon greeted him when he opened the glass door of the café. The loud chatter drowned out the music playing in the background. Oversized chairs in a wide array of colors cluttered the room.

O'Malley was sitting at a table in the corner reading the newspaper. There were already three empty cups pushed to the corner of the table and one in front of him untouched.

"That can't be good," Beck said as he sat down eyeing the black liquid in the cup.

"What?"

"You're on your fourth cup."

"You're late," O'Malley grunted.

"It couldn't be helped given the short notice."

"I didn't get permission to reopen your ex-wife's case." O'Malley folded the paper pushing it aside. "I didn't think I would."

"You could've told me that on the phone."

O'Malley pushed out a breath, looking around before he spoke. He picked up the coffee cup and drank.

"There are some things you need to know," he said then drained his coffee cup setting it carefully on the table. "When I got your ex-wife's case, I was coming back from a dark place in my life. I'd just come off a drug bust that went south, took a bullet in the thigh and got hooked on painkillers."

"Why are you telling me this?"

"Because I want you to know what happened."

O'Malley had that same tone in his voice as his father did when he had sat him down for a talk. Beck knew it was bad news. Then it came. His mother was dying and there was nothing else the doctors could do. He'd never forgotten the look on his father's face or the sound of his voice.

"What is it?"

"I want you to know I started out doing my job," O'Malley said looking towards the door when a woman carrying a dog in her purse entered the café. "I thought for sure you killed Monika or you had something to do with it.

You didn't pan out. Then there was another lead. I didn't follow through on because I was told not to."

"What?"

Beck couldn't believe what he was hearing. For months his life was turned upside down while the police conducted their investigation. They interviewed his parents and his friends. His home and office were both searched and now O'Malley was telling him it was all for nothing.

"What do you mean? Who told you not to follow up on the other lead?"

"I can't tell you that yet." His eyes finally met Beck's gaze.

"The hell you can't. What about this other lead?"

"I'm following up on it. That's all I can tell you right now."

"That's not good enough! You dragged me through hell and back four years ago because you thought I killed my ex-wife. I can't believe you had another suspect and did nothing."

If O'Malley was the least bit sorry for his oversight he showed no outward emotion. He sat across from Beck like a stone.

"I couldn't do anything. Monika came from money and her parents wanted someone to pay and you were the fall guy. I wanted to save my job. I was in no position at the time to stick my neck out for you."

"You're a cop. That's your job!" Beck slammed his fist on the table rattling the contents. Heads turned towards the table, but he didn't care. It was either that or reaching over the table and shoving the coffee cup down O'Malley's throat.

"I don't need you or anyone to tell me what my job is," O'Malley hissed. "What I did was wrong and I'll make it right."

"Where does that leave me?"

Beck slumped back in his chair, tired and on edge. For the past three months he'd been fighting to hold on to his company. He'd told himself it was a battle he was going to win.

Marklynn Brooks crossed his path. He didn't set out to fall in love with her but somehow, in all of this mess he had. His relationship with her was a struggle as well. It seemed as if she was holding on to a past she was not ready to let go of. But he was not going to give up on her either.

If Monika was still alive, then what? It didn't matter because they were divorced he reminded himself. That may be the case, but if she was responsible for Sydney's abduction or worse if she died…

"Is Monika dead?" He had to know. If she wasn't, where has she been all these years and why come back now?

"I'm looking into it. I believe what's going on at your company is somehow connected with Monika's death."

"How? She's supposed to be dead."

"She may have faked her own death."

CHAPTER NINE

Macy's house was a picture of southern hospitality. The white-bricked plantation styled mansion had a columned porch that seemed to extend around the exterior of the house. Plantation shutters covered massive windows and that was just what Markie's eyes could take in. She wondered what the back of the house looked like as she turned into Macy's driveway and thought it must be equally as impressive if all the species of flowers planted at the front was anything to go by.

The birds on the edge of the three-tier water fountain in the center of the circular driveway scattered as she pulled up beside Jamie's black jeep.

"Nice piece of real estate," Jamie said looking at the house as he came around and opened the door of her SUV and she got out.

"It's similar to the house in Sydney's picture." Markie glanced at the photo she pulled from her purse then at the house.

"Almost. That house," Jamie pointed to the left over his shoulder, "is four doors down the street on the right. I saw it on my way in. You missed it because you came from the opposite direction. We can take a look when we're finished with Macy."

She nodded. According to Carlos, Beck hadn't gotten back to him regarding the address. With every thing that was going on at his company maybe he'd forgotten. She didn't want to read more into it than that. They got the information they needed anyway.

"You look well rested this morning," Jamie said when they started up the steps towards Macy's front door.

Jamie kept staring at her with that knowing look *'that I know what you did last night'* look. Maybe she was being paranoid. Whether she was or not, she didn't want to discuss Beck with him.

"I'm well rested," she replied without looking at Jamie and rang the doorbell. She didn't have to look at him to know he was smiling at her.

A woman, with skin the color of caramel, dressed in a white linen pantsuit opened the door a few minutes later. She was on the cordless phone and the conversation with the party on the other end didn't seem pleasant as she shook her head rolling her eyes towards the ceiling.

She covered the mouthpiece of the phone with her hand and asked, "Markie and Jamie?"

"Yes," Markie replied.

"Come on in," she said to them. "Yes, they just got here," Macy responded to the person on the phone. She beckoned at Jamie and Markie to follow her. They proceeded through an arched doorway, the floor polished wood, as she led them into a front room.

Macy sat down behind a large desk that looked like it was carved from a tree trunk. Bookshelves lined the entire room from one end to the other.

"Please have a seat." She pointed to the two chairs in front of her desk. "I'm going to put you on speaker, Brad," Macy said hitting the speaker button as she put down the phone. "Brad Logan, Editor, *Upscale Design Magazine*. Marklynn Brooks and Jamie Wright are here."

"I heard that you two wanted to talk to me about Sydney. I don't know what for. As far as I'm concerned, she skipped out because she couldn't hack it. You can tell that to your other colleague Melanie as well. Sydney probably ran off with some man. Isn't that what women do?" The voice projecting over the speaker was nasal and loud.

"This is Marklynn Brooks. I disagree, Mr. Logan," she said trying to keep her instant dislike for the man from showing. "Sydney is my sister and she didn't run off with some man."

"I agree," Macy said combing her fingers through her hair. "If Sydney is missing then something happened to her. The fact that she disappeared after leaving my house is disturbing."

"You mentioned someone called Melanie," Marklynn said to Brad. "I've never heard of Melanie. You said she called you. What did she want?"

"I don't care. We have our own photographer for the magazine, but Macy wanted to use Sydney. Well, either we get the pictures by the end of the day or we go with someone else's house for the next issue."

He hung up and Macy shook her head in disgust. "I'm sorry about that. He's just as obnoxious in person I'm afraid."

Wanting to save Sydney's job Markie said, "Jamie retrieved some files on Sydney's computer that were erased. If we can find the pictures of your house we'll get them to you."

"Let him go with someone else. Sydney didn't like him anyway."

"Brad said he gave Sydney the job as a favor to you. I don't understand any of this. As far as I know, she didn't have a steady job. She had shown an interest in photography but I didn't think it went beyond that."

Macy looked at Markie confused. "When was the last time you spoke with your sister?"

"A few days before she disappeared."

"Before that?" Macy asked biting her thumbnail.

"I got the odd phone call when she dropped into town. The last time when we sat down together and talked was about a year or so ago at dinner."

"I remember. She didn't want to go. It was near to the end of Derrick's tour of duty," Macy said with a slight tremor in her voice. "

"Derrick?" Marklynn asked. "Who's Derrick?"

Macy hesitated as if not sure if she should divulge Sydney's secrets and Markie thought she wouldn't continue. Macy had every right. Markie didn't know her sister at all. It was clear Derrick was someone important in her life. What kind of sister was she? The disappointment must have shown on her face.

Macy got up and turned to the window behind the desk staring across a well-manicured lawn. The smell of fresh cut grass floated into the room on a gentle breeze through the open window.

"Derrick was my brother. He was in love with Sydney. They'd nothing in common. He was as straight-laced as they come being an army man and Sydney was unpredictable. To tell you the truth, I didn't like her at first. She didn't fit into our family."

"Why? Because Sydney didn't fit into the box you tried to put her in?" Markie asked sounding defensive and angry. She was also angry with herself. The same thing she accused Macy of doing was the same thing she'd done to her sister.

Macy turned from the window and laughed, then sniffled. "That's an understatement. Did you know she jumped out of Derrick's birthday cake wearing a bikini covered with pictures of the American flag singing the *Star Spangled Banner*? I'm sure when the man wrote the song that's not what he had in mind."

"That sounds like Sydney," Markie smiled, a wistful smile. Her sister danced to the beat of her own drum. She did whatever she wanted to without giving any thought to the consequences.

"There were military personnel there as well as our parents. He was livid at first then he broke out into laughter. We all did. You see, Derrick had seen a lot during his military career and he didn't laugh much anymore. Sydney brought laughter and hope into his life. I guess that's why he loved her." Macy rubbed the palms of her hands along her arms as if she was trying to keep warm. "He'd asked me if I could help Sydney with her career as a photographer since I had connections."

"You said Derrick 'was' your brother?" Jamie asked.

There were tears in Macy's eyes when she spoke. "He was killed by a road side bomb in Afghanistan a week before he was scheduled to come home."

"When?" Markie gasped.

"Thirteen months, two weeks, four days," Macy looked at her watch, "three hours ago our family was shattered."

"I'm sorry," was all Markie could say and it seemed inadequate.

"He'd told me he was going to ask Sydney to marry him when he came home." Macy shook her head. "I shouldn't have told her."

Markie looked at Macy in shock. Her mouth opened then closed again. The last time she saw Sydney, Derrick was alive. Sydney was happy which explained why she was thinking of settling down. She suspected after Derrick died things changed.

"I called her after Derrick's death, but she didn't return my calls until I contacted her about the assignment. I owed it to my brother."

"She never mentioned Derrick," Marklynn said softly. "And she never mentioned you."

"I'm sure she talked Derrick's ears off about you. As for me, she talked about you often enough. She was proud of you, but I got the impression from her that you were disappointed in her."

"Did she tell you anything else?"

"Only that you set high expectations and…"

"…and she couldn't live up to them," Markie finished for her. "I knew of her interest in photography, but thought it was a phase. Derrick didn't think so."

Macy's cell phone on the desk rang ending the silence that engulfed the room. She looked down at it but didn't pick it up. "I'm sorry, but I have to get ready for work. I just got in an hour before you arrived and I need to be on a plane to Israel in two hours. Will you keep me posted? My assistant can always reach me."

"I will. Thanks for all your help," Marklynn said as Macy walked them to the front door.

"I miss not having her around with Derrick gone. After you find her, maybe we can all get together for dinner when everything settles down?"

"I'd like that."

"You want the left or right side of the street?" Jamie asked as they walked down the steps, his hand shoved in his pocket. He glanced sideways at Markie.

"You go on back to the office and I'll do the canvassing."

They stopped in front of her 4Runner. Jamie cocked his head looking at her then blew out a puff of air.

"We can be more productive if we work together. You take the left side of the street and I'll take the right."

"I said no. I want to do it."

"No. What you *want* to do is to take what Macy told you and saddle yourself with guilt like a mother with a baby strapped to her side," Jamie said point-blank.

She remained quiet. Somewhere in the distant she heard a dog bark and the sound of children's laughter as they splashed into a nearby pool. Jamie stood there staring at her as if waiting for her to say something, but she had nothing to say.

"What happened to Sydney is not your fault, Markie. Sydney had a different life from yours. So what if you didn't know about her relationship with Derrick or of his death."

"Maybe if I was more accessible..."

"Accessible to what? Markie, your grandmother and your parents pushed this role of savior upon you. It's unfair for someone to carry such a burden. You can't save the world."

"I'm not trying to save the world, just my sister," Markie said and headed up the street.

Something was crawling on Sydney's face. She brushed

at her cheek and opened her eyes just in time to see a cockroach crawling on the mattress in front of her eyes.

"Ahhh." She swept the cockroach off the bed. When it hit the floor she jumped on it.

The cockroach was dead when she landed on it the first time, but that didn't stop her from stomping on it a half a dozen more times. She imagined it was Blondie and stomped on it a few more times for good measure before her head started to spin.

Reaching for the water bottle, she tipped her head back and drained the last drop of water from the bottle. She had finished the water hours ago but she didn't care. Her throat was so dry it felt raw.

Hunger twisted her stomach inside out and she slumped, exhausted, on the cot. When was the last time she'd eaten a real meal? She had dinner before arriving at Macy's. What was it? Seafood. Yes. Seafood chowder, garden salad and a glass of white wine.

It was a nice restaurant. They had even given her a mint with the bill. A mint she'd shoved in the pocket of her jeans. Then it dawned on her she was wearing the same pair of jeans. Along with hating to cook, laundry was at the top of the list and she hadn't gotten around to doing it. Who said procrastination wasn't a good thing?

Sydney stood up, patted down her pocket, and started to laugh when she felt the candy. The ropes had loosened just enough for her to wiggle her right hand in her right jeans pocket to retrieve the mint.

It was the size of a quarter, white with green strips, wrapped in clear cellophane twisted at the ends. Normally she couldn't stand restaurant mints. Some tasted like cough drops, cheap mints to be exact. But right now, cheap or not, the mint was her only food source and possibly, her last supper.

With trembling finger, she unwrap the candy. She was about to pop it all in her mouth but decided against it. With care, she put the candy between her teeth and bit into it. It broke into three small pieces. She placed one piece in her mouth and the other two pieces back into the wrapper sliding it back into her pocket. The mint tasted heavenly. Sweet. It felt cool in her mouth and soothing in her stomach.

She laughed and the laughter turned to tears. If she ever got out of this alive, she would not only be a better person, but also a better sister to Markie. Topping that list would be calling more often, and spending more time at home with Nan.

Sydney remembered one of the arguments she had with Markie about growing up and taking responsibility for her life. How could she live up to Markie's expectations or Nan's for that matter?

It was all about Markie and her accomplishments. She runs a successful private investigation agency. Sydney had lost count of the numerous awards Markie had won.

What did she have in her life? A string of broken relationships. But they weren't all bad. Derrick had been good to her. Good for her. She didn't have to be anyone but herself with him. Then he died and she had no one to be proud of her.

Don't think about Derrick. Think about something fun. Photography. She was a good photographer. Yet no one seemed to notice. Not the people that mattered. Markie was too busy with her life and Nan was too busy doting on Markie's life.

Anyway, why did she have to be good at anything other than photography? Markie was great at everything.

Markie can fix everything and she would find her.

Beck knocked on the door of Jamie's office and he glanced up from the computer waving him into the room. The office was a step away from the server room at Jamie's request. Beck didn't argue.

At first Beck had some concerns about Jamie's Mohawk and even wondered if the man would fit in. The man before him was neatly groomed from his trimmed Mohawk and beard, to the charcoal grey suit, down to his shoes.

Beck was taken aback by the complete transformation.

His concerns became a non-issue and the only thing that mattered was finding *Shadoe*.

"Hi Jamie," Beck said as he entered the office with his coffee cup in hand. Beck was on his way to his office when he'd decided to drop in on Jamie.

A desk and a wall covered with a white board was all Jamie had requested. On the white board were diagrams of what Beck assumed to be the solution as to how Jamie would solve his problem.

Jamie had brought in his own equipment and set up a stealth monitoring software of his own to track *Shadoe* and to watch him unnoticed.

Jamie knew more about computers than anyone Beck had ever met and that knowledge he was using to educate his team. His two hour meeting yesterday had led to an over whelming acceptance by everyone Malcolm had told him. Malcolm wasn't used to taking a back seat to anyone, but he had stepped aside, leaving Jamie at the helm.

"Is that for me?" Jamie's chin pointed towards the coffee cup Beck placed on the edge of the desk.

"Everyone around here gets their own coffee."

"Then why are you here?"

The corner of Jamie's mouth turned up into a scowl. A scowl Marklynn had told him not to take personally that it was a part of his character. Charm was also the word she'd used.

"You've regaled my staff with stories of famous hackers and I appear boring to them." Beck took the seat in front of the desk, leaned back in the chair crossing his legs at the ankles.

"I wouldn't worry. Once I leave, they'll worship you again."

Beck chuckled. He'd left half way through the meeting yesterday to drop in on an alarm installation job and wanted to catch up with Jamie. He could have gotten a full update from Malcolm, but he had an ulterior motive.

"Explain about this stealth monitoring software and how this is going to help catch *Shadoe*."

"As I mentioned in the meeting yesterday," Jamie began. "Erasing methods are not infallible. Whoever is uploading the virus is getting in and out of the system undetected. Often what are left behind are traces or fingerprints that can lead to another computer and this is how we'll catch our hacker. Plus, hackers are big on 'bragging rights' so we'll be monitoring the hack sites and blog sites as well."

"We're good to go then," Beck said then got up but sat down again.

Beck wasn't big on small talk. He'd gotten what he came for, a status report, but there was something else and he wasn't quite sure how to approach the subject.

Not that Beck had a problem with saying what was on his mind. It was the fact that he was in unfamiliar territory where Marklynn was concerned. Once again he turned to Jamie.

"Something else on your mind?"

Beck had been thinking about Marklynn since she'd left his place that morning, more so after his meeting with O'Malley. He knew she wouldn't voluntarily call and tell him about the meeting in Jamaica Plains.

"How did the meeting go this morning?"

"The meeting with Malcolm went well. I told him to put the word out to the team not to discuss what we're doing with anyone. That should be a given any way, but just a precaution in case *Shadoe* finds out. We don't want to spook him. We've to assume that this person is connected somehow to someone who works at Beck Security Systems."

"That's not the meeting I was referring to."

"I know. Discuss it with Markie."

"She won't tell me anything." He'd hit the brick wall, which was to be expected, but he had to at least try.

"That's too bad." Jamie turned his attention back to the computer.

Their conversation was over, at least the part about Marklynn anyway. Jamie was right. If he wanted to know about the meeting he should talk to Marklynn.

"You're right. I shouldn't be pumping you for information." Beck got up and grabbed his coffee cup.

"Why do you want your ex's boating accident case reopen?"

Beck's eyes widened in surprised. He should've known Jamie would find out. The man used to be a cop. He probably still had friends on the police force. Then something occurred to him. What about Marklynn? Did she know? He wasn't ready to tell her about his meeting with O'Malley or what he'd discovered.

"I didn't say anything to Markie," Jamie said twisting his mouth. "You better know what you're doing Beck because I sure as hell don't...Wait a minute." Jamie leaned forward and slapped his palm against his forehead. "It's about the picture, isn't it?"

Beck didn't answer.

Jamie swore. "You think your ex is alive."

"I don't know."

"But you suspect," Jamie said pushing for an answer. A deep scowl appeared on Jamie's face and Beck wasn't blaming it on Jamie's character.

"Yes."

"You should've told her. How do you propose to keep this from her?"

"I'm not trying to keep it from her. I want to help her. Help she would refuse if I came out and offered. Sydney is missing which is connected somehow with what's going on here. You're here to help me. I need to be doing something. Let me do this, please."

"I guess that explains why O'Malley hasn't called her back." Jamie shook his head looking at Beck as if he'd lost his mind.

Jamie became very quiet. Too quiet. He and Marklynn were close and Beck didn't know if he could convince the man to give him the time he needed.

More to the point, why should Jamie stick his neck out for him? They had come to mutually respect each others work, but that was all. Their friendship was a friendship in progress at the very least and that was probably because of Marklynn.

"I know what you're thinking."

"You have no idea what I'm thinking, Beck," Jamie said shaking his head.

"Don't worry none of this will touch you. I'm going to tell Marklynn everything as soon as I hear from O'Malley. I spoke with him this morning and we're meeting again. He should have some answers for me."

Jamie pushed out a breath. "I'm not worried about me, man. It doesn't matter what your intentions are. You lied to her and that my friend may not be so easy to overcome when she finds out. She doesn't trust a lot of people."

"Is that because of what happened when she was a police officer? What was the lawsuit about?"

Jamie shook his head. "If you want to know about that you'll have to ask her. I better get back to work."

"I asked O'Malley about the lawsuit and he didn't tell me either."

"Leave it alone. Why are you sticking your nose into something that's none of your business?"

"Because I care about her too."

"Only care about her?"

Jamie's gaze was hard. Beck thought about not answering his question because he didn't think it was any of Jamie's business. But then, he'd already pulled Jamie into his business by asking about Marklynn. He figured the man deserved an answer, an honest one.

"I love her." Beck turned towards the door, but Jamie's voice halted his steps at the door.

"Beck," Jamie paused, as if weighing his decision about the amount of information to share. "There were a lot of rumors when she left the force about a relationship with her Shift Commander. We never talked about it, but I don't believe it went down the way he said it did. More to the point – it's none of my business. If you want to know what happened then she'll have to tell you." Jamie's mouth twisted and a somber expression settled on his face. "I think she'll tell you when she's ready."

"From what I found out, she gave an interview to Michael Blake, the investigative reporter. Her interview was never aired because a settlement was reached between her and the police department. She won. I don't understand why she left her job?"

"You've been busy."

That wasn't the response Beck was hoping for but it seemed that was all he was going to get from Jamie. He pushed on anyway.

"According to O'Malley, Marklynn walked away with a truck load of money."

"She walked away with enough to start over." Jamie's hand cut through the air. "That's all."

A scowl settled on Jamie's face and he turned his back to Beck. It was a clear sign that he should back off, and leave well enough alone. He wanted to know more and wanted to ask the one question that had been bugging him since meeting Jamie.

"Why did you decide to partner with Marklynn? I could understand if you were close to retirement and you were looking for something until then. Brooks Investigations was a startup company with a woman at the helm. Not a lot of men would give up the job you had. Let alone, want to take directions from a woman."

The hard edge in Jamie's voice softened a little and a smirk appeared on his face. "You're like a dog with a bone."

"My father calls it creative intelligence," he smiled.

"He was being kind. To answer your question, I've always been a risk taker. I wanted a challenge…something different. I can go from a missing person's case to corporate espionage in a matter of months. What more could a guy ask for?"

Beck suspected there was something more behind Jamie's flippant response, but he didn't want to push any more. He could take a hint. He wasn't going to get any more information anyway. The scowl was back. He was dismissed.

"Can I get back to work? I'd hate to have *Shadoe* slip by

me because I'm distracted."

Markie didn't leave Jamaica Plains until about one that afternoon. Not until she canvassed every house within a four-block radius in the neighborhood where Sydney had taken the picture, the Bowman's house. They were still upset that their Renoir painting was stolen. All they talked about was suing Beck Security Systems and could care less about Sydney.

With nothing to show for her efforts except for sore feet and exhaustion, she decided to return to the office. First she had to make one call to tell Nan she had come up empty handed again. But Nan called her first on the ride back to the office to say, Sydney was still alive and they were close. Markie held on to that hope when she arrived at Brooks Investigations an hour later.

"Hi Cate," Markie said as she rushed passed Cate's desk and headed up the stairs to her office.

"I expected you back hours ago." There was an almost maternal tone in Cate's voice. "Are you okay?"

Markie paused half way up the stairs turning to face Cate. She had emerged from her office and was standing at the bottom of the stairs watching her.

"I will be once I get some good news for a change."

"You're in luck. The mystery woman has a face. The picture is on your desk. Carlos is running her picture to put a name to the face."

"Yes!" She punched the air, turned and ran up the stairs. "Tell Karter there is a bonus in this for him."

Markie saw the picture on her desk as soon as she walked into her office. Throwing her bag on the chair in front of the desk, she reached for the picture of Beck's ex wife in the file folder. She placed the two pictures side by side. Was it the same woman?

There were similarities between Monika and the blonde woman. Both were tall and willowy with the blonde having a little more muscle definition. Monika however, was the more attractive of the two with light green eyes and long brown hair. The other woman, there was something almost sinister about her. Her eyes were haunting, cold.

Even though there were certain similarities, she couldn't say for certain they were the same person. The woman could have changed her appearance. People do it all the time if they are on the run.

Reaching for the phone as she sat down behind her desk, she dialed O'Malley's number and got his voice mail again. She came to the conclusion he was avoiding her. Perhaps it was time she paid him a visit.

Kicking off her shoes, Markie began to massage the soles of her feet. Jamie was right. It would've been faster with the two of them, but she didn't want Jamie around. When he was right about something he would beat it to death.

Markie wasn't pleased about his comment that morning. Jamie had accused her of saddling herself with guilt over what Macy had told them and he was right. Because she was always pushing her sister to be what she wanted her to be she'd missed out on what was going on in Syd's life. If she had let her be, Sydney would have probably come to her sooner about the pictures and maybe her abduction could have been prevented.

Nan said she'd known about Derrick when Markie had asked about him during their conversation earlier. Sydney asked Nan not to say anything about Derrick to her. It shouldn't bother her but it did. Why was she upset about it anyway?

When she and Jared broke up no one knew the reason why. When you close people out of your life you miss out on their life and they miss out on yours.

She grabbed the phone and dialed Beck's number wanting to hear his voice.

"Good afternoon, Dalton Beck's office," the woman sang the greeting.

"It's Marklynn Brooks from Brooks Investigations. Can I speak with him, please?"

"He's on the other line. One moment please, Ms Brooks."

She was put on hold and a soothing jazz instrumental filled her ear.

"Hello Marklynn Brooks. I've been thinking about you all day. How are you?"

Hearing his soothing voice, she leaned back in her chair and propped her feet up on the corner of her desk. Smiling. She liked the fact that he was the only one besides Nan daring enough to call her Marklynn and she let him get away with it.

"It's been a good day. We finally got a clear picture of the woman in the photo."

Beck paused then asked, "Have you identified her?"

"We're working on it. I'll ask Jamie to get you a copy. By the way, FYI the Bowman's are on the war path."

"I know. Them and the Franklin's," he said sounding weary. "The legal department is having a field day."

"Sounds like it. How is it going with Jamie?"

She had a quick chat with Jamie after his first visit at Beck's office. It seemed as though he was settling in quite well at Beck Security Systems and she'd told him not to get too comfortable when he started beaming about Beck's Research and Development budget.

"He knows what he's doing. The IT guys as you know live in a world of their own, with a language of their own. They see Jamie as some kind of God," Beck laughed.

"Then he has died and gone to IT heaven. When he joined the agency I didn't think I would have enough of this kind of work to keep him interested. Then you came along. I'm thinking of expanding that side of the business once we find your hacker."

"Good business move," Beck said then fell silent.

Markie wanted to see him and was waiting for him to resurrect the dinner offer he'd made that morning but he didn't. Then she remembered she had told him to slow down—he had told her to set the pace.

She wanted to see him and cleared her throat before

asking. "Did you want to come by tonight? You have to bring dinner of course. I'm in the mood for Chinese."

He didn't respond and she knew what he was waiting for. Confirmation of what the evening would hold. What she wanted to happen. Then she stepped out of her comfort zone.

Why had she changed her mind? Because it felt good to have someone in her life even if it was only temporary and that was as far as she was going to analyze it.

"I can make you breakfast in the morning. Although, I don't have the leftovers required to make the Beck's Special."

"I'll come by and make dinner."

"In that case you should buy what you need."

"I plan on it. The only thing in your fridge is milk, yogurt and chocolate covered almonds." She heard the laughter in his voice and her heart did that little flip-flop thing again.

"You noticed. I should be home by six. See you then."

Marklynn hung up the phone staring at it as if it was some kind of foreign object. She reminded herself she wasn't going to analyze why she felt the need to be with Beck or to lean on him.

She wanted to and that was all there was to that.

"Jamie found something," Malcolm said when Beck answered the phone. For a split second he thought it was Marklynn calling back to cancel. She'd seemed a bit hesitant when she'd mentioned dinner.

"I'll be right there." Beck hung up the phone and leaped out of his chair running towards Jamie's office on the other side of the building.

Malcolm was hunched over Jamie's shoulder pointing at the monitor when Beck entered the office a few minutes later. The two men were staring at the monitor. Malcolm yanked at his tie, his expression sullen. Jamie cursed and turned to the laptop next to the other monitor, his fingers flew over the keypad.

"That's it," Jamie said, his gazed fixed on the laptop. "Gottcha."

"What are they doing?" Malcolm asked as he glanced from Jamie to the computer screen.

"Lurking. Nothing is being uploaded," Jamie replied, eyes still fixed on the monitor. I've put a program in place to counter anything that's uploaded."

Beck could have been invisible. No one noticed his arrival. The two men were lost in a game of hide and seek trying to find a person who didn't want to be found. From what he could figure out *Shadoe* had entered the network and this was the closest they'd come to catching him in three months. He held his breath waiting for them to tell him it was over. Tell him his life can go back to normal again. But no confirmation came.

"The IP address is hidden," Malcolm grumbled. "No matter what program we ran we couldn't find it. What about —"

"Hello? Remember me," Markie cut in, a trace of annoyance in her voice. "I'm still on the phone, Jamie."

Beck didn't realize Markie was on speaker. She sounded just as anxious as he was. Moments ago they'd made plans for dinner. Given the turn of events it didn't look like it was going to materialize.

"Sorry," Jamie said. "We're still waiting for Beck,"

"I'm here."

Jamie looked over his shoulder. "Oh, Beck just walked in. Good. I don't have to explain twice."

Beck pulled up a chair and sat down next to Jamie. "Hi Marklynn, I got here almost five minutes ago and they just noticed I was in the room."

"As I was saying the malware is written to mimic the monitoring software," Jamie said. "When it's uploaded it works with the software. The system has been hacked into at least a half a dozen times already based on the failed alarm systems. Right now, we have a visitor who is for lack of a better work just surfing."

"*Shadoe*. Can we trace it?" Marklynn asked.

"Yes, but it may not be so easy," Jamie replied shifting in his seat. "*Shadoe* has gone to a lot of trouble to upload the virus and he's not going to let us catch him. It's a game with him. He'll let you come close, but what we have to do is beat him at his own game."

"He may very well lead us to Iceland by the time we get a fix on the location," Markie said. "But you're going to try, right?"

"Yes. It's being done as we speak," Jamie said.

"*Shadoe* is in and surfing. Why? What does he want?" Beck already knew the answers to his questions. Whoever was sabotaging his company wanted him to know he wasn't untouchable.

"They are gearing up for something big," Malcolm replied. "They want to destroy Beck Security Systems."

"I agree," Jamie said. "But on the other hand, *Shadoe* may not know we know he has just accessed the system. Perhaps he was too eager to hack into the system and got sloppy."

Beck leaned back in the chair shaking his head. He didn't know what to say. Who would want to destroy him? He thought about his ex wife. By all accounts she should be dead. But he wasn't even sure of that anymore.

"You don't believe that *Shadoe* is sloppy any more than I do," Marklynn said echoing his thoughts.

"No," Jamie replied. "I agree with Malcolm. Whoever it is, is getting ready for a final showdown. "I can promise you this. I'll find your *Shadoe*."

"Will that be before or after I lose my company?"

Four minutes and thirty-two seconds.

Phoenix rerouted the signal and timed it down to the second. She had plenty of time before Jamie locked onto her signal. But she wasn't going to let him. Until then she could have some fun. She was smarter than him. Better than him. With all of his education credentials, he still couldn't catch her.

Three minutes and ten seconds.

Her heart raced in her chest. She loved the thrill.

One minute and three seconds.

Her heart pounded with the excitement of the chase as she watched the screen biting her bottom lip. Her eyes narrowed on the screen.

Jamie was getting closer. He can't be that good. Can he? Sweat broke out on her forehead.

One minute ten second.

One minute.

Then the smile slid from her face. He was right on her heels and then…

"Oh no!"

CHAPTER TEN

"I still have to make you dinner."

Markie smiled when she answered the phone and heard Beck's cheerful voice.

"Hang on."

She pressed the hold button and got up to close the sliding door of her office. There hadn't been much to smile about. Day six and still no word from Sydney.

Jamie had managed to locate the computer *Shadoe* used to break into Beck Security Systems. As it turned out, the computer belonged to a sweet little old lady in New Jersey, who had received the computer from her son. *Shadoe* hacked into Beck Security Systems via her computer.

Then the superintendent at Sydney's building had called after *Shadoe* have had broken into Beck's computer. A tenant had turned in Sydney's wallet to the management office. It had led to a second canvassing of Sydney's neighborhood that had turned up nothing.

The man found the wallet behind the dumpster when he had tossed his trash and it landed behind the bin instead of in it. He said he'd tried to return the wallet but was unsuccessful.

As much as she'd pushed Beck to the back of her mind, he was never more than a phone call away. He had called to ensure she was okay before and after the search. Nothing more. No pressure. All she had to do was go to him but she didn't.

"I thought you'd forgotten about dinner," she said knowing very well he hadn't.

She'd woken up this morning thinking about him after a restless night. As the morning went on she'd buried herself in work trying to identify the mystery woman in the photo but came up empty. Sydney consumed her thoughts pushing Beck out, but not for long.

"You know me better than that. Shall we try again for tonight? Hold on for a moment."

She heard him talking in the background and he returned a few minutes later. "That was Jamie at the door. He's monitoring the network and ordered Malcolm and I to take the night off."

"You always follow orders?" She felt like flirting.

"Only when it's in my best interest…and I'm rewarded for my efforts," he replied, jumping right along on the flirting train.

"What sort of reward are you looking for?" She held her breath waiting for his response. Her heart was beating so loud she thought for sure he could hear it.

"What are you offering?"

Time stood still. Seconds ticked by. Then she said, "We can start with dinner." She checked her watch. "It's almost six. I should be home in an hour pending traffic."

"See you soon," Beck said and hung up.

Chicken. He'd called her bluff and she choked. She knew what he wanted to hear and she clammed up.

Marklynn looked at the phone in her hand for a long while before a loud beeping noise jarred her out of her trance and back to reality. She hung up.

Beck had kept his promise. He'd called and offered words of comfort when the search of Sydney's neighborhood turned up empty. When he asked if she wanted to be alone after the search she had said yes and he respected her wishes.

No pressure.

With all that was going on at his company, he'd taken

the time to ensure that she was okay. He was kind and giving and…when she thought about the last time they were together her heart did a little summersault. Something was happening between them and she was afraid to name it. Didn't want to name it.

Why? She wasn't looking for love, but it may have found her. With all the craziness that had crashed into her life in the last few days, she'd found stability in Beck. Not only in his arms but also in his strength.

For all her talk about not going down that road again, she was already half way down and scared to death.

What if he walked away like Jared?

At 7:00 p.m., Beck arrived in Quincy, the "City of Presidents." Markie lived in the neighborhood of Wallaston a dense grid of residential streets and apartments.

This was his second trip to the city that had an amazing history and miles of shoreline that took your breath away. He never thought that he could give up his *Trump Tower*, as Marklynn has called his place, but found he liked the "Birthplace of the American Dream."

Beck pulled into Marklynn's driveway and grabbed the three paper bags of groceries from the back seat of his SUV. He balanced them in his arms as he made his way up the steps to Marklynn's front door.

He had gone a little overboard with the grocery shopping. It couldn't be helped. The woman had no food in her fridge just stacks of plastic containers in her freezer.

When they had made plans to have dinner together yesterday an invitation had followed for breakfast in the morning. She hadn't mentioned it when they had spoken earlier and once again he would step back and let her lead.

It tore at his heart every time he heard the disappointment in her voice over Sydney and even more so that Monika might have something to do with it. He'd wanted to be with Marklynn when Jamie had mentioned about someone finding Sydney's wallet, but she'd kept him at arms length lost in her grief.

She'd dropped her guard, if only for a moment. She wanted to see him and he was as happy as a kid in a candy store.

Beck juggled the bags in his arms freeing a finger to ring the doorbell.

"Oh my gosh!" Marklynn said when she opened the door and stood staring at him. "Did you buy out the grocery store?"

"A little assistance please or at least let me in."

"Sorry." Markie took one of the bags from him and stepped back from the door. "Come in."

He followed her to the kitchen and dropped the bags on the counter. She stood holding the bag as if not sure what to do with it. He took it from her, dropped it on the counter as well, pulled her into his arms and held her.

"I'm sorry you didn't find Sydney." He released her with a kiss on the cheek. "I'll get started on the food, and you unpack the groceries."

One of the bags contained all the ingredients for the stir fry which he laid out on the counter. She started emptying the other two bags staring at the groceries as if she wasn't sure where to put them and he couldn't resist.

"The can goods you put in there," he pointed to the cupboards along the wall, "and the dairy products in the refrigerator," he pointed towards the fridge.

She laughed and said, "I was wondering what I was going to do with all this food. I have to tell you...I don't really cook. You see, Nan, my grandmother makes dinner every Sunday. I usually get a care package to take home and it lasts for the entire week. I still have containers of food in the freezer."

"Ahhh a Nana's girl."

"This coming from a mama's boy or should I say a step mama's boy."

"Either way I'm proud of it," he added with a teasing grin. "Now, finish putting away the rest of the groceries and I'll start the prep work for the stir fry."

He watched as she put away tins of soup, crackers and all the other items he guessed at hoping she would like. Some of the foods he liked so he had an ulterior motive as well, to be invited back.

When she came to the box of chocolate almonds she looked over at him and her lips curved in a slow sexy smile. The chocolate was left out on the counter.

Marklynn was beautiful and she smelled pretty too, a floral scent. Beck didn't know what it was, but he liked it.

He watched as she moved around the kitchen. Her hair was in a ponytail tied back with a pink ribbon showing off her face. Only a faint dark shadow was left of the black eye. Her lips covered in a light pink gloss.

The black summer dress hugged her hips stopping just above her knees. Her feet were bare with her toenails painted pink. It was the sexiest thing he'd seen all day.

"Where do you want me?"

That question sent his eyebrows rising right along with his body heat. *How about naked and horizontal on the counter* he thought and she saw right through him.

"I meant – what do you want me to do." She blushed when she met his bold gaze and further clarified. "To help you prep, wash or chop? What?"

At least he wasn't the only one in over-drive. The moment he'd stepped through the door and laid eyes on her, instant replay. The last time they were together was the only thought that filled his mind. Every thing about her...the way she felt in his arms, the way she moved against him, and, oh yeah, she was a screamer.

"Alright if we must have food," he said with a lazy smile. "Start chopping the green onions."

The L-shaped kitchen was too small for two people to work comfortably without bumping into each other, but he didn't mind. A yellow stove was in the corner, a small table next to it, counter space then the sink, another tiny counter space, then a yellow fridge.

The cutting board was leaning against the wall by the sink and there were several knives in a chopping block on the counter. He retrieved a knife and the cutting board then placed them in front of her with the green onions.

"I don't have a wok," she said and turned on the tap to wash the green onions.

"A large skillet is fine."

"Here. Under the sink."

Marklynn stepped aside so he could retrieve the skillet. His hand brushed against her leg and he felt her shiver. The air was suddenly charged with sexual tension. She didn't look at him, but he knew she felt it too. He also knew she wasn't ready for what he had in mind at that moment. There was something shy and reserved about her tonight as if she was testing the waters between them and that was just fine by him. He would let her come to him.

Beck placed the skillet on the large burner and turned on the stove. The secret to great stir-fried rice is to use Basmati Rice, his father's recipe. By the time he had scrambled the eggs needed, peeled the cooked shrimp the rice was just about ready to come off the stove.

She finished chopping the green onion and stood quietly watching him. He found he liked having her to himself, standing there watching him. He wanted to know what she was thinking but didn't want to intrude. Recalling their last conversation to take it slow, he focused on preparing the meal.

"It smells wonderful," she said, looking hungrily at the plate of shrimp he added to the rice in the large skillet watching the steam rise up into the air.

"You wanted fried rice; your wish is my command." He snapped his fingers and pointed to the pan.

"Don't tell me, your stepmother moonlighted as a chef before she made it big in interior design."

Using a fork he speared a shrimp from the pan. "Have a taste." He brought the fork to her lips and she reached to take it. He shook his head. "Open your mouth."

Her mouth opened and closed around the shrimp. Then her tongue slipped out licking her lips. He had to summon every ounce of will power not to push the food aside, lay her on the counter and have his way with her.

"Mmmm. That's good."

"My father is the chef," he said bringing his mind back to the conversation. "It was a second career he found after my mother died from bone cancer. Somewhere in the midst of his grieving, he lost his passion as an architect and turned to cooking. Some of it rubbed off on me."

"I'd say. When did he marry your stepmother, Anika?"

"About eight years ago. Funny thing is she wouldn't know what a stove is if she bumped into it in a kitchen and dad wouldn't have it any other way."

"She sounds interesting."

"She is. I would love for you to meet her and my father."

That was about as subtle as a bull in a china shop and he wanted to take it back. Marklynn wasn't ready for a relationship with him let alone meeting his parents. She turned towards the sink and started washing the knife. It wasn't his intention to make her feel uncomfortable, but that was the result of his comment. He wouldn't make that mistake again.

He used the flat edge of the knife to gather up the chopped green onions from the chopping board she'd placed beside the stove and added it to the skillet.

"What else do you want me to do?"

"You can sit and talk to me if you like. Tell me about your meeting in Jamaica Plains."

Markie watched Beck as he added the green onions mixing it together with the other ingredients in the skillet. He had the dishtowel thrown over his right shoulder watching her. She focused on the spot on his jean shirt just above the breast pocket where he'd spilled the soya sauce when he opened the bottle. Of course, if she owned an apron his shirt wouldn't be soiled.

She didn't see his scars when she looked at him and she did, while he whisked around her kitchen like the Galloping Gourmet. He looked so comfortable like he belonged in her kitchen, in her bed and in her life.

"If you don't want to tell me about Jamaica Plains, that's fine."

It was her way out and she decided to take it. However, her brain hadn't discussed it with her mouth and she opened up to him like it was perfectly natural as if they had known each other for years.

"It's difficult for me to talk about it. I found out my sister had a life I knew nothing about." She told Beck what Macy had said about Sydney and Derrick. "Sydney is a photographer. She had a boyfriend, Derrick. He wanted to marry her, but he died."

"Are you hurt because Sydney didn't tell you about him?"

"She told Nan." She was hurt but she couldn't explain why. "I don't even know why that bothers me. It's not like I confided in Sydney. We argued all the time. If I said white she said black. When I left the police force, I didn't even tell…"

Markie's voice trailed off as she leaned against the counter, arms folded across her chest. She didn't look at Beck, but knew he was watching her. She could stop right now and he wouldn't push her.

For some reason, she wanted to confide in him and tell him about Sydney. She wanted to tell him things she hadn't wanted to share with anyone.

Markie started on a shaky breath looking down at her feet at the brown vinyl floor and the day of the shooting came to mind. It was hot that day, a day she'd relived a thousand times. She remembered everything about that day. She and her partner were about to go off duty when the call came in, robbery in progress.

"I'd been on the force for about five years at that time.

They tell you about it in training, but when it happens to you and you pull the trigger for the first time, it's almost surreal. It was the first time I'd ever shot and killed someone. He was a kid, maybe sixteen if that. He'd robbed a gas station and killed the attendant. When he pointed the gun at me, I knew he was going to kill me. I could see it in his eyes."

Markie unfolded her arms and gripped the counter for support. Running her hands along the edge of the counter she could feel the smooth surface against her palms. She'd seen that kid's face in her sleep, woken up too many nights in a cold sweat until she was finally able to live with it.

"Did he hurt you? Is that how you got the scar on your pelvis?"

He had seen the scar when he kissed her there.

"No." She shook her head. "Bullet wound yes, but that happened when I was nineteen. I was in the wrong place at the wrong time."

Markie had gone to a club to celebrate her friend's birthday and some idiot opened fire in the middle of the dance floor. Her friend had died that night and she'd taken a stray bullet right in the reproductive organs.

Thirty-six hours later, one ovary was destroyed with bleeding and scaring, the other traumatized the doctors had told her. More than likely she would not have any children. Markie hadn't realized she'd stopped talking until she heard Beck's voice.

"What happened after the shooting at the gas station?"

"My Shift Commander, Jeffery Booker, took me out for a drink to talk right after it happened. I thought it was nice of him. The evening was going well until he dropped me at home and came onto me. His version of the evening ended with me in his bed with vivid details he decided to share with his buddies. When I got wind of the rumors, I told him he needed to correct it or I'd file a complaint. He became belligerent and tried to force me not only out of the department but off the police force as well. You see, I wasn't a team player."

When she looked up at Beck, he was staring at her, his

body tense. Anger flashed across his face as he stirred the fried rice. He remained quiet and she was glad.

"One drink had destroyed everything I'd worked hard for. I was mad at myself for allowing it to happen. I should've stuck with the department shrink, but I guess I wanted to be one of the guys. A few weeks later when nothing was done by him to retract the statements he made, I filed an internal complaint and the "powers that be" sided with him. So I retained a lawyer."

"That must have been difficult." Turning off the stove, Beck grabbed the two plates from the counter where she had laid them out, filled them with fried rice, and sat them on the placemats on the table. "Time to eat."

Beck took out the bottle of wine she had placed in the fridge, poured two glasses and set them on the table.

"It looks delicious."

"I aim to please." He nodded for her to sit and join him. "What happened after you retained the lawyer?"

"A lot of mud slinging. I was called a tease, a whore you name it. Then I met Michael Blake."

"The investigative reporter. Don't look so surprised. You aren't the only one that can find out information. How did you meet him?"

"My partner, Randy and I pulled him over one night for speeding. That was another catastrophe. Randy attacked Michael and Michael broke his nose, which resulted in a suit against Michael. I testified on Michael's behalf."

"That couldn't have helped you," he said his eyebrows raised.

"No. You see there is this unwritten code that you can't testify against another cop. Not everyone follows it, but …but what Randy did was wrong. We should be held accountable for what we do. Jeffery Booker included. That's what I told Michael when he asked me why I stuck my neck out for him."

"Was it his idea for the story?"

"Yes. As it turned out, I wasn't the only female officer Booker had harassed. Then all of a sudden a settlement offer was on the table with a promotion to detective. I took the money and was naive enough to think the settlement would make everything okay." Her voice cracked and she stopped taking a deep breath staring at the plate in front of her.

"What do you mean by everything?"

"I guess I wanted things to be the way they were before the shooting and the harassment. It all changed. I had the money, but lost friends or rather the people who I thought were my friends."

"You landed on your feet."

"Barely," she said remembering how hard it was just to get clients. All the money had gone into the company. "Everything was such a struggle getting Brooks Investigations up off the ground. When Jamie asked to join me I was floored. He said I had guts." She shook her head. "Terrified was more like it. I had to start all over again proving myself to people that I could do the job they wanted me to do. Most of all, I had to prove to myself that I was good at what I did. That was the hardest part. I couldn't let myself fail."

"That's a lot of pressure to put on yourself."

"It's what I had to do. I had employees depending on me. Then there was Nan. She had a stroke. I thought I was going to lose her. Sydney and I had a big blow out after that. I shouldn't have gotten on her case," she said thinking about what Macy had told her. "She was just trying to find herself. And in the middle of it all, Jared cancelled our wedding. The one stability I counted on walked away."

"I won't walk away, Marklynn."

She looked at him from across the table. Well, not really at him per say, the soya sauce stain on his shirt. She didn't know how to respond except just to nod.

"Why can't you have children?"

Markie knew that question would come up and wondered how she would handle it. Should she tell him? She told him more that she had wanted to tonight and felt almost vulnerable. At the moment, she didn't want to hear how brave she'd been or talk about the money she'd received.

And, she didn't want to talk about why she couldn't have children.

"You can tell me when you're ready," he said as if sensing her reluctance.

She met his eyes then and he smiled. The smile that she'd come to love, where the corner of his mouth lifted and laugh lines fanned out from the edge of his eyes. That smile told her he understood how she felt. Nothing more was needed.

"I hope you're hungry."

"Yes. Thank you."

"Bon appétit," Beck said.

"This is fantastic," she said after the first mouth full of fried rice. The Beck's Special paled in comparison to this. She had never tasted anything so mouth watering. Maybe she did, but his lips didn't count.

Again, she thought she could get used to being taken care of, get used to this man sitting across from her whose dark eyes told her the kind of relationship he wanted, yet she wasn't sure if she wanted to take that risk.

They ate in silence. It wasn't an uncomfortable silence, but an understanding silence. She didn't want to talk anymore and he understood. When the meal was over she said, "Since you cooked I'll wash up."

"I'll help." He stood up taking his plate to the sink.

"No. Sit down and I'll wash up." She took her plate from him when he reached for it.

"At least let me dry."

"Okay you're on dry duty."

Reaching for the box of almonds on the counter, she opened the package and popped one in her mouth savoring the chocolate. She didn't realize she'd made a noise until she heard him chuckle.

"Shall I leave you two alone?" He nodded towards the box with a smile watching as she licked the chocolate from her fingers.

She laughed offering him the box. "Try one."

"Not a fan of chocolate."

"No?" She plucked a partially melted chocolate covered almond from the box. He reached for it, but she shook her head. "Open your mouth."

Beck obeyed his eyes locked with hers. "Nice," he said as he ate the chocolate. Then she outlined his lips with her fingers giving him a chance to lick the chocolate from them.

"What is nice? The chocolate or my fingers?"

He turned towards the sink and said, "I think we better get to the dishes."

"I think we better get to the dishes?"

Where did that come from? A Casanova he was not at the moment. What he wanted to do was introduce her to the horizontal mamba and dance until morning.

He'd waited in silence while she'd confided in him, told him about her life and her relationship with Sydney. That couldn't have been easy for her. All he'd wanted to do then was take her into his arms, but it wasn't the right time.

She had asked for space and he had told her to set the pace. Tonight she was giving off all the right signals with the dress. And the chocolate, oh that was a nice touch. Her finger had skillfully outlined his lips and she'd waited for him to lick the melted chocolate from her finger and that had nearly done him in. That was the green light he was waiting for, right? Wrong.

What was he waiting for? He wanted her to say the words. None of that action speaks louder than words business. He wanted her to make the first move and ask him to stay, inviting him into her bed.

So, what if she doesn't ask you to stay Casanova? What then? A lonely ride back to Boston and a very long cold shower.

Markie handed Beck the last of the plates and he put them away in the cupboard. After he dried the skillet, he put it away under the sink then he leaned over, his lips gently caressing hers. Her hands crept up locking behind his neck pulling him closer deepening the kiss. He tasted of chocolate and wine.

"I should go," he said pulling away.

Markie didn't want Beck to go and she knew he didn't want to go. But if she wanted him to stay she would have to say something. Asking him to stay was inching further down that road again and at that moment she didn't care. She didn't want to be alone. It wasn't because she was afraid of being alone. She wanted to be with him. To touch him with her hands and lips, and have him touch her.

"I believe the original dinner offer came with breakfast," she said with a shy smile. "I *want* my Beck's Special."

She took his hand leading him to the bedroom. Tonight she would take what she wanted living only in the moment with this wonderful man who wanted to be with her. This wonderful man allowed her to talk. He listened and most of all didn't push. She wanted him to know she appreciated his kindness.

The dim light from a lamp on the nightstand cast a shadow across the room. Closing the door, she moved into his arms running the palms of her hands up his chest. She unbuttoned his shirt pushing it off his shoulders and he made no objections. His jeans were discarded next along with her dress.

He laid her on the bed, covered her body with his and she scrambled from beneath him reversing their positions, surprising him.

"You like being in control in every aspect of your life, don't you?" She asked teasing.

"I can be sub—" he groaned when she pressed her hips into him "—missive when the mood calls for it."

"I don't believe you," she said, kissing him smiling against his chest.

He loosened the ribbon from her hair running his hand through it. "Try me," he challenged, eyes burning into hers.

"Okay. Let's play a game."

"I love games. I'm very competitive, you know." He ran

his hand along her inner thigh and she shuddered.

"Ground rules...I can do what ever I want with your body and you can't," she removed his hand, "touch me."

"Define touch. I mean, can I kiss you like this." His lips touched hers, soft sensual then demanding. His tongue slid into her mouth, exploring, tasting, and feasting then pulled away, eyes laughing. "Or touch you like this." His hand found her inner thigh again and she covered his hand with hers stilling its movement against her thigh trying to regain the control she started off with.

"You're right. I should *define* touch. You can't touch me like this with your lips." She mimicked the kiss he'd given her and laughed when he groaned. "And you definitely can't put your hand there, removing his hand dropping it on the bed. Is that clear?"

"Crystal," he smiled, a smile stolen from the devil. "Any other *rules* I should know about?"

"You only get three strikes and you're out."

"What if I win? What do I get?"

"You're assuming you'll have the will power to control yourself. I like a man with confidence," she laughed.

Clasping his hands behind his head, he closed his eyes and smiled with smug male confidence. "Piece of cake."

She straddled his hips running her hands down his stomach, followed by wet kisses liking the feel of his skin against her lips. Sucking...kissing...biting playfully. Her tongue outlined each scar it encountered because she was sorry that he got hurt. His eyes flew open and she felt the gentle caress of his hands on her bare shoulders.

"Strike one," she said pushing his hands away. He didn't put his hands back behind his head, but placed them next to his hips on the bed. His eyes never left hers. He flexed his hands as if fighting for control then grabbed the sheet in his grip.

"Strike two," she giggled when he shivered and grabbed her shoulders stilling her movement when her tongue dipped into his navel. She looked up at him shaking her head wanting to taste him, wanting to continue the game as heat swirled like wild fire around them. Liking the power she had over him…Liking the way he groaned out her name as if he was in pain…Liking the way he was coming undone. She was going for the prize.

"Shall we go for strike three? Wait, I'm—"

He rolled her beneath him and she screamed with laughter. Pinning her to the mattress, his mouth covered hers in a kiss of pure dominance. He was in charge now and wanted her to know it. She pulled her lips away.

"What happened to 'a piece of cake'?"

"I'm eating it," he said with a wicked smile that told her he was nowhere near being submissive tonight.

"You're supposed to…" and that was the last coherent thought she remembered before he took her breathe away. She was lost in him and when they came together it was fireworks and symphony all rolled into one.

"What other games can you play?" He asked when their breathing returned to normal. He held her while he stroked her back.

"Why?" She lifted her head up off his chest and his eyes were playful, teasing. "You want another shot at redeeming yourself."

"Do I need to redeem myself?"

"Not in my book." She rested her head on his chest feeling the cool breeze from the ceiling fan against her damp skin.

He brushed her hair from her face then ran his finger along her cheek. "I love you."

CHAPTER ELEVEN

Phoenix slipped out of the bed when Malcolm rolled off her onto the bed towards the window thankful to get his dead weight off her body. He always fall asleep right after sex. The first time they had sex she thought she'd killed him, but she'd just worn him out.

Earlier she had pulled out all the toys and props she had because he loved them, not because she did. She didn't like sex. You used sex to get what you want. She learned that early from a great teacher.

She watched him from the foot of the bed, the moonlight shining through the sheer curtain across his face. She felt something for him, but it wasn't love. Love didn't exist in her world. It didn't take long before the snoring that could wake the dead started and she left the room. He would be out for the rest of the night and she could attend to business.

Phoenix turned on the computer. The blue glow from the laptop screen lit up the small den just off the bedroom she used as an office. She glanced towards the bedroom when she didn't hear his snoring then back at the computer screen when the foghorn sound started up again.

She hadn't expected Malcolm to come by her apartment tonight. He'd called and wanted to spend the night because her place was in town. He lived in Mansfield, Massachusetts in the south-southwest suburbs of Boston.

She took to the idea wanting to know more about what was going on at Beck Security Systems and more about Jamie Wright. Malcolm was in a talkative mood when he arrived a little after midnight, but wasn't saying anything she wanted to hear. What was even more infuriating was he didn't want to talk about his work at all.

Love and marriage were the only two things on his mind. What made her want to gag was when he said he could see them married. Phoenix had to bite her tongue to keep from laughing. She'd played her role to such perfection that she deserved the *Oscar* for Best Actress and laughed at the thought.

Phoenix had gotten cocky earlier and was almost caught. She'd lost sight of the end goal and became overconfident. Hacking into Beck Security Systems was easy and she'd done it because she was bored. Not because it was a part of her plan.

Oh, she knew Jamie was tracking her movement and should have gotten out of Beck's network before he locked onto her. But no, she wanted to see how good her opponent was. She had to admit he was better than she expected. She had never met anyone that had come so close to catching her. Too close for comfort.

Malcolm had mentioned that they'd hired Brooks Investigations and the Mohawk man was leading the project. He didn't tell her anything else. After a quick search, she'd found the ex-cop a worthy adversary, but she was better than Jamie…smarter than him. She was smarter than all of them at Beck Security Systems and when she delivered her final blow she would have her revenge.

Phoenix heard the toilet flush and then the tap running. When she looked over her shoulder a few minutes later, Malcolm was at the door of her office dressed in slacks with his belt unbuckled and shirt in hand.

The plan was to get back to bed before he'd gotten up. She hadn't expected him to be up so soon.

"What are you doing up?" Malcolm asked looking at her through sleepy eyes. A wide grin splashed across his face as he shrugged into his shirt. She had made him happy earlier. The way he was looking at her suggested he wanted a repeat performance with the honey and whipped cream.

"I couldn't sleep." Phoenix switched to another document that was open on the screen and got up to meet him at the door. She pushed him towards the bedroom. "Go back to bed. I thought I would get some work done while you were asleep. You don't have to leave. Go back to bed and I'll be in to join you in a minute. You can arrest me again," she grinned.

"I would love to," he said with regret in his voice. "But I can't stay. I have to go back to the office. When I come back later you and I need to have a serious talk."

She didn't care about his serious talk. Beck Security Systems was the only thing she wanted to talk about. What was Jamie up to? She needed inside information and Malcolm was the only one that could supply that. His answers would determine how quickly her plan would unfold.

"It's after four in the morning. What's so important that you can't take a break and let your favorite lady take you on one more ride?"

Malcolm shook his head. "As tempting as that sounds, I can't stay, babe."

Babe. Phoenix hated it when he called her that. That wasn't important now. What she needed was information.

"What's going on at Beck Security Systems?" She asked hoping he would be more forthcoming than earlier. "You've been so tight-lipped since Jamie what's his name was hired. You always said that I don't care about your work. Well, I do sweetheart," she cooed.

"I can't discuss it. Any way, I missed an urgent call from the office."

"Come on tell me." Phoenix ran her long red fingernail up his chest and down stopping at the belt buckle. She was begging. It made her sick, but she had to know about the phone call. It was probably from Jamie. It could have been because she'd logged into the system using Malcolm's ID not ten minutes ago.

The plan was to log in a few more times as Malcolm and eventually throw suspicion onto him. They would waste valuable time pointing a finger at Malcolm.

It didn't take long to figure out his password. Malcolm was a creature of habit. He ate at the same restaurant, took the same route home to and from work everyday and he liked sex. Strike that, loved sex.

When they first met, he loved talking about his work. Now he had decided to change his habits. Something she hadn't counted on.

"I can't talk about what's going at work."

"Tell me, please."

"You know I can't. We had this discussion already several times tonight," he said sounding almost irritated. Why are you bringing it up again?"

"You can't or you won't," she said frustrated, pushing him away hard when he tried to touch her. "You used to tell me everything. It's as if you don't trust me any more."

"It has nothing to do with you."

"Then tell me."

"We'll talk later. I have to go," he said turning away from the door.

"It's as if you think that I'm the one that uploaded the virus. You won't even be able to find the damn thing anyway."

He turned around slowly. "Why did you say that?"

Malcolm stared at Phoenix as if he was seeing her for the first time, eyes widened, lips pursed. His gaze fell on the computer. She knew she'd said too much. He flipped on the light and grabbed her arm dragging her into the room towards the desk. Hitting the enter key on the computer had brought up a blank word document. He closed the document and the secure page of Beck Security Systems filled the screen. Disappointment replaced rage.

He cursed under his breath. "Tell me you're not responsible for what's going on at Beck Security Systems." He shook her. "Tell me."

Phoenix didn't respond. She stood there looking at him waiting. His fingers bit painfully in the flesh of her forearms where he grabbed her. The shaking stopped but he didn't let her go. She waited for the blow to come and braced herself in silence. It never came, only anger.

"My God," Malcolm said staring at the computer as if something occurred to him. He opened his mouth then closed it again. He turned his face away for a moment. "That day when you backed your car into mine, it wasn't an accident. You planned it. You planned all of this."

She could lie to him denying the truth, but he'd already seen through her. He wanted answers she wasn't ready to give him, answers she didn't want to give. He was a means to an end. That was his role. He wasn't important anymore. The wounded puppy dog look on his face almost made her want to apologize.

"I guess this is you." He showed her a picture he pulled from the pocket of his slacks.

"I thought you said you couldn't see the woman's face." She stared at the picture, but didn't take it from him as he pushed it towards her.

"Our tech guy removed the shadow."

"It's amazing what we can do with technology." She took the photograph when he pressed it into her hand, studying it. Then a smile spread across her lips. "It's not one of my better pictures, is it? I think it's the blonde wig. It makes me look too old. That's why I got the blonde extension. It looks more natural. Don't you think?"

"I didn't want to believe it. On my way over here, I'd convinced myself the resemblance was a coincidence. I defended you."

He shoved her away from him like she was garbage. The wounded puppy dog look was gone. He was angry, unpredictable now. She couldn't control him with sex anymore and she scrambled trying to figure out what to do next.

It was too soon, she thought beating the heels of her palms against her forehead. She needed more time.

Think.

"You're using me so you could destroy the company. I love you. How could you do this?"

"Don't be so melodramatic darling. It's not the worst thing that has ever happened to you. There will be enough money at the end of this and we'll both be rich."

"Rich? How do you propose to get money out of Beck? By holding his company hostage? I know Beck. He won't give you a dime."

"He destroyed my life." She beat her fist against her chest. "He needs to pay and he will pay!"

"Who are you?"

Phoenix didn't like the way he was looking at her as if there was something wrong with her. She had to make him understand. Then maybe he would change his mind and be on her side. She needed someone on her side. Someone to love her not hurt her. He didn't hurt her when he could have.

"Don't you want to be rich, Malcolm? You said you did. We can get married. Isn't that what you want? I can make you happy. Didn't I prove that tonight?"

Malcolm didn't care about her any more. He looked at her as if she was nothing. He was like all the others. They said they loved her and then turned on her.

"You're responsible for Sydney's disappearance." Malcolm said as if he had some divine revelation. "Where is she?"

"Sydney's safe. She's my get out of jail free card," Phoenix grinned.

"The attempts on Markie's life...you could've killed her."

Phoenix shrugged. "There are casualties in war."

Contempt seeped into his voice. It was directed at her. She'd show him. She'd show all of them. She wouldn't allow anyone to push her around anymore.

"This isn't a bloody war. You're sick," he spat, shoving her away when she tried to grab his hand. He reached for the phone on the desk. "I'm calling the police."

Phoenix rubbed her hands together and began pacing the floor. Monika called her delusional. Her mother said she was crazy and her father called her mad. Now Malcolm was calling her sick after his confession of love.

There was nothing wrong with her. Why was everyone telling her there was something wrong? Because they wanted to put her back in that place with the white walls and force medication down her throat. She rubbed her knuckles against her temples trying to relieve the sudden pressure building up in her head.

No. She wasn't going back to the hospital. Monika had tried to force her to go back and…well she was Monika now. Monika Beck was married to Dalton Beck and Malcolm was trying to ruin everything. He wanted her for himself and because she doesn't want him he was trying to ruin her.

Picking up the heavy granite paperweight from the desk, she put all her weight behind the stone and brought it down on Malcolm's head when he reached for the phone. When the stone connected to his head, it made a thud and he slumped over onto the desk with a loud groan. She watched the blood flow from the gash on the back of his head pooling onto the desk turning the papers crimson.

She pushed the chair under his legs and he fell back into it. His head hung over the headrest with his arms stretched out on the elbow rest.

"The *Oscar* for Best Actress in a leading role goes to Phoenix…no, Monika Beck for her role in Hide and Seek," and she began to laugh and laugh because they would never find her. Then she had the perfect idea as she wiped the tears of laughter from her eyes. It was time she had a conversation with her husband.

She fished through Malcolm's pocket for his cell phone and searched through the missed calls and found what she was looking for.

"What's going on?" Beck asked when he opened the door of Jamie's office. The office was quiet except for the humming of the computer equipment and Jamie's fingers clicking on the keyboard.

The 911 4:30 a.m. call had jarred him from sleep and away from Marklynn's warm body. Beck had broken all the speed limits to arrive at the office only to be greeted by Jamie's deep dark scowl. He didn't even get a chance to sit down let alone take off his jacket before Jamie jumped on him

"Where is Malcolm?" he growled.

Jamie had made the office his home away from home with a rolled up sleeping bag in the corner and food within reach. After sending the team home, it appeared as if he'd hunkered down for the night, but something had set him off. Had the network been accessed?

Decked out in full combat gear all the way down to his boots laced up at the calves, it was as though he was gearing up for war and it appeared Beck would be the first casualty.

"Did you call him?" Beck asked calmly trying to defuse the situation.

"He's not picking up at home or on his cell phone. Yet, he logged into the network just after four this morning."

Beck went still. He needed coffee, something to cut through the fog in his mind. But Jamie's comment had done just that.

"What do you mean?" Beck asked but then he already knew what Jamie meant.

He and Malcolm had left the office together. There was no reason for him to log into the system when Jamie was monitoring it.

Beck reached for the phone in his jacket pocket then realized he'd left it on the front seat of his SUV. He grabbed the phone on Jamie's desk.

He tried Malcolm's home then his cell phone number. "He's not picking up," Beck said to Jamie. "He may be at his girlfriend's house. I don't have her number."

Jamie's mouth twisted. Then he asked, "What do you know about his girlfriend?"

"Not much. I've spoken to her on the phone a couple

of times. What are you getting at?"

"You and Malcolm are good friends, yet you've never met her. How did he meet her? Did he at the very least tell you that?"

"They haven't been seeing each other that long." Beck tried to remember when Malcolm had met her but couldn't. His friend was happy. Why should he question the relationship? Malcolm's relationship was his business.

"Malcolm said six months. The funny thing about your right hand man is that he loves to blow his own horn. Perhaps his girlfriend enjoys his music."

"What are you implying?"

"I'm not implying anything, I'm saying it. We did a complete security check on everyone from management right down to the cleaning staff including their partners."

"You did a security check on me?"

"That was my idea. We've ruled you out and cleared everyone on your team including Malcolm. However, that may be tainted."

"Tainted? How?"

"The identity of Malcolm's phantom girlfriend has not been cleared to my satisfaction. Malcolm said her name is Phoenix. Not *Phoenix* as in *Phoenix*, Arizona, but *Phoenix* as in Greek Mythology *Phoenix*. That's what Malcolm told me."

"So?"

"When I asked how he met her he became defensive. He didn't like my line of questioning. That's when the red flag went up. I started digging."

"What did you find?" Beck asked not sure if he wanted to know.

"Nothing. Phoenix Jackson, if that's her real name does not exist. She has never filed a tax return. There are no credit cards issued in her name anywhere and she has no driver's license."

"Have you told Malcolm?"

"Just got the report." Jamie tapped on the folder on the desk. "I did however show him the picture of the mystery woman."

"And?"

"The picture is gone. I'm thinking he's in on it with her."

Beck wanted to see the report, but Jamie didn't give it to him right away. He didn't believe Jamie's accusations about Malcolm. Malcolm was there when he needed money for the company. Asking his father wasn't an option for he had done enough after the car accident.

Malcolm was a source of support when his marriage to Monika ended. How could he believe what Jamie was saying? Malcolm had a weakness as far as women were concerned, but would he jeopardize the stability of the company over a woman?

Beck wasn't going to address Jamie's concerns until he'd spoken to Malcolm. But Jamie wouldn't let up. He turned in his swivel chair shoving the report in Beck's hand. Jamie was determined and wanted Beck to see what had to be seen. That was Jamie's job.

"Do you know what Social Engineering is, Beck? It's manipulating people into performing actions or divulging confidential information. How is it done? By using trickery or deception for the purpose of information gathering, fraud, or computer system access."

"I know what Social Engineering is," Beck said not in the mood for a lecture. He would not address any of Jamie's questions until he'd spoken with Malcolm. "I know Malcolm. He may have his faults, but he's careful. I can't see him letting someone get so close to him, manipulating him that way and putting the company at risk."

Jamie wasn't convinced with Beck's defense of his friend. This was his job – to find the breach within the organization. And it looks like he had. Could he be right about Malcolm? With the evidence in the file, it looked like he was.

"In most cases with Social Engineering the attacker never comes face-to-face with the victim." Beck dropped the folder on Jamie's desk and then massaged the back of his stiff neck. "If you're right about Malcolm, then the woman in the picture could be his girlfriend." Or Monika, that went unsaid but Jamie knew what he was thinking.

"We'll find out soon enough. I've been doing this job a long time and I always trust my gut. We'll either hear from her or Malcolm."

No sooner had Jamie made that declaration the phone on the desk rang. Beck looked at the caller ID and said, "Let's get some answers." He hit the speaker button. "Malcolm where are you?"

"Not Malcolm, darling, it's Monika."

Beck's heart just about stopped. He couldn't believe his ears. Yes, it did sounded like Monika, but she was dead. He rubbed the back of his hand across his forehead.

How did he know she was dead? Based on the type of explosion and the current at the time, Monika's body could have been washed away, was washed away. The investigation concluded that she was dead. If she was still alive….No. He refused to believe it.

"Monika is dead," Beck said when he found his voice.

Beck's eyes fell on Jamie. He was trying to trace Malcolm's cell phone location using GPS tracking software, as Malcolm's phone was company issued.

"You can call me Lazarus if you like," the woman said with a throaty laugh.

"Where is Malcolm? Let me talk to him."

"Okay, Dalton Beck," she said sounding bored. "I'll play your little game and give you time to trace the call. You haven't found me yet, but go right ahead and try. Oh, Jamie Wright, you're a worthy opponent. However, I'm much better."

Jamie glanced at the phone, but didn't rise to her bait.

"Where is Malcolm," Beck asked again.

"Malcolm is resting. We were up rather late."

Beck had to assume two things at that moment. Malcolm was in on the sabotage or he was dead. By the woman's deadpan tone, he concluded the latter. He knew Monika and didn't think she was capable of murder. Yet this woman on the other end of the phone clearly was. What if it was Monika? The question plagued him.

Beck looked down at Jamie and Jamie shook his head. He couldn't get a fix on the call.

"The signal is bouncing all over the place," Jamie whispered.

Since Jamie wasn't getting anywhere with the trace Beck asked, "What do you want?"

"Beck Security Systems. It's mine and you took it away from me. You will sell it and give me what's mine."

Beck felt cold. Numb. He didn't think it would happen again, but it was happening. Except this time there were no lawyers battling it out around a table in a conference room just a mad woman making demands. No face. Just a voice, a very angry voice.

"Assuming you are Monika, you got everything in the divorce settlement. I ended up with nothing."

He wasn't going to bow to her request. For three months she'd invaded his life, lurking in the shadows. She has now surfaced with demands. He wasn't going to walk away from his company. If it was a fight she wanted then so be it.

"Not everything. You're still alive and that…that woman you're sleeping with has taken my place. She's like a damn cat with nine lives. Well, she's on her last."

"If you hurt her—"

"You'll do what?" The voice that exploded over the speakerphone was filled with venom.

Beck stared at the phone in silence. For the first time in his life that he could remember, he was afraid, afraid for Marklynn, himself and afraid of losing his company. His head began to pound, his heart raced.

"What's the matter? Cat got your tongue? No problem. All you need to do is listen sweetheart."

"I am *not* your sweetheart."

"You are what I say you are. You've taken everything away from me. I'm going to take everything away from you and Marklynn including her sister."

"No!"

"Yes! You give me my money or I'll kill Sydney and then your precious girlfriend."

The woman hung up and the dial tone echoed throughout the room. Jamie hit the end call button. Beck felt sick to his stomach. He had to physically steady himself before he picked up the phone and punched in the number.

"O'Malley, we need to talk, now!"

Markie had the two pictures side by side laid out on the kitchen table. Monika Beck and who?

"Who are you?" She asked aloud over the groaning of the refrigerator and the clanking of the window unit air conditioner in the living room. She made a mental note to call the repairman and order a new fridge then turned her attention back to the picture.

Karter had done a great job removing the shadow from the woman's face. It was almost as if the woman was looking at her. She was a step away from calling Nan to do some sort of psychic reading on the picture. Yeah, she was that desperate.

They had a face but no name to put to the face. She was hoping that they would've gotten lucky with the prints that were lifted from the Bowman's house in Jamaica Plains. No such luck. Beck had said the only prints found were that of the homeowners.

When Beck was called into the office earlier that morning she would have gladly gone with him for they were still up. He had told her that one of them sleepwalking was enough. The bed had felt lonely after his departure and she'd gotten up in search of the pictures. That was four hours ago.

She didn't want to think about their love making, but it consumed her. Beck said he loved her. Jared had told her he loved her also, but it meant nothing. He'd walked away with her heart when she couldn't give him what he wanted.

It felt different with Beck. He said he wouldn't walk away, but she couldn't be sure. Was she willing to take that chance? Sydney would. Sydney was never afraid to do what she wanted to do. Markie wished she were more like her sister.

Her heart sank as she swallowed back her tears. She knew the odds of finding missing persons. The longer it takes to find them the least likely they will be found alive. She wasn't going to think about the odds. Nan keeps insisting Sydney was still alive and that was enough for her.

After a strawberry yogurt and a bowl of cereal, Markie turned her attention back to the pictures trying to figure out what it was about the blonde woman's picture that troubled her.

Jamie had included several pictures of Monika in the file and Markie had those out as well comparing them to the woman with no name. They could be sisters?

Sisters.

Markie had never thought to check if Monika had a sister. Besides, Beck would have told her if he had suspected something. Since he didn't recognize the woman in the picture then he had no cause to say anything about her.

She had taken Beck at his word. Doubt plagued her. No one else would have gotten off that easily with her. Had her relationship with him clouded her judgment? She reached for the cordless phone on the kitchen counter.

"Peter Kingston, please," Markie said when a man with a gruff voice answered. "Yes, thanks. I'll hold."

"Detective Kingston." The voice boomed in her ear.

"It's Marklynn Brooks."

"Hey Brooks. Hang on for a minute."

Markie had helped him when his sixteen-year-old drug addicted daughter ran away from home. Kingston was one of her first clients when she started the agency. He had wanted to keep the troubles with his daughter quiet and asked her for help. His daughter was now a mother of twins and married to a senator. Markie wanted to collect on the IOU he'd promised.

"Sorry about that. How are you? Kingston asked. "It's not the same around here without you."

"I'm fine," she said not wanting to talk about the past.

"As you know, things happen."

"It wasn't right."

"Don't lose any sleep over it. We have more cases than we can handle at the moment. I'm actually calling because I need a favor."

"Shoot."

"I want to know if there has been any recent activity on the Monika Beck case. It was a boating accident about four years ago. The investigating officer was Detective Samuel O'Malley."

Kingston lowered his voice. "What do you mean?"

"You're stalling. Come on Kingston, you owe me." Markie got up from the table to throw the empty yogurt container in the recycling bin and put her bowl in the sink. She balanced the phone between her ear and shoulder while she turned on the tap to rinse the bowl and spoon.

"Jamie already used that 'you owe me' card."

"Wait. You spoke to Jamie?" She turned off the tap reaching for the towel to quickly dry her hands. "When?"

"I'll tell you the same thing I told Jamie. Samuel O'Malley reopened it unofficially at the request of Monika's ex-husband, Dalton Beck. He was investigated at time for her murder, but they couldn't make anything stick."

"Because they couldn't prove it or because he did it?"

"Talk to Jamie."

Beck a suspect in a murder investigation? Markie couldn't breathe. "What happened?"

"What happened to what?"

"The investigation O'Malley opened up."

"It was shut down. That's all I know. We're even now."

Markie's head reeled after she hung up the phone. Why didn't she know about Beck being a suspect in his wife's boating accident? Had she dug deeper she would have known instead of ending up in bed with him.

Why did Jamie keep his conversation with Kingston from her?

The ringing of the phone jarred her out of her shock and she reached blindly for it. "Marklynn Brooks."

"Are you okay?" Jamie asked sounding worried.

"I want to talk to you. I just spoke to Peter—"

"I'm at Beck's office," Jamie cut her off. "Carlos should be arriving at your house in about ten minutes to get you."

"Why? Have you heard from Sydney?" Jamie didn't answer and her heart leaped in her chest. "Jamie—" The doorbell rang and she looked towards the door and saw the large shadow through the frosted glass window part of the door. "I think he's here."

"Good. He'll fill you in," Jamie said and hung up the phone before she could get another word in.

"What's going on?" Markie asked Carlos when she opened the door. He was dressed in a pale green mesh T-shirt under a lime green leather jacket, jeans and cowboy boots. Not one of his better fashion decisions. Then she remembered he was working as a bouncer at a nightclub where a run away girl was spotted. He probably came straight from the club.

"The Ryder case," he said when he caught her checking out his outfit. "She was a no show."

As much as she was concerned about the missing thirteen year old, Sydney was the only person she wanted to know about.

"I just got off the phone with Jamie. He said you would fill me in."

"We can talk on the way," Carlos said pushing her gently towards the bedroom. "Get dressed."

Ten minutes later Markie was dressed in jeans and a white shirt. When she emerged from the bedroom Carlos was coming out of the kitchen with the pictures she'd left on the table.

"Ready." He handed her the pictures.

She nodded securing her gun in her shoulder holster then grabbed her handbag.

Carlos opened the front door, stepped out onto the veranda and stopped. She ran into his back and had to grab onto his jacket to keep from falling backward. He didn't seem to notice as his eyes searched the street watching the passing cars and pedestrians all the while his body guarding her. He was on hyper alert and she wanted to know why.

"Are you going to tell me what's going on?" Then she noticed Beck's SUV parked in her driveway. "Why are you driving Beck's vehicle?"

He didn't say a word until they were inside the Navigator and after he put in a call to Jamie to tell him they were on their way.

"Well?" Her patience stretched to the limit.

"We heard from a woman who we believe kidnapped Sydney."

Markie felt the color drain from her face. She willed herself to remain calm as she focused on Carlos' words. They had heard from a woman who *they* believed had Sydney. The *'they'* she assumed would be Jamie and Beck. There was nothing definite. They were still unsure.

"Why do you believe this woman kidnapped Sydney?"

"She called Beck. The conversation between them was recorded. Jamie wants you to hear it. One more thing, Sam O'Malley is involved. You'll know more about his involvement when we get to Beck's office."

Markie snapped her head around to look at Carlos, but he kept his eyes focused on the road. It appeared that was all he was going to say and she didn't press him.

Carlos merged onto I-93 North heading to Boston as Markie sat back reflecting on the events of the last seven days. From Sydney's disappearance to her relationship with Beck, everything seemed to be spinning out of control.

She was used to being in control and not having decisions made for her. Yet that's what was happening. They were driving Beck's Navigator and if she was a betting person she would lay odds that Beck had something to do with it. Not just something, a lot.

Why did she need an escort to Beck's office? They could've called her and she could've found her way there by herself. What was Sam O'Malley doing at Beck's office? Markie had a feeling that Beck could answer all her questions.

Then it all came together in her mind. Beck recognized the woman in the picture and called O'Malley that would explain why Monika Beck's case was reopened. Peter Kingston said so.

Another revelation hit her like a head on collision. The woman in the picture was Monika Beck. Beck recognized her and he kept it from her.

He lied to her. Why? The woman in the picture, his ex, had Sydney. Monika had changed her appearance and Beck knew it from the beginning.

That had to be it. Monika Beck was still alive. Markie felt sick to her stomach.

CHAPTER TWELVE

Beck looked up from his conversation at the table with O'Malley when Marklynn entered the conference room. O'Malley had arrived half an hour after Beck's call and they had been locked behind closed doors trying to figure out the best plan of action. O'Malley and Booker were at odds about something so they were on their own.

Six hours after Phoenix's call they were still scrambling to catch the woman and locate Sydney. They were close. O'Malley was waiting for a call. Beck wanted to wait until O'Malley had the woman's address before he called Marklynn, but Jamie wouldn't allow it.

Jamie had said she would be angry. Angry was an understatement. Marklynn had taken one look at the surveillance equipment and O'Malley and came to the conclusion that they had excluded her from something important.

Soft brown eyes that had been filled with laugher when they were making love last night were cold and unyielding. He should have understood what finding her sister meant to her and the responsibility she'd placed upon herself to do so.

"I see I'm late, gentlemen." Her voice matched her chilling tone and Beck immediately regretted his decision about not calling her earlier. Jamie wasn't immune either.

Beck looked over at Jamie who was sitting in front of his laptop. Jamie said nothing, but his eyes spoke volumes with the "I told you so." He was on his own.

"You're right on time," Sam said and got up from the table to greet Markie when she entered the room. He extended his hand to her. "I'm afraid I commandeered Beck's boardroom, but it couldn't be helped."

"It's been a while and several phone calls I might add," she said and shook his hand.

"You look well," O'Malley said and flashed her a smile that lit up his face. It seemed as though he was trying to turn an awkward situation around but Marklynn wasn't having any of that.

"As well as one can be with a truck load of money," Marklynn said.

Surprise registered on O'Malley's face and she gave him a knowing look. Markie had mentioned to him about what some of her former colleagues had said about her settlement.

She dropped her handbag on the table and sat down in the chair turning to face O'Malley. The detective sat at the edge of the table beside her, his arms folded across his wide chest.

Dressed in black combat gear, complete with boots and cap, O'Malley looked like a man on a mission and they needed him right now. Phoenix was on the loose and the threat of more violence had everyone on edge.

Silence engulfed the room. It was as if everyone knew what needed to be said, but no one wanted to go first. No one wanted to tell Marklynn that Phoenix had taken her sister.

"You want to tell me what you're doing here?" Markie asked not wasting any more time.

O'Malley looked at Beck before he spoke. "Beck came to me with this picture." He placed the picture on the table in front of Marklynn. "He thought he recognized the woman."

"His ex-wife." Markie rubbed her temples. She raked her hand through her hair then dropped her elbows on the table. "Monika Beck is still alive."

There was a sharp edge in her voice when she spoke.

She didn't look at him. Hard eyes fixed on O'Malley. Beck knew then that things would never be the same between them again.

"It's not Monika. It's Melanie her sister."

"Melanie? I've heard that name. She called the publisher of the magazine." Markie looked over at Jamie for confirmation and he nodded. "She has Sydney. Why?"

"Marklynn—" Beck attempted to join the conversation but Jamie cut him off.

"Yes. We believe so but we haven't spoken to Sydney," Jamie said. He got up from the laptop and stopped a few feet away from Marklynn at the table. "What proof do you have, O'Malley that the woman in that picture is Melanie? We were able to remove the shadow from the woman's face in the photo, but we still don't know who she is."

"It's Melanie," O'Malley said. "She has been in and out of mental institutions since the age of sixteen. According to the report I got from the last hospital she was committed to four years ago, before she disappeared, she suffers from delusions and hallucinations. Schizophrenia was also thrown in the mix. Bottom line — she has mental issues."

O'Malley handed Marklynn a dossier on Melanie. Beck already knew what was in the file. Monika had gone to see her sister after their divorce. The hospital verified the visit. After Monika's visit, Melanie disappeared and Monika was dead.

The report went on to say Melanie didn't have much contact with other people when she was growing up, just her computer. Their parents, Roberta and Kennedy Daniels didn't spend a lot of time with their two daughters, Monika and Melanie. They were raised by nannies.

The two sisters were close growing up until Monika befriended a boy in high school. Melanie tried to kill the boy. It was then the family realized that something was wrong with Melanie and shipped her off to a mental institution. They'd forgotten about Melanie. Now she wanted to ensure that everyone remembered her.

Melanie showed all of them, Beck thought. With her

father's money, Melanie earned a degree in computer science. With her *mental issues*, as O'Malley had called them, she was able to get an education and worked for a computer company until she was fired. Details of her firing were not disclosed.

According to O'Malley, the last time the Daniels' heard from Melanie was when Monika died, right before Melanie disappeared from the hospital. It was Melanie who informed them of Monika's death, not the police.

The woman was his sister-in-law and he never knew she existed. Monika had kept it from him.

Marklynn looked up from the file in front of her and stared at O'Malley. Beck knew that look. He had been on the receiving end several times. She was ready for battle.

"Is Monika still alive?"

"No," O'Malley replied glancing at Beck.

Marklynn wasn't finished with O'Malley yet and they all knew it. They didn't have long to wait for the fireworks.

"Are you sure? Based on the police report I've seen you weren't so sure four years ago. You had no dead body to prove your case," her eyes challenged.

"My hands were tied back then. I'm sure now."

"How?"

Beck thought O'Malley would fill her in on their discussion at the café but nothing was said.

"I know. You can't say," Markie said. Can you at least tell me where you got all this information on Melanie?"

"Most of it from the hospital."

"Can you tell me why Melanie told her parents about Monika's death before the police? That would mean—"

"Melanie killed her sister," O'Malley concluded. "If that information had come out at the time then Melanie would have been a suspect as well as..."

"Beck," she finished shaking her head not hiding the bitterness in her voice. "I just found out about that. It says here," Markie pointed to a paragraph on the page in front of her, "she goes by the name of Phoenix. Greek mythology? The mythical firebird?"

"That's the information I got from Jamie. He also said Malcolm is quite taken with her," O'Malley said.

Markie turned to the next page in the file and Beck watched as her hand paused on the page. She stiffened.

"What is it?" Beck asked moving closer to Marklynn. He wanted to put his arms around her, to protect her. Yet, with every piece of information she uncovered had widened the distance between them even further. She wanted nothing to do with him least of all comfort and it broke his heart.

"Monika's birthday was three months ago. Is that correct?"

"Yes," Beck replied wondering where she was going with her line of question.

"I believe that's when Beck Security Systems started having problems."

"I don't understand." Beck said. Then it hit him like a fist in the gut. What they had been trying to figure out all along, the "why now question" was staring him in the face.

"That's it," Jamie said slapping his forehead. "We just found our connection. Why Melanie started when she did."

"Monika's birthday is the trigger. It seems Melanie has been reborn into her sister's identity and has taken over her life," Markie said agreeing with Jamie. "Which means in her mind she believes she is married to Beck." She turned her gaze to O'Malley. "Tell me you know where she is, O'Malley or at least you have a starting point."

"I got a lead from the hospital. We found a post office box that led to an address in Chinatown. We're waiting for a search warrant. Oh, another thing," O'Malley reached for a file folder behind him on the table and flipped it open. "The pickup that tried to run you over, we found it abandoned yesterday. There were two sets of fingerprints taken from the pickup. One matched the set taken from Sydney's apartment. There is an APB out for a Frank Wang and Lee Kane."

"Anything else?" She said to O'Malley. He shook his head.

"Yeah. The recording," Jamie said.

Beck didn't agree with Jamie about playing the

recording of his conversation with Phoenix back to Marklynn. He thought it would do more harm than good and O'Malley agreed. Jamie dug his heels in and when he started the tape, Beck saw the color drain from Marklynn's face.

The boardroom was a sleek design from the cabinets to the massive mahogany table. They were in a room where multimillion-dollar deals were made, but not today.

Today, Markie sat up straight in the chair listening to the exchange between Beck and Phoenix as a chill ran down her spine.

Phoenix's voice sounded normal at first, like she was chatting to an old lover. She kept calling Beck darling as if she was on intimate terms with him, but with each rejection from Beck her behavior became more erratic and hostile.

Markie froze when the woman ended the phone conversation with, *"You give me my money or I'll kill Sydney and then your precious girlfriend."*

She felt lightheaded and grabbed the edge of the table for support. The woman wanted to kill Sydney over what? Money? Even though she was already sitting down she felt as though she was going to pass out. Jamie rested his hands on her shoulders.

Markie shrugged his hands off and turned in her chair to face Beck who had wandered over to the window, his back faced them. The outside world had captured his attention while she listened to the message from his sister-in-law. He hadn't wanted her to hear the message and was visibly upset when Jamie played the recording.

"How long will it take for you to liquidate the assets of Beck Security Systems?"

Phoenix didn't just want money. Her parents were rich according to O'Malley and Markie was sure there was a trust fund somewhere with Melanie's name on it.

No. Melanie wanted money that came from the sale of Beck Security Systems. Something had happened to Melanie and she wanted to hurt Beck by taking away the one thing he had managed to hold on to after the divorce.

"You can't be serious." Beck turned abruptly from the window shaking his head. "There has to be some other way, please. It's all I have. Besides, I can't sell the company overnight."

"You have to do it, Beck," she pleaded.

This was her chance to save Sydney, to be there for her sister. She didn't care how long it was going to take. She wanted him to do it.

They knew who had Sydney. All Beck had to do was give Phoenix what she wanted. Markie wasn't thinking like a cop or a private investigator. She wasn't even thinking rationally.

Sydney was going to die and she needed to do something. But Beck wasn't going to give into Phoenix. He raked his hand through his hair and began to pace the length of the wall-to-wall window. Beck Security Systems was his life and he wasn't about to give it up for Sydney. He had said he loved her. She hadn't wanted to think about it and had pushed it to the back of her mind, until now. Did he really love her?

"That's not fair, Marklynn," Beck said, his voice raw with emotions. He stood staring at her his eyes begging for understanding, but she couldn't give him any. It was a choice between him and her sister.

It suddenly became about the two of them in the room and the fragile string that held their relationship together. Jamie and O'Malley faded into the background in silence.

"Fair?" She jumped up out of her chair facing him. "Your sister-in-law has kidnapped my sister. You knew about Phoenix/Melanie whatever her name is and didn't tell me."

Something else occurred to her. With the hatred that laced the woman's voice and her willingness to hurt anyone around Beck just to get back at him, this was personal. Very personal. Then a thought occurred to her. Before she even had a chance to process it she voiced it.

"My God, did you have an affair with her while you were married to Monika?"

It was the question that hung in the air that no one wanted to ask. All eyes fell on Beck, but he only looked at Marklynn.

Disappointment, hurt and anger all played out on his face. She was accusing him of infidelity.

"I can't believe you asked me that. We never had a relationship of any kind. I never knew Monika had a sister until O'Malley told me about her today. Monika was never close with her parents. We rarely saw them and when we did, they never talked about Melanie."

Relief fought with anger and anger won hands down. Although she believed him about not having a relationship with Melanie she was still angry. He didn't want to help in getting Sydney back and he'd deliberately lied to her.

"The picture was familiar to you and you suspected something. Instead of talking to me, you ran to O'Malley. You lied to me."

O'Malley opened his mouth to speak and Beck cut him off. "I wanted to help and made the decision to do so."

"It wasn't your decision to—"

"Time out!" Jamie did a time out sign like a referee calling a game. "We're all on the same side." He didn't try to touch her again, but he stood close like a guard between her and Beck.

Beck moved back towards the window dragging his hand across his face. He started to pace again. Hardness settled over his features.

Markie was breathing so hard she was shaking with anger, which was now directed at Jamie.

"No. We're not all on the same side. We all want different things here. I want Sydney safe at home. Beck wants to keep his precious company and O'Malley gets a second crack at catching the one that got away. I don't know what *you* want out of this. Perhaps your name on the door."

Jamie drew back as if she had struck him. He had been with her from the beginning and had always been honest with her. He had never kept anything from her. Yet, he sided with Beck. He knew what Beck was up to and didn't tell her. She was probably making more out of Jamie's involvement than it was, but she couldn't help it.

The three men stood staring at her. They all looked at her as if they wanted to say something to ease the fear that was tearing her apart, but nothing was said.

The woman could kill Sydney and there was nothing anyone of them could say that could ease the pain she felt. She knew it and they knew it.

The ringing of O'Malley's cell phone broke the silence that had settled over the room like a blanket.

"Yes," O'Malley turned away and barked into the phone. "I'm on my way. There may be two hostages. They may or may not be on site. Have a couple of ambulances standing by just in case."

Markie turned towards O'Malley when he requested the ambulance. He was covering all the bases she told herself. *Don't panic. Sydney is fine.*

When he got off the phone he turned to Markie and said, "We got the search warrant. You can come along, but I call the shots."

She didn't respond to O'Malley's words. Her heart beat in her chest like a drum. They were close to finding Sydney.

Markie turned to Jamie as he was packing up his laptop ready to go with them. "You stay here and finish what you've started. You said Melanie is getting into Beck Security Systems through some sort of back door. Find the door and shut it!"

Grabbing her handbag from the table, she was behind O'Malley when he opened the door and followed him out of the conference room. Carlos was leaning against the wall and he pushed away when she stepped into the hallway.

"You're with me, Carlos."

He looked past her shoulder to Jamie with a confused looked on his face. His eyes were asking what was going on, but she didn't have time for his questions. Markie was half way out the door when Beck caught up with them just before they reached the elevators.

"I'm coming O'Malley and don't try to stop me," Beck said with a determined look on his face.

"Fine. You ride with me and as I mentioned to Brooks, I'm in charge."

They all rode down to the underground parking lot in silence. Carlos and O'Malley found a spot on the wall staring straight ahead. Markie stood behind them watching the light move from floor to floor while Beck leaned against the control panel in the corner willing her to look at him. The elevator doors opened and everyone rushed out. Markie followed Carlos to his red Bronco.

"Marklynn wait," she heard Beck call. He ran to catch up with her, but she kept up her brisk pace. She didn't want to talk to him.

"Beck, let's roll," O'Malley yelled and a long curse followed.

"Gimme me a minute," he hollered back.

"Now!"

She climbed into the Bronco and slammed the door. Beck yanked it open ignoring Carlos' glare.

"We have nothing to say to each other."

"When this is over, you and I *will* talk," Beck said leaning in close to Markie's ear. "And that's a promise."

He slammed the door and ran over to O'Malley's car.

"Sydney."

A voice called to her out of the darkness but she ignored it. The darkness was a source of comfort to her and she didn't want to leave it. There was no pain in the darkness.

She couldn't feel the throbbing in her head or the pain in her side. And the stinging of her wrists caused by the rope burn, yes that was also forgotten.

She was going to die and accepted it. Yes, there was fear, but she would not give in. That would make it worse.

Was this how Derrick felt when he stepped on the roadside bomb?

Derrick.

In the darkness, she could be with Derrick. They could get married and have kids. Lots of kids. He was going to ask her to be his wife when his tour of duty was over Macy said so. But he never got the chance. They never had a chance at a life together because he never came home. She was so lost without him. He was the only one that understood her.

Derrick didn't want her to be anyone but herself. He loved her for who she was. She was unique. He said so and she believed him.

"Sydney, Sydney baby open your eyes."

The voice was stern yet gentle. Although it sounded familiar, she ignored it.

"Please talk to me." The voice begged for a response and she did.

"Nan?" Her eyes fluttered open and focused on the light in the corner of the room by the door. No, it couldn't be Nan. She had to be hallucinating.

Closing her eyes, she rolled over to the other side of the cot and grimaced in pain. Her head pounded as nausea rose up in her throat.

"Yes baby, it's Nana."

Sydney opened her eyes again squinting at the light shining in the corner of the room as she tired to sit up, but couldn't.

"Nan? Is that really you? How did you get here?"

"Yes baby. You know I'm always with you. No matter where you go. Help is coming."

"I don't feel so hot," she groaned. "My throat is dry and it hurts when I swallow."

"I know baby. Hang on."

"I can't," Sydney said closing her eyes again welcoming the darkness. In the darkness, it was safe.

No pain.

No fear.

She could be who she wanted to be and not worry about disappointing anyone. Hot tears flowed. She'd hurt Nan and Marklynn too many times to count. In the darkness she didn't have to worry about hurting anyone.

"Yes you can. Hang on for a little longer. Marklynn is coming."

"I don't know why she would," Sydney mumbled. "It's not like I was there for her. It was always about me." Hot tears rolled down her

cheeks. "I wasn't there for anyone but myself."

Sydney had started out wanting Markie to come and rescue her, but not anymore. Thoughts of the woman with the taser gun changed her mind. What if she came back when Markie was trying to rescue her? Her sister could get hurt and she would rather die than see Markie get hurt. She didn't want to put her in danger.

She wanted Markie to be safe, to be happy again. They were all happy once. It seemed so long ago. Death had stolen her parents, Derrick and it was knocking at her door.

"You're not the only one baby. We all depended on her a little too much because of fear I guess."

"Fear?" The light moved towards her.

Nan afraid? She had always been so strong.

"That's right, Sydney. But we're going to make it right. To do that, you need to hang in there. You want to make it right, don't you baby?"

"Right? Yes, Nan. I want to make it right."

The light faded. Sydney felt a warm hand on her forehead and closed her eyes.

"Make it right," she mumbled and slipped into darkness. She wasn't alone someone was holding her hand.

"Fools!" Phoenix slammed down the cordless phone on the kitchen counter after her conversation with Lee Kane. She breathed in and out slowly counting to ten between each breath trying to stop from shaking.

The only thing he and his cousin had to do was to get rid of the pickup. Nowhere in her instructions had she told them to park it at a gas station. Did she have to do everything herself?

Yes! When she depended on other people they messed things up. Reaching for the bottle of pills, with trembling hands she twisted off the cap. She needed one but shook out two into her sweaty palm, tossed them in her mouth. No water. Then waited for the shaking to stop.

With the police impounding the truck, it was safe to assume that they dusted it for prints and the two idiots would be picked up soon. She didn't hire them because they were choirboys.

They both had criminal records and that meant the police would be busting in her door soon, or she had to assume that they would find her somehow. The two idiots didn't know where she lived, but precautions must be taken.

She had slipped away once before and had a life along with a job. Back then no one knew she existed. Sam O'Malley had found a trail. He'd contacted the hospital according to her source. It was safe to assume he was out to get her.

Phoenix paused for a moment before pushing away from the counter heading for her bedroom. She should eat something. But she couldn't. Her stomach was in knots.

"You can still finish this." She assured herself when the shaking finally stopped.

For a split second Phoenix thought about calling her parents, but chased the thought from her mind. They didn't want to be around her let alone help her. They had made that clear.

She remembered the day when Monika came to visit her at the hospital to tell her about her engagement. Beck had just given her a ring. Big and sparkly.

Monika had asked her to be the maid of honor. They'd talked about it all day. The colors for the wedding were simple. Her dress would be the color of espresso and the bridesmaid's cream and espresso. But she could only participate in the wedding and meet Beck if she took her meds and stayed on them. She'd promised Monika she would because she wanted to be in the wedding…to feel like a part of the family.

Two days before the wedding they all came to see her. It was the first time she'd seen her parents in six months.

"What's wrong?" she asked, packed and ready to go when they came into the room. Monika didn't answer or even look at her. It was their mother that had started off the conversation.

"We don't think you're well enough to attend the wedding or even meet Mr. Beck and his family."

"Really mother," Monika said. "It's just one day. I promised."

"You shouldn't make promises you can't keep. You should have consulted with us first." Her mother looked at her father, who nodded in agreement. *"She's sick, Monika and this is where she belongs. Here she can get the help she needs. Remember what happened with that boy?"*

"That wasn't my fault mom. He tried to—"

"They were friends of ours which we lost because of your lies. You'll stay right where you are, where you belong with your kind."

"Monika you promised," she cried. *"I took all my meds. You promised."*

"I'm sorry," Monika said and mom pulled her out of the room. She needed their money to pay for the wedding. That was how their parents controlled them with money.

Dad stayed back in the room. He took her hand and stroked it. *"You know I love you, don't you? I'm the only one that loves you just the way you are. It's best that you stay here for now as your mother suggested. After the wedding, you can come home for a weekend and we'll see how it goes."*

She dragged her hand away. *"Get out!"*

Three weeks later Monika returned after the wedding and honeymoon with pictures. The wedding she wasn't allowed to attend. Her mother had said she couldn't go because she would bring shame upon her family. Everyone was at the wedding except for her. There were pictures in the society pages the following day with people she didn't recognize.

She hated her parents. When she'd called to inform them of Monika's death they had told her back then they wanted nothing to do with her unless she was back at the hospital.

Her father had given her another option. She could come home, but she knew what that meant. There was one way she could go home. No. Don't think about it. She would never go back to that house.

Since she had chosen none of her parent's option, she couldn't touch her trust fund. They had taken away her money because they couldn't break her. She didn't need their money. She was a survivor.

Monika didn't know what the word survivor meant. She'd allowed Dalton Beck to use her and then discard her like trash. Well, he wouldn't get away with throwing her aside and replacing her.

"He will pay," she vowed as she packed. Throwing a couple of jeans and T-shirts in a backpack, she headed to her office to grab the laptop.

Phoenix looked at Malcolm slumped over in the chair, he was barely breathing. His role was complete. By the time anyone found him or Sydney they would be dead.

Placing the laptop carefully in the backpack, she took the only picture she had kept of Monika, tossed it in the wastebasket and headed out the front door. She had no one.

Stepping out onto the sidewalk into the bustle of Chinatown, she put on her sunglasses. Chinatown was located in downtown Boston. One of the reasons she liked Chinatown was because people minded their own business especially where she lived. They didn't look at you unless you talked to them and she talked to no one unless they were a part of her plan.

Phoenix had chosen Chinatown because of its close proximity to Beck's office. Now she would have to find another place to finish what she'd started.

What she needed was a place to regroup and she knew just where to go. If she were lucky, Marklynn Brooks would come to her.

Markie jumped out of Carlos' Bronco when the vehicle screeched to a halt in front of a three-story apartment building. It had only taken ten minutes to arrive at Phoenix's apartment, but it had seemed a lot longer with every stoplight and stop sign.

All she could think about was Sydney. What if she was too late? How would she live with herself? She had promised Nan and had made a promise to her parents that she would take care of Sydney. She couldn't go back on her promise.

Three police cars with sirens blaring and two ambulances arrived at the same time. One of the cars blocked the street. She joined O'Malley, ready to enter the building but she had to wait for him to get organized. He was doing what he was trained to do but to her it was taking too long. They were wasting time.

"You two take the back entrance," O'Malley pointed to two of the six uniformed officers that had gathered around him awaiting instructions. The two he'd given orders to sprinted down the alley to the rear of the building.

"You two," he pointed to two of the four officers left, "stay here at the front entrance. No one enters or leaves the building until we're done. As for you two," he said to the last two officers. "You're with me and Brooks. Someone get Brooks a vest."

Markie thanked the officer who brought her the vest and secured it tightly around her torso with the wide Velcro straps. Markie checked her gun and nodded. She was ready and waiting for O'Malley.

The front entrance of the building was deserted. She didn't see an elevator, just three flights of stairs through the large glass window to the left of the building.

"Beck, you and the Jolly Green giant *wait* here."

Markie saw O'Malley motion to the officer he assigned to the door to ensure his orders were carried out.

"O'Malley—" Beck started to object.

"Brooks can handle herself and she is armed. This is as far as you go. Don't make me sorry I allowed you to come along," O'Malley warned.

Beck held up his hands and backed off. Markie could tell he wasn't pleased but too bad. He can kick up a fuss, but he would be a lot safer away from that crazy woman. She didn't want to worry about him getting hurt.

"When this is over we will talk."

Breathing deep, she focused on the task ahead pushing Beck's words and the disappointed look on his face from her mind.

"Markie?" Carlos shot her a questioning look ignoring O'Malley's orders. He didn't like being referred to as the *Jolly Green Giant*. Carlos' face was set in a stubborn line. He was gearing up to enter the building with her despite O'Malley's orders.

"Take care of him, Brooks or I'll have him arrested," O'Malley warned.

"It's okay, Carlos. Stay put," she laid a hand on his chest. "I'll be fine."

O'Malley turned the beak of his black cap to the back of his head and shouted, "Apartment 220. Let's move!"

Feet pounded on the steps as they raced up the stairs. The two officers that were with them approached the door on the second floor. One was a blond jock O'Malley called Parker and the other a red-haired freckled face man who looked like he should still be playing in a sandbox, not cops and robbers. O'Malley called him *Opie*. Markie didn't think it was his real name.

Parker opened the door on the second floor and they moved into the hallway of the unit. The once beige walls were now the same color as the worn out brown carpet.

The heavy food scent of something Markie didn't recognize hit her right in the gut. She swallowed hard to keep her breakfast down.

Unit 220 was to the left of the stairwell door a few feet away. O'Malley followed the officers and she was right behind him.

"Clear," Parker said chomping on a piece of gum he popped in his mouth. She wasn't the only one trying to keep her breakfast down. They moved towards 220 with precision and speed. A man opened the door to exit his apartment unit across the hall and O'Malley waved him back inside.

"Police! We have a search warrant. Open the door!" The red-haired officer's voice boomed in the corridor as he banged his fist on the door. What he lacked in appearance he definitely made up in lung power.

A crashing noise came from inside the apartment and the red-haired officer reared back and kicked the door in on

O'Malley's orders. Markie followed O'Malley when he entered the apartment holding her weapon in a firm two-handed grip. Let Sydney be okay, she prayed and adrenalin took over.

The kitchen and living room was cleared with one sweep of the eye. There was a small balcony that could be seen from the living room window. It looked like there were stairs leading from the balcony to a fire escape.

"See where the stairs lead to," O'Malley said to Parker pointing with the barrel of his gun.

The rest of them headed to the bedroom just steps from the living room. Markie could see the inside of the bedroom from the living room. Nothing fancy just a bed covered with a white sheet. Her heart rolled over in her chest when she saw a large red stain on the sheet.

Blood?

"No." O'Malley stopped her with a firm hand on her shoulder when she started towards the bedroom.

Markie followed O'Malley. The bedroom was empty. In a room off the bedroom Malcolm lay bleeding on the floor. From the blood on the chair and desk it appeared he'd fallen out of the chair. That may have been the noise they had heard outside the front door. She didn't see Sydney. Whose blood was on the bed? Her heart pounded in her chest as the blood rushed to her head.

"Sydney's not here," Markie said willing herself to stay calm.

O'Malley dropped down on his knees to check Malcolm's pulse. "I need a paramedic in 202!" O'Malley shouted in a radio unit attached to his bulletproof vest. "I have a male, late forties, his breathing shallow."

"Malcolm," Markie said when O'Malley looked up at her. "His name is Malcolm Rivers." The last time she'd seem him he was grinning at her. Now he was clinging to life. Phoenix had done this to him. Her eyes searched the room again. "Where is Sydney?"

"There is a storage unit in the basement. The stairs on the other end—"

Markie raced out of the apartment towards the back stairs.

"Brooks!"

CHAPTER THIRTEEN

"We need a paramedic on the second floor," the officer with the brush cut manning the door said.

"What's going on?" Beck asked but the officer ignored him. Along with guarding the door like it was the Holy Grail, the officer didn't let him or Carlos out of his sight.

Beck hated waiting. Half an hour had passed since he had watched Marklynn walk through the door into the apartment building and disappear from sight. He'd wanted to follow and would have if it weren't for the threat of being arrested by the gatekeeper.

"Move, move it!" The officer motioned to the two men standing beside the ambulance and held the door for them.

"What's going on up there?" Beck asked inching closer to the open door.

"I'm here with you. How am I supposed to know?" he said and closed the door when two paramedics ran pass them into the apartment building.

Beck stood by the front door of the apartment building eyes fixed on the wall of glass window as he watched the men hurry up the stairs carrying the gurney. No one else had been allowed to enter or leave the building since they arrived and residents of the apartment complex started to complain. A crowd began to gather outside the building and Carlos was pulled on duty to help with crowd control until more officers showed up.

The mid-day sun beat down on the back of Beck's neck, but all he could feel was the chill that had taken over his body. In the last three months, his relatively calm life had turned into a nightmare with each passing day. He could very well lose everything – his company and Marklynn.

Who was he kidding? Marklynn wanted nothing to do with him. He had chosen his company over her sister's life and she would not forgive him for that. It couldn't end this way between them. He wouldn't let it. She needed to understand why he couldn't give up his company.

The front door of the apartment building burst open fifteen minutes later and Malcolm was wheeled out on a stretcher towards one of the waiting ambulances. His face was gray, swollen and covered in blood. What about Sydney?

"Parker where are you?" Beck heard O'Malley yell over the radio. "Brooks is heading for the basement."

"Brooks! Wait!"

Markie heard O'Malley's voice. It sounded far away in the distance instead of two flights of stairs above. His footsteps pounded on the steps echoing in the narrow stairwell as he raced to catch up with her.

Markie reached the basement and yanked the door open. There were several storage areas with items behind chain-linked fencing.

The basement was dark and dingy and the smell of mildew hung in the air. The only light source came from under the door of the storage room at the end of the long narrow hallway. As she neared the door she noticed the deadbolt.

Markie turned her head away and fired one shot. The lock broke and fell off the door on the ground. Sydney was curled up in a fetal position on the cot when she entered the room. The noise from the gunshot blast hadn't aroused her and she feared the worst.

"Sydney. Can you hear me?" Markie lay her gun down

on the cot and checked for Sydney's pulse. "Oh God." She worked frantically to loosen the rope from her wrists but couldn't. A tear slipped down her cheek and she wiped it away quickly.

O'Malley entered the room and swore. He yelled for medics in the basement in his radio.

"I got it." He took a small knife from his vest.

"No. Let me do it."

"I got it, Brooks." With one swift slice of the knife the ropes fell away from Sydney's wrists. He checked her pulse. "She's still alive."

Within minutes the small room was filled with some of the officers he had given orders to earlier.

"Where are the paramedics?" Markie yelled at O'Malley. She couldn't get this far and loose Sydney. Not now. "Call them again."

"Right here."

"She's barely breathing," Markie said to the dark-haired man as she moved out of his way so he and his partner could attend to her sister.

Sydney lay like a rag doll on the cot, head to one side, her breathing labored. The deep red marks around her right and left wrists stood out against her pale skin. Markie had never seen her sister so wan and frail.

The feeling of wanting to do something but couldn't left her feeling empty inside. She watched as Sydney was hooked up to an IV.

"She's dehydrated," the other paramedic said. "We need to get some fluids into her and get her to the hospital. She seems like a fighter. I think she'll pull through."

Markie let that sink in then drew in a ragged breath. O'Malley gave her shoulder a gentle squeeze then turned to Parker to fill him in.

"She's long gone," Parker said looking apologetically at Markie. Then he addressed O'Malley. "We found nothing. Opie is still checking the units on her floor."

"We need to get the forensic guys up in her apartment to see if we can figure out where she went."

"Let's go," one of the paramedic said. Markie walked beside the gurney as they pushed it out into the narrow hallway. She helped as they tried to get it up the stairs from the basement. After what happened to Malcolm, it was a miracle that her sister was still alive.

Yes, Sydney was alive, and was going to be okay. She had been found a week to the day she'd disappeared. Markie wanted to laugh and cry at the same time. Fear overwhelmed her. Would Sydney survive this emotional experience?

Then there was the woman that had caused all of this emotional upheaval. She was still on the loose and no one knew how to find her. That more than anything left an unsettled feeling in her stomach.

Beck jumped when he'd heard the gunshot over the radio. Moments later O'Malley's voice had boomed over the radio for the paramedics. In went the paramedics and one of the officers guarding the door. That was ten minutes ago. Marklynn's face appeared before him, and on impulse, he started towards the apartment building.

"Stay put and keep calm," the officer guarding the door said with a hand on Beck's shoulder.

"Can't you at least find out if anyone is hurt?" Beck asked, anxious. Marklynn was still inside the building. There was no way he was going to be anywhere near calm until he saw her walk out the door.

"If someone was down they would have said so."

It had to be about Sydney. His mind raced. Carlos made his way over to Beck and stood beside him, arms folded across his chest. Reinforcements had arrived to relieve him from duty. He too had heard the call for medics in the basement.

Beck wanted to go to the hospital with Malcolm, but he also wanted to be there for Marklynn if she needed him. If they found Sydney then she would need him. There was a chance it may not be Sydney, he thought trying to convince himself.

"It may not be Sydney," Carlos said a few minutes later mirroring his thoughts.

"You're right. It could be someone else."

They both knew the odds of it being someone else was slim, but it was better than facing the truth.

Carlos followed his gaze as he watched while they placed Malcolm into the ambulance.

"I'll go with Malcolm and you wait for Markie."

"Thank you."

"Nan?" Sydney moaned.

Markie turned from the window watching her sister. She was sleeping, but it wasn't a peaceful sleep. Her head turned from one side of the pillow to the other. She'd even cried out a few times.

Sydney had been that way since they had brought her into the hospital a little after one in the afternoon. That was almost seven hours ago. When Markie had called Nan to tell her about Sydney, she knew. It didn't matter how Nan knew. All that mattered was that Sydney was okay.

Moving towards the bed, Markie sat down on the chair taking Sydney's hand between hers. It was as cold as ice and she began to rub her sister's hand, first the left then the right. Sydney's eyes were still closed, yet her head turned from side to side on the pillow. Then she bolted up screaming.

"Nan!"

"Shh. It's okay. You're safe." Markie folded Sydney into her arms and held her until she stopped screaming. "Nan went to get something to eat. She'll be back soon. Okay?"

She nodded and calmed down.

"I saw her in the light," Sydney said and lay back down in the bed.

"What light?"

"I'm sorry she's dead. It's my fault."

"You've nothing to be sorry about. Nan is very much alive and we're both glad you're okay."

"Nan is alive?" She asked looking confused. "Are you

sure?"

"Positive. Now get some rest."

"Thanks for coming for me," and with that Sydney closed her eyes again.

"You don't have to..." before she could finish Sydney was asleep. She smoothed Sydney's hair from her face, "...thank me."

Markie heard voices in the hall and turned her head towards the door. For a moment she thought it was Beck.

Beck.

She remembered seeing him briefly when the paramedics had placed Sydney in the ambulance, but she wasn't close enough to tell him Sydney was okay. But she figured he knew by now.

His friend was dead. Carlos said Malcolm had died on the way to the hospital. She'd caught a glimpse of Beck in the hall when she left the room in search of the washroom earlier, but they still hadn't spoken.

Markie wasn't ready to talk to Beck. There were too many things whirling around in her mind clouding her judgment and she wanted time to sort it all out.

She looked at Sydney, her chest rising and falling gently. The doctor said she would be fine physically, but it was too early to comment on her emotional health. Would she pull through?

Then there was Jared. As much as she'd tried to suppress his memory, he kept pushing through whenever she thought about Beck. He hadn't been a part of her life in a long time, yet since meeting Beck he'd become a ghost between them.

Jared wasn't honest with her. He had said she was enough when they had the discussion about children. Then he changed his mind. Not being able to have children was something she'd told herself over and over again that she could live with. Even accepted it.

Yet the question that was always in the back of her mind whenever she met someone was would he change his mind? It wasn't about anyone else. It was about Beck. Would he change his mind? That she could not take and she wasn't willing to take the risk no matter how much she loved him. And she did love him.

"Go grab a bite," Nan said as she came into the room with a bottle of water. Worry creased her brows. "What's wrong?"

"I'm tired," Markie lied. It wasn't a total lie. She didn't want to get into it with Nan.

"Mmm," Nan said not believing her for a minute, but she didn't press the issue. "I got some water for Syd. Did she wake up?"

"Briefly. She asked for you and something about seeing you in the light."

"She'll be fine," Nan said looking at the red marks on Sydney's wrists. "My baby will be just fine."

Markie got up from the chair so Nan could sit down, but before she did Nan hugged Markie.

"What was that for?" Markie asked when she pulled away.

"To thank you. Because you needed it. Because whatever is bothering you I hope you sort it out. Take your pick. Now go on and get something to eat."

Markie wasn't hungry, but she left the room in search of the lounge to be alone. If she was honest with herself, she didn't really want to be alone. She wanted to be with Beck, but he had lied to her.

She had always tackled problems head on, not allowing her fear to paralyze her. Yet, this was different. Very real. More real than any battles she had fought.

And because he did lie to her, she was afraid to trust him. Afraid to want him…Afraid that if she gave him her heart, he would leave her.

Beck saw Marklynn enter the lounge and hurried to follow her. After he'd called his office to get the number for Malcolm's parents, he called them. It wasn't something he had ever had to do and hoped he would never have to report the death of a loved one to a parent again.

He had met the Rivers' when they visited him in the hospital after his car accident. They had flown in from Texas to see him because he was a friend of their son. They didn't deserve this.

Once that call was completed to Malcolm's parents, he then notified his parents. Malcolm had an open invitation to his father's annual barbeque. His father was in shock. He wanted to come and pick him up. Any other time Beck would have told his father he wasn't fifteen any more, but he understood the cause of his father's concern.

When someone close to you dies it changes everything. Even though his father had remarried, he still mourned the dead of his mother.

"I'm going to be here for a while dad," he had told his father.

And the reason why had just walked into the family lounge area, right across from the nurse's station. He didn't want to leave the hospital without her.

"Hi," he said hesitating for a brief moment before entering the lounge.

A lamp on an end table in the corner of the lounge lit up the room. A worn brown leather couch was pushed up against a wall with a wooden coffee table in front. A vending machine hummed in the background.

Marklynn turned from the window and glanced at him over her shoulder.

"Hi," she said turning her attention back to the window. "I'm sorry about Malcolm."

The sadness he heard in her voice tore at his heart. Sydney was alive. She should be happy. Yet, she wasn't. Had Sydney taken a turn for the worst?

"I'm sorry about Malcolm too. How is Sydney?"

"She's doing better," Markie said running her hands through her hair. "She's sleeping."

She breathed in deep lifting her shoulders letting them drop. Weary. It was as though she was carrying a heavy burden and he wanted to pull her into his arms.

"Marklynn, look at me."

She turned around slowly to meet his gaze. She'd built up a wall between them closing him out and he wanted to tear it down.

"I'm sorry I lied to you," he said with regret in his voice. "I should've told you the truth about the picture or what I suspected."

"Doesn't matter anymore." She shook her head. "You did what you had to do."

She faced the window again looking off into the darkness at something only she could see. He came up behind her and turned her around to face him holding on to her arm. It mattered if she was going to use what he'd done as a roadblock to distance herself from him.

"Why don't we have it out now?" Beck wasn't going to tiptoe around her anymore. He was tired and hurting. He didn't want to be pushed away.

"Let me go." She pulled her arm away.

"I think it's time you leave, Beck."

Carlos was standing in the doorway. Big and menacing. They were friends when the day began during the raid at Melanie's apartment. Now Beck felt like the enemy and Carlos was protecting Marklynn, from him?

Hell no. Everyone was trying to protect her. What about him and how he felt? He'd made a mistake and wanted to make it right. This had nothing to do with Carlos. It was between him and Marklynn.

"This is personal and does not concern you," Beck said pointing a finger at Carlos who started to advance into the room. Carlos halted his steps looking at Marklynn as if waiting for her to say something. When she didn't, Beck said, "Back off."

Carlos looked at him and Markie for a moment as if assessing the situation. He must have concluded Markie was not in danger, turned on his heels and left the lounge with a grunt disappearing down the hall.

Beck focused his attention back on Marklynn who seemed surprised at Carlos' sudden departure, yet made no comment. He figured if she wanted him gone then he would have been gone, not Carlos. She wanted him to stay. He could feel it, even if she wouldn't admit it.

The only thing he wanted to do at the moment was pull her into his arms and he did just that. With her head on his shoulder and her arms around his waist, she clung to him, shaking.

"It's going to be okay," he whispered in her ear while caressing her back feeling some of the tension leaving her body.

"Is it?" He heard the tremor in her voice.

"Come home with me," he said softly wanting to take her home and to ease his pain and hers. Most important, he wanted to keep her safe. Melanie was still out there somewhere and O'Malley couldn't find her.

Marklynn stiffened. "I can't do this again," she said pulling away from him, but he wouldn't let her go.

"Do what again, Marklynn?"

"I don't want to talk about it."

He could see the struggle within her. She wanted to be with him, but something was holding her back. It had to be her ex and he wasn't going to let the man's ghost stand between them.

"I love you, Marklynn. I'm not your ex who broke your heart. Give me a chance. Give us a chance. I'm sorry I lied to you. I wanted to help."

She didn't say anything just stood there staring at him, lost. He didn't want to let her go for fear he would lose her.

"After Monika, I never thought I could be with someone without thinking about the scars. When I'm with you it doesn't matter. We can work it all out together."

"No." She shook her head.

"Why?"

"Because of you my sister was almost killed. I'll never forgive you for that."

Beck knew that was coming and he deserved it. In a way he was responsible for what happened to Sydney. When he could have helped he didn't. He gambled and lost. All he was concerned about was his company. He had his company and Marklynn wanted nothing to do with him.

Beck didn't say anything else because there was nothing left to be said. He let her go, turned and walked out of the lounge without looking back.

Markie reached for the gun on the night table when she heard the doorbell and shoved it in the back of her jeans pulling her shirt over it. She had sent Carlos back to the hospital after he'd dropped her home last night. With Phoenix still on the loose, she wanted Sydney protected.

She had also gotten permission for Nan to stay at the hospital with Syd. That way Carlos can keep an eye on both of them. Besides, after her confrontation with Beck, she didn't want to run into him again.

Now she was back to protecting herself. Something she was very capable of doing. Then that mad woman who thought she was some mystical creature came into her life and turned it upside down.

With Sydney and Nan safe, it was time to get back to her life and her job. There was some unfinished business she had to take care of first…a visit with Melanie's parents for one. They needed to know what Melanie was up to. She had to get their address first and was waiting for Cate to call her back.

She wasn't expecting company. The doorbell rang again and a sharp knock followed. For a moment she thought it might be Beck. But after last night, the way she'd hurt him she didn't think so. Whoever it was, she wasn't shying away.

This was her house, bought and paid for with money she'd worked long hours to earn. If it were that flaming bird, she thought as she left the bedroom, then she would put a bullet in her beak and be done with it.

As she neared the door she saw the shadow through the frosted glass. Male? Beck? Taking a deep breath she paused before she opened the door. Her eyes widened with surprise and a little disappointment crept in when she saw who it was.

"Are you lost, O'Malley?"

He chuckled but didn't comment on her abrasive tone. "It's nice to see you too again, Brooks."

"May I come in?" She didn't move and he said, "Or we can talk out here if you like."

Gotta give the guy credit, Markie frowned. He knew that with Melanie still on the loose she wasn't going to carry on any conversation with him on the verandah.

"Come in." Markie closed the door and they stood in the entranceway. She didn't offer him a seat or something to drink. That was for invited guests. "What do you want?"

"Mind if I sit down. I've been up for the past twenty-four hours and I'm pretty much running on fumes right now."

"How about I whip you up some breakfast and round it off with a nice pot of coffee?" Her voice dripped with sarcasm, but it went right over his head.

"No breakfast. I could go for the coffee," he said swallowing a yawn.

Markie opened her mouth to say something, but changed her mind when she saw his red tired eyes. He moved into the kitchen and she followed.

She retrieved a mug from the cupboard and poured him a cup of coffee.

"How is Sydney?"

"She's fine." Markie set the cup down in front of the empty chair. "Did you drop in to ask about Sydney because you could've saved yourself the trip and called."

Yeah she knew she sounded snippy, but she was still a little annoyed with him. However, since he was instrumental in finding Sydney she should at least hear him out to see what he wanted. She'd heard of O'Malley when she was on the force. A renegade cop they'd called him, but she had never had the opportunity to work with him.

"Thanks." O'Malley nodded towards the coffee and sat down at the table. "I was on my way to see the Melanie's parents today. I thought it would be a good idea if you came along." He looked up from his coffee mug at her when she didn't respond and shrugged. "I figured you were going to see them anyway so we might as well go together." He drained the coffee mug and set it on the table. What do you say?"

"I don't need you by my side." Leaning her hip against the counter staring at him, she was wondering why he was here. Now she knew. No was on the tip of her tongue. Although it wouldn't be a bad idea, she mulled over the thought.

"I need you. If you tell them what happened to Sydney then they might want to help us locate Melanie. By the way, thought you'd like to know, we picked up Frank Wang and nabbed his cousin at the airport, Melanie's partners in crime. They don't know where she is."

"And?" There was something else he wasn't telling her. She could sense it. Now she was turning into Nan.

"Booker is riding me on this," he said staring into the empty cup. "I'm on my own.

Jeffery Booker.

At the sound of the man's name Markie straightened up. The man had turned her life into a nightmare when she was a police officer and what did he get for harassing her? A promotion, and she had to start all over again.

"As far as he's concerned, the Monika Beck case is closed. We have no real evidence against Melanie to warrant even looking for her, his words."

"What? She's responsible for her sister's death. Malcolm is dead and Sydney is in the hospital. What more proof does he need?"

"I carried out the search on Melanie's apartment without his blessings yesterday and he has it in for me."

"I don't get it. How does Booker fit into this? Why is he riding you on this?"

O'Malley dragged his hand over his face and got up, leaving the kitchen. "Maybe I shouldn't have come."

"It's a little late for coulda shoulda isn't? Talk to me, O'Malley." She pushed passed him and blocked the front door. "You came here to say something. Say it."

"I'm sorry I didn't call you back. When Beck came to me with the picture, I wanted to fix my mistake. I didn't want you involved."

"News flash – I was already involved."

"I reopened the Monika Beck's case and Booker shut it down. We got into it yesterday after Melanie got away and he more or less told me I'm finished as a cop." He paused. "A Jane Doe had washed up a week after Monika's death. I just found the file on it. It's Monika Beck. She didn't die in the boating accident. The autopsy said blunt force trauma to the back of the head. Booker buried the file."

"Why?" Markie asked stunned. "I don't understand his interference in this. Booker doesn't do anything unless he gets something out of it."

"He and the Daniels' are tight."

"How tight?"

She watched as O'Malley closed his eyes for a moment then turned his head to one side before facing her again. He began twisting the button on his jacket then unbuttoned it and shoved his hands into the pockets of his slacks.

"When I was given Monika's case, I'd just kicked a drug habit and was trying to prove that I could still play with the big boys."

"Let me guess, Booker used your addiction to cover up the fact that Melanie had called her parents and told them about Monika's murder. She didn't die in the boating accident because Melanie killed her. Why would she kill her sister?"

He shrugged. "When I found out about Melanie's phone call four years ago, Booker told me to forget it and focus my investigation on Beck. If I didn't, he would make my drug use very public. I couldn't afford to lose my job. It was all I had."

"You were clean by then. If you had kicked the habit as you said, then you should have done something."

"Don't you think I know that? Malcolm would still be alive if I had. Your sister wouldn't be lying in a hospital bed.

I can't change the past, but I can do something about it now. I choose to do something about it. When we find Melanie, I'm turning in my badge."

"What do you want, sympathy?"

Markie realized he wasn't looking for sympathy. He was simply trying to fix a mistake he'd made, a mistake that by the looks of it had been eating away at him for a long time. She wondered if finding Melanie would be enough for him.

"Not your sympathy, just your help to find Melanie." He was silent for a while. Then said, "There was a rumor circulating at the time of Monika's death that Booker had gambling debts. I'm starting to think it wasn't a rumor after all."

"You think the Daniels' paid him off," Markie said wondering how Booker could get away with all that he'd done.

"Had to. Could still be. In the end it probably won't matter anyway because no one can touch him. You were the only one that tried to topple him off his ivory tower and almost succeeded. The way I look at it is I've nothing else to lose by bringing Melanie in. Booker would bring up my drug use and I'll be out of a job so I might as well quit."

"You're going to walk away from your job and Booker gets away free, again."

"You can't win them all. Besides, he limped away from you remember?" He actually smiled when he said that. "He wasn't as lucky with Jamie."

"Jamie? What does Jamie have to do with Booker?"

"He didn't tell you?"

"Tell me what?"

"Water under the bridge. The Daniels' are playing golf today. How is your handicap?"

Phoenix walked around the apartment touching and moving objects in the cramped space. Collectable spoons and little bells from all over the world were displayed on little shelves on the wall. The woman didn't look like a world traveler yet all the memorabilia scattered around the room suggested she was.

If it weren't for the boarded up window in the bedroom, which she had slipped through, one would think the occupant was out in search of another bell or spoon. Jealousy rose up within her. She'd never been outside of Boston because they had kept her locked up.

The apartment was clean. Free of broken glass. Everything was put back in its place. Markie had done it. Sisters did that. They took care of each other and loved each other.

She and Monika were close until Dalton Beck took her away. He used to come to her room at nights. It started when she was nine. The heels of her hands pounded on her temples.

No.

She was getting confused again. It was Dalton Beck that took Monika away and then there was no one to protect her.

Yes. That was it. That made sense. It was all his fault and he deserved to lose everything. He destroyed Monika and threw her away. But Monika didn't know how to survive. She knew how to survive. Malcolm was dead. Sydney was dead. Soon, Markie would be dead. Then she and Beck could be together.

CHAPTER FOURTEEN

O'Malley came to a rolling stop outside of the gated entrance of Lord Manors Country Club in Jamaica Plains and a low whistle escaped his lips.

It hadn't taken Markie long to decide to accompany him to visit the Daniels'. Sydney was alive because he'd found the woman's address. Bottom-line: She wanted Melanie and another shot at Jeffery Booker.

O'Malley had insisted on driving. A drive, that left Markie wondering, how on earth he had passed a driving test and acquired a valid driver's license.

He didn't believe in slowing to a stop and was oblivious to the concept of a red light. The red light, she had pointed out to him, he'd barreled through a block back to which he had given her a "what" stare.

The trip was done in silence. A silence that started when he'd asked what was up with her and Beck. She'd replied it was none of his business. That shut him up, but not before he'd gotten off what was on his chest.

"All I want to say is that I don't think Beck meant to hurt you, not in the way you think. Things just happen sometimes," he'd said with a far away look in his eyes.

Things just happen sometimes: That was code for: he blamed himself for Melanie's rampage and it was eating away at him. Since his statement had not required a comment she left him to his demons. Although, she wondered if finding

Melanie would be enough to clear his conscience.

"How much do you think a membership in this joint cost?" O'Malley asked.

"If you have to ask you can't afford it," Markie replied looking over at the rolling hills beyond the gate.

"You're probably right."

"You sound disappointed. I didn't think this was your cup of tea."

"Far from it. This is just a place where rich people get together with other rich people and snub their noses at the outside world."

Markie didn't agree with O'Malley and chose to ignore his comment. No matter what he thought, the establishment was impressive. She had been to country clubs before, mostly for client meetings, but this was no ordinary country club. It was a sprawling estate, which spanned about five acres that sat on a well-manicured lawn as far as the eyes could see. The manmade lake with a water fountain shooting up from the middle was the most impressive feature of the country club.

A well-dressed Hispanic man, in black and white attire, emerged from the glass booth, opened the gate and approached the car looking at it with disdain. Markie wasn't knowledgeable on cars by any means but she knew that O'Malley's pride and joy was a diamond in the rough. His corvette was a project car. It looked like he'd put a lot of time into it and is doing so, looking at the worn leather seats. It could use a coat of paint and the door panels needed fixing. A coat of paint outside would restore it back to the beauty it once was.

"Snob," O'Malley grunted and wound the window down. At least that was the only part she heard.

"Can I help you?" the man looked down his long nose at O'Malley and O'Malley shoved his badge in his face.

Markie suppressed a laugh. It appears O'Malley didn't care to be looked down on and he didn't care much for the gatekeeper either.

"It's Detective O'Malley. We're here to see Roberta and

Kennedy Daniels."

The gatekeeper bent to look into the car over at Markie. She had changed into a black pantsuit and blue shirt, but it wasn't up to par with the dress code of the club. Neither was O'Malley's gray suit.

"This is a member's only club, sir." He zeroed in on the crack in the dashboard.

"It's police business. Either they come out or we go in," O'Malley said one hand resting on the steering wheel as he revved the engine ready to move forward. Was he going to ram the gate? Markie wouldn't put it past him.

The man turned on his heels, entered the glass booth and picked up the phone. A few minutes later he returned with a look on his face as if he'd bitten into something sour.

"It seems you're expected, but," he said looking over at Markie, "she'll have to wait at the gate."

"She's coming in with me. Do we have a problem?"

One look of disdain deserves another and O'Malley gave as good as he got daring the man to challenge him.

"Someone will meet you at the main entrance," the man said with a forced smile.

"Thanks, Alfred," O'Malley said.

"Alfred?" Markie looked at him as he drove through the gate. She wasn't sure where he'd gotten the name from, as the man wasn't wearing a nametag.

"He looks like an Alfred, don't you think? You know, one of those stuffy butlers you always see on T.V.," he said with a smirk.

Another man, a clone of the one in the glass booth, met them at the grand entrance of the club after O'Malley parked. Then they were ushered to a private patio overlooking the pool to wait for Mr. and Mrs. Daniels.

A waiter came in and placed four glasses of lemonade on the table and left without a word. They were not welcome.

From the patio she could see members playing golf in the distance. They were surrounded by the lush beauty of nature as the warm breeze rustled through the trees.

Tranquility.

How long had it been since she'd sat back and just enjoyed life. She couldn't remember. It was always one project after another.

For some reason she thought of Beck. This country club scene wasn't his thing. Yet, he would fit right in, but she couldn't picture him playing golf or…Never mind what Beck would like or dislike she told herself. She was here to work not to daydream about him.

Markie wiped the sweat from her forehead squinting against the sun as she took off her jacket. She sat beside O'Malley, reaching for the lemonade. The cool refreshing liquid hit the spot and she almost finished the glass.

"I think you could get used to this place, Brooks," O'Malley chuckled as he got up to crank the lever adjusting the umbrella to shade the table from the sun. "Maybe their lemonade anyway."

"This place has a certain draw. You have to admit, this has got to be the best lemonade—"

"Jeffery Booker informed me you were coming to see us," Mr. Daniels said when he strolled out onto the patio, hand shoved in the pockets of plaid navy walking shorts his white polo shirt stood out against his dark skin. He was talking to O'Malley, but he was looking at Markie's chest. "My wife will join us shortly."

He was tall, distinguished and handsome. He knew it too. Probably used to getting anything he wanted, but not from her, Markie thought as his eyes traveled down the length of her body and settled on her chest when she stood up to greet him. He smiled at her and she immediately felt the need for a shower.

"This is Marklynn Brooks, a private investigator."

"A private investigator? And an attractive one too."

O'Malley saw where Mr. Daniels' eye's landed and stepped in front of Markie and extended his hand forcing Mr. Daniels to shift his gaze.

"I don't know what else I can tell you except to reiterate we don't know where our daughter is. She has cut off all ties with us."

A few minutes later a woman floated onto the patio, tennis racket in hand, resting on her right shoulder. She looked like she was peeled from the cover of some sports magazine with her white tennis skirt and polo shirt. Toned and tanned, she seemed annoyed that her tennis game was interrupted.

"My husband is correct. If that's all then I'd like to return to my game. The court is reserved," she said looking at Markie, as if she was something stuck on the bottom of her shoes.

"No, that's not all, Mrs. Daniels," Markie said not hiding the annoyance in her voice.

Was this woman for real? With her hair in a neat bob and her makeup flawless, it didn't look like she was playing tennis at all. More than likely lounging by the pool she would guess.

She and her husband were in their sixties and it was about time they started taking responsibilities for someone other than themselves. That responsibility should start with Melanie.

"You've ten minutes," Mrs. Daniels said, looking at her watch as if she was starting a count down.

They all sat down around the patio table. Mr. Daniels shoved the lemonade aside when the waiter appeared with a scotch. Markie made a point of putting her jacket back on before taking her seat to avoid his wandering gaze.

"Melanie is a troubled young lady and we've done all we can for her. She belongs in an institution. Until she decides to accept our help there is nothing we can do for her," Mr. Daniels said glancing at his watch.

"Are we keeping you both from something more important?" O'Malley asked a hard edge in his voice. "I would think that your daughter is worth more than *ten* minutes of your time."

"No one talks to me like that, not even an underpaid cop like you."

"We mean no disrespect, Mr. Daniels." Markie gave

O'Malley a look that told him to simmer down. "Melanie is more than troubled. She kidnapped my sister. We found her yesterday barely alive. Your daughter has also killed a man I'm told she was fond of. That makes two murders. The first one you covered up."

"Get out!" Mrs. Daniel sprang up from the chair she'd folded her slender frame into pointing to the door. "Now!"

Markie didn't budge. "You already lost one daughter," she said looking up at the woman. "Why won't you try and save the other? I understand Melanie has mental issues, but all that will be taken into consideration if she turns herself in. We need your help to find her before she hurts someone else."

"And you're not going to get it. My baby doesn't need your help," Mr. Daniels replied inspecting his nails as if he'd just had a manicure.

It was the way that he said *my baby* that got Markie thinking and it wasn't a pleasant thought.

"When did you start?" Markie pinned him with a disgusted look.

"Start what?" Mr. Daniels asked, brows drawn together.

"Molesting Melanie."

O'Malley, whose gaze had drifted down to the pool, whipped his head around to look at Markie then to Mr. Daniels. Mrs. Daniels picked up her glass of lemonade and threw it into Markie's face.

Markie jerked back when the cold liquid hit her face, squinting when the lemon juice stung her eyes. Hatred blazed in woman's eyes when she glared at Markie and stormed away from the table.

"You two are finished," Mr. Daniels hissed.

"Not yet," O'Malley said when Mr. Daniels pushed his chair back and got up from the table. "A Jane Doe was identified as Monika Beck. If you're interested, I can tell you where she's buried."

"Monika died four years ago and we buried her."

They both watched as Mr. Daniels ran from the patio to catch up to his wife.

"I think we've outstayed our welcome," O'Malley said dabbing the napkin along the arm of his jacket where the lemonade splashed.

"You think?" Markie wiped her face with the napkin. She removed her jacket and dabbed at the wet shirt then threw the soiled napkin on the table.

When they got to the car, O'Malley paused for a moment before starting the engine. "How did you know he molested Melanie?"

"I didn't, but Mrs. Daniels did. It was the way she looked at me and I knew."

"Do you think he molested Monika as well?"

"If I had to guess, I'd say no. Melanie has problems so it was easier to manipulate her than Monika. If he'd been hurting Melanie since she was a child, which I suspect he was, she has escaped into a world inside her head."

"She'll kill again," O'Malley said with a grim look on his face.

"I know," Markie said wondering if Beck would be next.

"Be careful," he warned.

Beck didn't even know why he came into the office. After a sleepless night, productivity was not the name of the game this morning.

He couldn't think straight. The fight with Marklynn at the hospital had soured his mood. Bringing himself to the task at hand was proving to be an undertaking. All of Malcolm's files were brought to his office. He sat there staring at the Lincoln Heights file. They had agreed not to pull the account. He could have asked someone else to go through the files to see what was pending. Peta Ann had offered, but he wanted to do it.

At least he had opened the file, but after Malcolm's parents had telephoned him upon their arrival at the hospital an hour ago that was as far as he had gotten. They had caught a red-eye after their conversation yesterday and were preparing to take Malcolm's body back home.

The funeral would be in a couple of days if they could get the body released by then. O'Malley was helping them with the paper work.

Beck had called O'Malley to thank him for all his help. He had a lot to say. More than Beck wanted to hear.

After four long years of assuming Monika was dead, he was assured she was dead. They had evidence. Her body was identified. Since her parents could care less or maybe they were in denial, he didn't know, he'd asked O'Malley to ensure she had a proper burial. He would pay for it and finally have closure.

Beck looked up from his desk when the door opened and Jamie walked in. No suit today just a sport shirt with the Brooks Investigations logo and jeans.

"Hey, you okay? You didn't answer my knock so I came in."

"Sure." Beck pushed the folder aside leaning back in his chair. "What's up?"

"You wanted an update."

"Sure. Sit down." He vaguely recalled sending the email request earlier for a meeting. When he'd sent the email he also wanted to ask about Marklynn, but decided against it. How could he walk away? He didn't have a choice. She pushed him away and shut him out.

"Beck?"

"Sorry. What did you say?"

"We're just about done," Jamie said looking at him funny. "We found the backdoor. It's been closed. Melanie's access to the system has been cut off. The monitoring software is being rewritten and will be uploaded by the end of the day. Sooner if testing goes well. Your team has been great."

"You must be relieved you're done?"

Beck was glad yet a part of him was saddened. The completion of the job meant he wouldn't see Marklynn again. Brooks Investigations would stay on as a security consultant, testing to ensure that Beck Security Systems would not be vulnerable to attacks again, but nothing else.

The contract was clear about that.

Jamie shrugged. "It's bitter sweet. I can't believe Malcolm is gone."

"I know what you mean."

"What's next for you?" Beck knew that Marklynn and Jamie hadn't spoken since the meeting in the conference room and he felt responsible. She felt Jamie had betrayed her.

"A new challenge who knows."

"Does that include Brooks Investigations?"

Again, Jamie shrugged. "Anything is possible."

"You shouldn't let her push you out," Beck said. "She needs you."

"What about you? It's been a long time since I've seen her so wound up about someone. She needs you as well."

"She blames me for what happened to Sydney."

"And you're going to let that stop you?" Jamie snorted.

"I could say the same to you. You've been together a long time."

"There's a big difference between you and I. I'm not in love with her."

Beck didn't respond just stared off into space thinking about the last time he and Marklynn were together.

"Bottom-line: we have control of Beck Security Systems. No need to hang a "For Sale" sign on the door."

"You understand why I couldn't even consider it, right?"

He kept replaying that moment in his office when Markie had wanted him to honor Melanie's request to sell the company. He could still see the look of disappointment on her face. It was more than disappointment. It was betrayal. She believed he had betrayed her and for that he would not be forgiven. The fight at the hospital that night confirmed that.

"Beck, you did what you had to do."

"Would you have chosen differently?"

"I didn't when I found out you had your ex-wife's case reopened. I chose not to tell her. I wanted to give you the time to do what you had to do. I guess we're in the same boat. Until she tears down that wall there's nothing we can do, is there?"

"Hi Cate," Markie said when she walked by her office. O'Malley had dropped her off at her house an hour ago. She'd changed and headed straight for the office. It wasn't work she had on her mind. She wanted to see Jamie.

"Hi, how is Sydney?" Cate's voice stopped Markie before she headed up the stairs.

"Sydney's fine. Thanks for asking. She should be out of the hospital today, if not then tomorrow."

"That's wonderful." Cate clapped her hands together. "Jamie told me about Melanie. They still haven't found her?"

"No and her parents were no help at all."

"Perhaps she's gone for good." She had a hopeful look on her face.

"I don't think so." Markie shook her head remembering what O'Malley had said about Melanie killing again and thought about Beck. She wanted to call him. Thought about it on the drive back from Jamaica Plains but hadn't acted upon it. "She planned all of it, the sabotage and the murders. She has an ultimate end in mind. I'm not sure what that is, but I don't think she's finished yet."

"Sydney?" Fear registered in Cate's eyes.

"Carlos is at the hospital."

"Good. You better be careful," Cate warned, her maternal nurturing kicking in as it often did.

"Count on it." She turned her head towards the stairs. "Is Jamie around?"

"He just got back. He was at Beck Security Systems all morning."

"Is he with anyone?"

"Not as far as I know."

"I'm going up to see him. Oh, could you clear my calendar for the next couple of days. I want to spend some time with Sydney."

"Already done, and an update report listing what

everyone is working on is on your desk." She smiled. "So you can take off on a clear conscience."

"Thanks. What would I do without you?"

"I hope we never find out," Cate laughed and went back to her desk.

Jamie's office was a couple of doors before hers at the top of the stairs. She knocked on the glass door and he waved her in.

"Hi."

"Hi," he replied twisting his mouth, staring at her in silence.

She could always count on a smile from him, but not today. His trademark scowl was directed at her in spades.

"Got a minute?"

Jamie indicated for her to sit in the visitor's chair with the point of his chin then leaned back into his chair. Moving the laptop to the corner of his desk, he gave her his undivided attention. He'd told her once he liked order at the office and it showed.

Files were laid out neatly on his desk of various projects he was working on. The bookshelves were lined with computer books, and his degrees were hung upside down on the wall behind him. A private joke which he had not shared with her.

"I'm sorry about what I said in Beck's office. I was angry and afraid. I took it out on you. It wasn't fair." Jamie opened his mouth to speak but she held up a hand to stop him. "Let me finish. Please."

Jamie nodded for her to continue.

"I don't want you to leave." Jamie's eyebrows raised in surprise as if wanting to know how she'd found out. "If you had treated me the way I did you, then I would be thinking about leaving or at the very least questioning our friendship."

"I see."

He didn't, but she went on anyway. "I've given this a lot of thought and I want you to be an equal partner."

Curiosity flickered in his eyes nothing more.

"Set up the Security Consultant side of the business.

Run it however you see fit with no interference from me." He gave her a 'yeah right look'. "Don't give me an answer right now. Think about it."

Jamie didn't say anything for a long moment. He sat there staring at her and she knew he'd decided to leave. And why wouldn't he? She had messed up big time.

No, she wasn't going to let him go without a fight. She took one last run at him hoping to change his mind.

"I'm making you the offer because you deserve it not just because I don't want you to leave. You've always been there for me and I guess I never realized how much I leaned on you until we started working with Beck. I trust you and want you to stay."

A raised eyebrow was his only response. He was coming around. She could tell, but he was going to make her beg.

"You're the closest thing I have to a best friend," she continued. "You're not going to make me go out and find another one, are you? You know, I don't have time for that."

"I couldn't allow you to mess up some poor soul's mind like you've done to me over the years."

"Does that mean you're staying?"

He cocked his head to one side and a slow smile settled on his face. "Do I get a raise?"

Screaming with excitement, she jumped out of the chair, ran around his desk to hug him.

"Alright, alright. No need to get mushy. Go sit down." He pushed her away gently clearing his throat.

She dropped back in the chair with a big smile on her face. The smile slid from her face when Jamie asked, "Have you spoken to Beck today?"

The last time she'd spoken to Beck was at the hospital. Then she'd thrown herself into work pushing him out of her mind. Well, she tried to.

"No." She hesitated. "Why?" She'd wanted to ask how Beck was doing. Wanted to know if he'd asked about her, but the only thing that came to mind was, "Did Melanie resurface?"

"Not in Beck's network. The monitoring software has been rewritten and his team is testing it as we speak."

"She actually published the source code on how she'd broken into Beck Security Systems on one of those *How to Hack* sites? Why would she do such a thing?"

Before she left the house, Markie had scanned the email update that Jamie had sent. The backdoor into Beck Security Systems Melanie had used to bypass the normal authentication and secure access undetected had been found.

"It's a rush. You don't think you're going to get caught."

"Are we still talking about Melanie or do I need to start worrying about you?"

Jamie laughed. "No more than usual. You know, it was actually Malcolm's idea to start checking out those sites. I didn't think she would be daring enough to do it. That's how we were able to trace it back to her computer and eventually uncover her IP address. She may be good, but we're better."

"Too bad Malcolm is not here to get the credit."

Markie could still see him on the floor in Melanie's apartment with the gash on the back his head. She couldn't image what his parents must be feeling right now. They were lucky Sydney made it out alive.

"Beck's getting ready to leave for Texas," Jamie said watching her.

"Oh," was all she could think of to say. *Oh,* how original. She figured since Malcolm was from Texas that was probably where he would be buried.

"Want to grab some lunch and we can talk some more?"

"Lunch?" Markie looked at her watch. "It's almost three."

"Okay early dinner then."

"Can't, been on the go since this morning. I'm heading over to the hospital. Sydney said that she might be released today if all goes well with her test results. If that's the case, I'm going to be off for a few days."

"Say hi to Syd for me," Jamie said.

"Will do," Markie said as she headed for the door then turned around. "One more thing." She filled him in on the visit with the Daniels' and told him what O'Malley had told her about Booker.

"Booker is scum," he spat.

"Tell me something I *don't* know." Jamie understood exactly what she meant.

A thoughtful expression settled on his face for a moment. "I put him in traction during a charity football game. His face broke into a smile. You know, the one the precinct used to do for that children's charity."

"Yeah. Why?"

"Booker screwed up and made a bad call. Two good police officers died and the bastard blamed my team. Said he received wrong information. Wrong information my eye. He was just coming off the lawsuit with you and he couldn't be caught with his hand in the cookie jar again."

"So that's how you ended up on my doorstep," she said rubbing her chin thoughtfully.

"Yeah," he said looking almost apologetic. "I started out just wanting to piss Booker off. What better way than to rub it in his face. The two people that he hated the most teaming up together to build an empire." He swept his hands around the room with a smile.

Markie threw back her head and laughed. It felt good to laugh. There hasn't been much to laugh about lately. "I wouldn't call it an empire."

"You did one helleva job with Brooks Investigations. I'm proud to be a part of it. Having my name on the door doesn't hurt either. Brooks and Wright Investigations. It has a nice ring to it, don't you thing?"

"Mmm…"

"I know that look," Jamie leaned forward, elbows on the desk watching her closely. "What are you thinking?"

"I'll tell you later. Gotta run."

Markie made a quick stop into her office and found the number for Michael Blake. She dialed.

When his voicemail kicked in, she said, "Hey Michael,

it's Markie. Hope you and Angela are doing well. Yes, it's been a while," she smiled into the phone, "we need to talk. Subject: Jeffrey Booker."

Beck rubbed his eyes as he stepped off the airplane. They felt like he had sand in them. Forty-eight hours had passed since he had actually lain on a bed and slept. Yet sleep, was the furthest thing from his mind.

Malcolm's funeral was over. His friend was gone. Dead. A senseless death. But when did death ever make sense? When his mother died, he could remember his father sobbing.

There were things he should have told his mother. Like thanking her for being there for him or even telling her he loved her instead of causing her grief. He figured he had time, but she got sick. Then she died and things were left unsaid.

Maybe there were things he should have told Malcolm as well. Who knows? Beck made his way out to the passenger pickup passing people, but not really seeing their faces.

Pulling out his cell phone, he sat down on one of the iron benches by the door and punched in the first number that came to mind.

"Marklynn Brooks." When she answered his mind drew a blank. He didn't even know why he called her or what he wanted say to her. He just wanted to hear her voice.

"Hello? Is anyone there?"

"Malcolm was buried this morning," he said before she hung up. "It was a small funeral."

A minivan pulled up to the curb. The rear door opened. A man jumped out from the driver side, kissed the woman and the two little boys, then loaded the luggage sitting on the curb.

Marklynn was silent on the other end of the line and he rambled on. He never rambled. Didn't need to, but he felt lost.

Alone.

"There is something about death, you know." He watched the van drive off. "It can't be undone. If you forget to…" His voice trailed off.

"Beck, where are you?" Concerned registered in her voice.

"Airport. I just flew in from Texas on the 6:00 pm flight. I left Boston last night. I was…I wanted to…"

"I'll come and get you."

He told her the airline. Half an hour later she drove up stopping in front of him. Tossing his small travel bag onto the back seat, he slid into the front passenger seat.

"You okay?"

"No." He laid his head on the headrest, closed his eyes and fell into the sleep that had eluded him for the last two days.

"Hey, wake up." Beck felt a warm hand on his cheek and woke with a start. "We're here."

He didn't know where here was until he saw his building. Marklynn had stopped at the entrance of the underground parking lot of his condo. Reaching into his wallet, he took out the security card and handed it to her.

Watching her as she maneuvered her way through the under ground parking, he kept thinking he should say something. They hadn't spoken since the fight at the hospital and yet when he called her she came and picked him up. Why? Again the thought occurred to him that he should say something, but he couldn't think of anything. So he remained quiet.

She slipped her hands in his and they walked from the underground, to the elevators, then from the elevators to his unit, all in silence while his mind raced. He wanted the last three months of his life back. He wanted Malcolm to be alive and Sydney to be well again.

Gripping the woman's hand that held his, he wanted them to go back to the last time they'd made love. But nothing would ever be the same again. It was the loss that shook him then isolation. It was more overpowering than when Marklynn released his hand to close the door of the condo.

At that moment, it didn't matter that he couldn't go back to the past, he just wanted to. He wanted to hear her laughter. He wanted to touch her, feel her body against his and hear her cry out his name in the height of passion.

"Want something to eat?" she asked looking at him. The concern that was shown on her face was also evident in her voice.

"No. I want to go to bed." He held out his hand. She took it without hesitation and he lead her to the bedroom.

Unzipping the black jersey knit, he pushed it off her shoulders and down her body. It fell to the floor and she stepped out of it, and then kicked off her black pumps.

Beck sat on the bed and pulled her down on his lap. "Thank you for coming to get me. I didn't think…"

"Shh." She placed her finger on his lip. "I'm so sorry about Malcolm."

He held her face in his hands and kissed her hard bruising her lips wanting to recapture what they had the last time they made love. She returned the kiss with the same feverish intensity, but something was missing between them.

He knew she felt it too.

The last time they were together it was playful and erotic. The way Beck kissed her was out of need and fear and loss.

She felt it too. That's what had driven them to seek refuge in each other's arms. When she had heard his voice on the phone, picking him up from the airport was the only thing to do.

She didn't think they would end up in bed, not after the way things had ended between them at the hospital. He was hurting and she felt it in the way he held onto her like a drowning man.

He laid back on the bed taking her with him as he

worked to get them in the center of the bed without letting her go. That was okay because she didn't want to let him go either.

Pulling away for a moment, he discarded his clothes quickly and returned to her with the same urgency.

Skin to skin.

The roughness in the way he'd kissed her before was gone when he came to her again. Something else had taken its place. Something she couldn't quite put her finger on. They were two people desperately trying to hold on to a fragile connection that had somehow developed between them and trying to keep it from slipping away. But it was too late.

Nothing would be the same between them. Yet they both wanted it to as they struggled to reach fulfillment. Murder had touched their souls and lies divided them. That was enough because there was no climax.

Beck collapsed on top of her his body drenched in sweat. Panting in the dark. No words were said as they both clung to each wondering what the next step was as sleep claimed them.

CHAPTER FIFTEEN

It was the vibration of Markie's cell phone in her bag that pulled her from sleep the following morning. She turned her head towards the night table and glanced at the digital clock. It was 7:55 a.m.

Beck's arm was draped across her waist. Slipping out of bed, trying not to wake him, she grabbed her handbag, clothing and headed for the bathroom. She flipped on the light switch, dropped her clothes on the marble counter then dug into her handbag for the phone.

"Marklynn Brooks," she said with the phone tucked between her neck and ear as she started to dress.

"It's the superintendent from Sydney's building."

"Yes." Markie figured he was calling to tell her the window was fixed. She had asked him to notify her, but at this hour.

"I wanted to tell you that your sister is back just in case you didn't know."

Her hand paused as she was zipping up her dress. A million thoughts raced though her mind, but only one stuck.

Melanie Daniels. It had to be her.

"Did you see Sydney?" She asked her voice calm not wanting to alarm him. She didn't want him confronting Melanie if indeed it was her. But Markie had no doubt that it was.

"No. The guys are here to replace the window, but I

can't get access to the unit because the chain lock is on. I knocked but she's not answering. That's why I called. Maybe something is wrong."

He sounded concerned. Concerned enough to enter the apartment and she didn't want that. She didn't want him to get hurt. Killing had become second nature to Melanie. Markie didn't want him added to Melanie's body count.

"Sydney is in the hospital," she said deciding to be honest with him.

"Who is in the unit?"

"Please don't go back to the unit. I'm on my way.'

"What about the job?" He didn't sound too pleased that he would have to reschedule. "It's going to cost money to have them come back."

"I'll foot the bill. Look, I know it's inconvenient for you, but if you could reschedule the window installation I would appreciate it. Thank you."

Markie couldn't believe it. Melanie was crashing at Sydney's place. No wonder they couldn't find her. No one thought of looking for her at Sydney's apartment. Why would they?

No sane person would do what Melanie had done. She wasn't exactly playing with a full deck of cards now was she?

She washed her face and brushed her teeth. Beck had brought in the tooth bush from the guest bathroom she had used on her last visit. She didn't want to think of the implications or Beck for that matter.

Melanie crashing at Sydney's apartment concerned her more. Why? Because Melanie knew someone would find her and it would get back to Markie. The woman wanted a showdown.

Her killing spree ends now Markie vowed dropping the phone in her bag. She reached behind to zip her dress and felt Beck's hand against her bare back.

He zipped up the dress while looking at her in the bathroom mirror. "Good morning." He kissed her neck.

She hadn't heard when he entered the bathroom. How could she? The bathroom was the size of her entire house.

Her skin was still tingling from where he had kissed her.

"I have to go," she said abruptly.

He frowned. She knew he wanted to talk about last night and probably a whole lot more by the look on his face. They had no future together and the more she kept entertaining the idea the harder it was going to be to walk away.

"I thought we could talk about us this morning," Beck said running his finger along her arm. "Maybe finish what we started last night."

She grabbed her brush from her bag and started brushing her hair. She didn't want to talk. Had no time to talk.

"Not now. I need to use the washroom."

Markie closed the door when he stepped out. She turned on the tap ran her hands under the water, then combed wet fingers through her hair and brushed again. When she came out of the washroom, Beck was waiting by the door.

"We need to talk."

It looked like this time he wasn't going to take no for an answer. He put his arm out blocking her exit from the bathroom.

"I have to go to work." She ducked under his arm.

"Marklynn?"

"I have to go," she said on her way out the front door. "I'll call you later."

"Tell me Markie is with you," Jamie said when Beck answered. "She's not picking up her cell phone. Carlos is at her house. She's not there."

"She left about ten minutes ago," Beck said hiding his disappointment. He had hoped it was Marklynn calling to say she'd changed her mind. That was wishful thinking. When she made up her mind, she rarely changed it.

He had wanted them to talk about their relationship, but she didn't seem interested. Maybe she didn't care about him at all.

"Did she say where she was going?"

"Work. Is there a problem?"

Beck picked up on the urgency in Jamie's voice, putting the milk back in the refrigerator, breakfast forgotten.

"What's going on?"

The only thing he could think of was that Melanie had found a way back into the network.

"If you call someone trying to hack into Brooks Investigations network a problem then I'd say we have a big one."

Beck cursed. "Melanie is going after Marklynn."

"That's what I figured," Jamie said. "Are you sure she said she was coming into the office?"

"She didn't mention the office. She got a call, said she was going to work and left."

"Think, Beck. Who was she talking to? A man or woman."

"I don't know."

"Did you hear what she was saying?"

"I got bits and pieces of the conversation. I think she was talking about Sydney. She mentioned the hospital and something about staying away from the apartment."

"She's on her way to Sydney's place," Jamie concluded. "Why would—"

Fear gripped Beck. "Melanie."

"I'll meet you there."

Markie reached for her cell phone to punch in O'Malley's number when she stopped at the traffic light at the end of Beck's Street and realized it was turned off. She didn't remember turning it off. She turned it on and saw the message icon. When she scrolled the directory she saw the missed calls from Jamie and Beck. She would deal with that later.

She called and got O'Malley's voice mail. She left a message to let him know she was on her way to Sydney's and for him to meet her there.

Twenty minutes later she was parked across from

Sydney's building. She made a quick call to O'Malley again, but didn't bother leaving a message.

Markie checked her gun then dropped it in her handbag. After she scanned the street, she made her way towards the building.

The building was quiet. There was no one in either the lobby or the corridor as she tiptoed quietly down the concrete hall to Sydney's apartment. Using her key, she opened the door slowly, listening before entering the unit.

Melanie had removed the chain lock. Markie wasn't sure if that was because Melanie had left or she was in hiding. Either way, she was not going to underestimate the woman and pulled out her gun.

Who would have thought Melanie would have ended up at Sydney's place?

Melanie wanted a showdown. She wouldn't have gone through all that trouble if she didn't. It was clear to Markie that only one of them would walk out of the apartment alive and she'd decided it was going to be her.

The apartment was quiet. Too quiet. Like the crucial scene in the movie when the music swelled then all hell broke loose. And then it did.

Melanie rushed out of the bedroom firing her weapon. A bullet zinged by Markie's head and lodged into the door. Markie hit the floor hard landing on her stomach with a grunt. More bullets splintered the door. She rolled for cover behind the sofa and lost a shoe in the process then kicked off the other one.

"You ruined everything!" The woman screamed.

"What did I ruin, Melanie?" Markie figured if she distracted Melanie enough with conversation she might get a clear shot off instead of feeling like a trapped animal.

Markie was pretty much running on adrenalin and her only thought was trying to stay alive.

"My name is Monika."

"Monika is dead."

Markie belly crawled to the corner of the sofa to see where Melanie was, but the woman fired again. That was how many shots? She tired to count how many shots Melanie had fire, but it wasn't working. Stick to psychology, she told herself. Keep her talking.

"She's dead because she didn't protect you. Isn't that right? She left you."

"Shut up!" The woman hissed. "You don't know what you're talking about."

"I think I do, but you didn't have to kill Malcolm," Markie said and tried to do a belly crawl to the front door. That idea was scrapped when she heard Melanie moving towards her and rolled back to the sofa.

"He loved you," Markie said continuing to engage Melanie in conversation.

"He loved sex. Just like…like…"

"Your father," Markie finished for her. "Monika and Malcolm didn't hurt you. It was your father."

"Shut up!" She said and fired off another shot.

Markie had never felt such hatred as she did for anyone at that moment than she did for Mr. Daniels. This was the result of his handiwork. Melanie was a very angry and confused woman. He was supposed to be her father, her protector. Her mother did nothing to help her as well. There was no one to protect her.

"What happened when Monika visited you at the hospital? Is that when you decided to kill her?"

"You don't know what you're talking about."

"Why did you kill her? She was your sister."

"She said we could be together, but I had to get better first. There's nothing wrong with me."

"You killed Malcolm," Markie said inching towards the door again.

"He deserved to die."

"What about your sister?" Then Markie remembered what O'Malley had told her. "Monika wasn't on the boat when you blew it up."

"That was her idea. She wanted to get even with Dalton. We faked her death so he would be blamed for it. It would have worked, but she changed her mind wanting to go back to him. I told her it would be okay that I wouldn't fail like the car accident."

"You're responsible for Beck's hit and run?"

"Monika freaked when I told her. I couldn't let her leave me again and go back to him. She deserved to die."

"Why? Because she loved him?"

"She had everything and didn't know how to keep it. That was her fault. I have everything now. I'm Monika. With you out of the way Dalton and I will be together."

Markie had to give her head a shake. Melanie didn't know who she was. It was as if she was Monika one minute and Melanie the next. She wasn't going to get her hands on Beck. Not if Markie had anything to say about it and she had plenty.

"I love Beck and you can't have him," Markie said. "I won't let you hurt him either."

"No!"

Markie pushed her head up above the sofa back just as Melanie lunged towards her over the sofa. She fell backwards taking Melanie with her.

Stars, in a rainbow of colors exploded behind Markie's eyelids. Giving her head a quick shake to clear it, she rolled to a squat on her feet, her hand sweeping the floor to find her gun.

"Did you lose something?" Melanie was pointing the gun at Markie's head. She felt the cold steel against her forehead. The woman was quick on her feet.

Markie felt something trickling down at the corner of her mouth and wiped at it with the back of her hand. Blood. Out of the corner of her eye she scanned the floor and saw her gun sticking out from under the sofa.

"Get up! Move." She shoved Markie towards the bedroom when she stood up slowly. "You're going to die like the rest of them."

Markie stumbled and turned towards Melanie. "You don't want to do this, Melanie."

"It's Monika! What makes you think—"

Markie hiked up her dress swung her right leg in a

semicircular motion. Striking with her foot in a roundhouse high kick, her foot connected with Melanie's chin. Melanie went down with a thud on the floor. Before she could recover, Markie dove for her gun scraping her knees against the parquet floor. Her gun trained on Melanie.

Anyone would have stayed down with that blow, not Melanie. She grabbed her gun and sprang to her feet. Whatever drug she was on, she was higher than a kite.

"It doesn't have to end like this, Melanie. Drop your weapon and we can both walk out of here. I can get you the help you need. I promise."

Melanie laughed. "I don't want your help."

"I don't want to hurt you."

Markie had seen the eyes of death before in the boy at the gas station, and they were staring at her again. She fired one shot through the heart and Melanie fell back against the bookshelf. She also saw the boy's face again at the gas station as he cried out in pain and fell back onto the glass wall. She would now see two faces in the dark at night.

It was so quiet she could hear herself breathe. Her hand started to shake as she looked down at the gun in her hand.

Markie dropped down on the floor on her knees staring at the woman's body, her heart still pounding in her chest. A large red stain formed on Melanie's white T-shirt. Markie turned her heard quickly towards the door when she heard voices. She raised her gun and aimed at the door. Then it busted open.

It was O'Malley, Jamie, and Beck with a terrified look on his face.

"Are you okay?" Beck rushed to her side. He was looking at the blood smeared on her hand. He knelt down and his hand went to her face. She moved her head away from his touch.

"I'm fine," she said, her voice hoarse. Her eyes shifted to Melanie's body.

Jamie tapped Beck on the shoulder and he got up. He

whispered something in Beck's ear and they both moved towards the door in conversation.

"She's dead," O'Malley said as he got up from over Melanie's body. Six officers appeared at the front door. They were the same officers involved in the raid at Melanie's place. One of the officers extended a hand to help her up off the floor. She looked over at O'Malley. "Booker doesn't speak for everyone."

She took the officer's hand. "Thank you."

"You haven't been formally introduced," O'Malley said. "Parker say hello to Marklynn Brooks."

"Nice to meet you, ma'am. You alright?" Parker asked after seeing all the bullet holes in the door.

She nodded. After she'd given her statement to Parker, O'Malley said, "Go home. We don't need you anymore. We can take it from here."

"Thanks."

"I'll drive you home," Beck volunteered. He picked up her handbag from the floor and handed it to her.

He'd stood by the door watching while she'd given her statement as if he was her protector. Markie didn't want him to take her home. She was not in the mood for a discussion. She wanted to be alone.

"That's not necessary."

"I just want to take you home. That's all. Okay?"

She nodded and walked out of the apartment praying that her legs wouldn't buckle under her. He held out his hand for the keys she retrieved from her purse and handed them to him. Their hands touched, their eyes met. Warm kind eyes.

All she had to do was to reach out to him and he would hold her. She saw it in his eyes. She needed to be held. But she didn't want to reach out to him. History had taught her that when you reach out you get burnt.

It was a little after one in the afternoon when they made their way from Cambridge towards Quincy. The sun had disappeared behind the clouds and it started to rain. A song by the Manhattans, *Kiss and Say Goodbye* played on the radio and she turned it off.

The only thing she could hear after that was the whistling noise coming from the engine caused by a crack in the drive belt. It needed to be replaced. The mechanic had told her so the last time it was in the shop.

She could do that tomorrow and started planning her schedule because she didn't want to think about the shooting. Maybe if she dropped it off first thing in the morning she could get a rental then head over to the hospital. Sydney was being released tomorrow.

Markie didn't want to think about Beck either, but it was hard since he kept staring at her every time he stopped at a traffic light or slowed down. What did she tell Melanie? *I love him and you can't have him.*

Yes, she did love him, but she wasn't going down that road again. No discussion required. He could go find someone who could give him a house full of babies. Did he tell her he wanted a house full of children? No, but neither had Jared. Yet that had stopped them from getting married.

Beck pulled into her driveway. She jumped out and said, "You can take it. Let me know where to pick it up later."

"I'm coming in with you." He turned off the engine and got out after her.

"I didn't invite you in." She slammed the of the SUV door. Beck was right behind her by the time she reached the verandah.

"Dammit! You just killed someone."

"Yes and I don't want to talk about it." She wanted him to go, but it didn't look like he was planning on doing that.

"I don't want to either. I want to be here with you, Marklynn."

"For how long?" She flung the door open and it smashed against the front hall closet. She wrapped her arms around her body to keep from coming apart.

"What do you mean *for how long?*"

Looking at him she realized he didn't know what she meant. He really did just want to be with her and she didn't want to accept it. He would change his mind later and she couldn't live with the hurt.

"Nothing."

"Don't give me that nothing. I want to know why you said it. Talk to me."

Silence filled the room except for the *tick tick tick* of the wall clock above the mantel. Funny, she'd never heard it before or had even paid any attention to it.

"Why is it so hard to get through to you?" he asked. Frustration was evident in his voice as he raked his hand through his hair. It seemed as if he wanted to shake her. "Talk to me."

Her nerves were raw. She was hurting and not just from the shooting. They should have this conversation when they both had clear heads. But it was never going to happen. How did she protect herself from getting hurt again? She would do the pushing.

"I don't know if I can do this again."

"Do what, Marklynn?"

"Do you want children?"

He blinked slowly then stared at her as if he finally understood. "Is that what this is all about?"

She looked down at the floor afraid to hear his answer.

"I'm not going to lie to you and say no. Becoming a parent was something I had considered when the time was right."

Her heart shattered in a million pieces because even though he had considered it he would eventually want children, and she couldn't give him what he wanted. The time would never be right for them.

"Well I can't. It's that simple. The bullet I took in my pelvis destroyed one ovary and traumatized the other." She swallowed back the tears. "There is something inside me that hurts when I think about it. It's not fair to you or me to proceed with this. You'll only end up changing your mind."

"Since we started *this* I haven't changed my mind about my feelings for you. I gave you the time you needed because I love you. You on the other hand, have been clutching onto the past. You're terrified of letting it go and reaching out to me." Beck paused when she turned her back to him. "Okay," he said taking a deep breath. "This is not the time to discuss this. Let's talk about this tomorrow."

"No, Jared we can't."

"It's Dalton Beck!" With a hand on her shoulder, he spun her around to face him. "Dalton Beck," he said again, nostrils flared.

"What?" Markie stared at him oblivious to what she had said.

"You called me Jared."

It was the hurt that reflected in his eyes that tore at Markie's heart. She hadn't meant to call him Jared.

The roller coaster week…the shooting…Sydney. Everything collided together at that moment in her mind. And with that, the realization of what she'd set out to do…what she'd accomplished.

She felt a sense of loss, but the damage was done. There was nothing left to say. Tears shimmered in her eyes.

"I'm…"

"It's okay." Beck dropped his hand from her shoulder. "I finally get it."

He backed away from her, turned on his heels and headed towards the door. Markie jumped when he slammed the door. She stood staring at the closed door as tears streamed down her cheeks.

CHAPTER SIXTEEN

"Look at you," Markie said when she entered the hospital room the following afternoon.

It had taken the rest of yesterday afternoon, and a sleepless night to pull herself together after Beck had left. This morning she plastered a smile on her face as she entered the hospital. It was all about Sydney today.

Sydney was up and dressed in a red halter-top summer dress sitting on the bed applying a red lipstick shade to her lips. The doctor said she could go home today.

The marks were still visible from the rope burn around her wrist, but her honey brown coloring was back. Her eyes were brighter with full eye make up.

"I was tired of the hospital get up. Since this is my last day in this wonderful establishment, I might as well leave in style."

"Where can I take you to lunch dressed like that?"

"Do you like it?" Sydney stood up and did the walk of a model strutting her stuff on a catwalk from the bed to the window. "Nan bought the dress for me."

"Very nice. You look great."

"More than I can say for you. You look like you haven't been to bed yet." Sydney sat down on the bed and patted a spot beside her. Tell me, were you and the dishy Dalton Beck getting it on last night?"

"How did you find out about him?"

"Pleeease. Nan keeps sprouting her proverbs and," she pointed to the bouquet of calla lilies on the window ledge. "Who sends calla lilies?"

"Dalton Beck," Markie replied missing him. Wanting to undo what she'd done last night but feared it was too late.

Beck was different from everyone else. Never leaving anything to chance. Knowing Beck he probably asked Nan what kind of flowers Sydney liked before he even set foot in the flower shop.

"He and I are not seeing each other anymore."

She thought about the conversation they had last night and had convinced herself that she had made the right decision for both of them. The only problem was she wasn't certain of that anymore, but he got the message loud and clear. Her SUV was in the driveway this morning and the key in the mailbox. He had returned it without a word.

"What happened with Beck?"

Markie didn't want to talk about Beck and changed the conversation to a safer topic.

"Where is Carlos?"

"The threat is gone so Nan tells me and I sent him home," Sydney said staring off into space for a moment. "He asked me out and…"

"…you turned him down. Carlos is very persistent. Trust me, he will ask you again."

"Maybe I'll be ready by then." Sydney took Markie's hand. "Tell me what happened with Beck?"

"Wasn't meant to be."

She looked at Sydney and it was as if she was seeing her sister for the first time. Sydney had changed. There was something more settled about her. She had told Nan that she wanted to be around more and she meant it.

Right there and then in the hospital where doctors were being paged, laughter and cries drifting into the room through the open door, Markie told Sydney everything. She began with why she left her job as a police officer, which led to her broken engagement with Jared and a life without children, and it ended with her fight with Beck.

"I'm so sorry."

Sydney's sorry covered a whole spectrum of things. Markie could tell and at that moment they finally connected after years of being emotionally estranged. Nothing mattered any more because they had found each other again.

"I know. What about you? Nan said Macy came to see you. There is a job offer on the table for a six-month assignment in Israel. You're going to be a photojournalist or rather an assistant to one anyway."

"I'm not interested."

"Why?" Markie already knew the answer before she asked the question. Sydney was afraid. She had survived her ordeal, but she'd lost the one thing that made her Sydney...her free spirit.

"I'm not up to it."

"It's a great opportunity." Markie paused for a moment. She didn't want to push Sydney into something she wasn't ready for. "Does your decision have anything to do with Derrick?"

Sydney looked down at the floor, her eyes watered. "I wanted to tell you about him, but when he died it didn't matter any more."

"Tell me about him anyway. Don't even *think* about leaving out the part where you jumped out of his birthday cake wearing a string bikini."

Sydney screamed with laughter. "How did you know about that?"

"I'm a P.I., remember?"

"It was his thirtieth," she said still laughing." I had been seeing him for about six months when I'd planned that. After two of his men were killed in combat, he didn't smile any more."

"How did you meet him?"

"He stole my parking spot at the mall and I blocked him in." A smile settled on Syd's face as if she was remembering that day. "He had *me* towed. I couldn't believe it. Then he had the gall to ask me out and I said yes."

"I would've liked him."

Sydney closed her eyes for a moment. "Derrick was everything I wanted in my life…order…stability. He saw me at my best and worst and loved me anyway."

"I'm sorry he died. I wish I'd known him."

Sydney wiped her eyes with a tissue she retrieved from her makeup kit. "Can we stop all this sorry business and get out of here. My priority right now is finding a new place to live. I'm not going back to that apartment, not after all that drama."

"You don't have to rush into finding a place. You can stay with me as long as you like."

"That sounds great now, but it won't be long before we drive each other crazy."

"Fair enough. Just promise me one thing. Think about the assignment in Israel."

"I will."

"My two girls are back together again," Nan said when she breezed into the room wearing a green and yellow floral dress down to her ankles. The straw hat she'd placed strategically on her head had a big sunflower on the brim, and on her arm, a yellow sunflower straw bag to match the hat. White laced gloves covered her hands.

"Why are you dressed up like a flower garden?" Sydney asked.

Markie smiled, lightly elbowing Sydney in the ribs.

"What? You were thinking the same thing."

"You're back to your old self, Syd," Nan laughed and when she did her whole body shook. "If you must know, I'm having afternoon tea with a dear friend."

"Afternoon tea?" Markie and Sydney asked in unison.

"Yes. You know, it requires a kettle, boiled water and a tea bag."

"Tea eh?" Markie asked. Was it possible that Nan was going out on a date? "What's his name?"

"Why should I give you two something to talk about?" Nan stood hands on her hips and cocked her head to one side looking at them both.

A ray of emotions spread across her face. It was the

sadness in Nan's eyes that tugged at Markie's heart.

"My two girls have survived the last week of hell and now they're afraid to live."

Both Markie and Sydney looked at each other then at Nan. They said nothing. Nan took their silence to mean that she was indeed correct. That sadness that Markie had seen in Nan's eyes was replaced by sheer determination. She would have her say.

"Sydney, your Derrick is gone, but you can't stop living because he is. That's not right. I should've said something to you before. I guess it wasn't the right time," Nan said, pulling off her gloves. "Life is too short. Grab it." Nan opened and closed her fingers together in a tight fist. "Live it with as much zest as you used to. Follow your dreams. Hiding is not what you do."

Markie remained silent because she knew she was next in line. And she didn't have to wait long.

"Marklynn..." Nan came and stood in front of Markie, touching her face. "You are the most giving and selfless person I know. You are as smart as a whip and for the life of me I don't know why you can't see that Dalton Beck is a good man. If you stop running long enough and let him catch up to you, you will be pleasantly surprised. I guarantee it."

"Hope I'm not interrupting."

They all turned towards the door and Sydney's mouth dropped open. An elderly man with snow-white hair, white goatee, dressed in a white suit and shirt with a black bowtie stood at the door, leaning heavily on his cane.

"Not at all. See you girls later. Oh, and don't forget dinner next Sunday. Remember to invite Macy, and whom ever else you wish."

With a quick peck on their cheeks Nan was gone.

"She didn't even introduce us," Markie said, pretending to be offended.

"He looks like the man in the chicken commercial Colonel something," Sydney whispered and they both began to laugh.

"I heard that," Nan's voice drifted from the hall.

It had taken Markie a week to figure out that Nan was right. Arriving at that conclusion was no easy task. She'd analyzed all the conversations she and Beck had since they met. Reliving all the times they had spent together trying to figure out if there was anything about Beck that made her believe he was anything like Jared.

She arrived at two conclusions. One, Jared was not the man for her. He had made the decision to end their engagement based on what he wanted. In the end it wasn't her. Two, if he hadn't let her go then she wouldn't have met Beck.

Dalton Beck.

She had messed up the best thing in her life and for what? Because she was afraid.

Fear wasn't something she had ever given into in her life. Yet, she'd walked away from Beck without at least giving him a chance. That was about to change.

Markie had decided to swing by Beck's condo after dropping Sydney off at the airport half an hour ago. After a week of going back and forth, Sydney was on her way to Israel to meet Macy.

It was her turn now. The only thing was she couldn't bring herself to park and leave the confines of her vehicle.

"You're a coward," she told herself on the fifth drive by and decided to park before she ran out of gas.

She turned on the interior light and checked her lipstick in the rearview mirror. She was nervous but ready.

Markie headed for the building silencing the voice that kept telling her it was too late. She wanted to find out if it was too late for them.

"Hi, I'm Marklynn Brooks," she said to the security guard sitting at the desk when she entered the building. "I'm here to see Dalton Beck."

"One moment please." He dialed the number and waited. Then said, "Yes sir. I'll send her up. Go on up."

She smiled inward. He wanted to see her. Good sign. Beck's door was ajar when Markie got off the elevator and it was a woman's laughter she heard over the Temptations' song, *Ain't too Proud to Beg*.

Dressed in the outfit she had worn the night he had made his stir fry was part of her plan on winning him back. He'd liked the dress. Told her it was sexy. She went further, paired it with the black stilettos Syd had given her and was pretty much all legs. He liked her legs. It didn't matter if he had found someone else. She would have her say and beg if need be.

Markie pushed the door open and saw a woman swaying in a man's arms. The man was the older version of Beck. His father? The woman screamed when the man dipped her.

Markie heard Beck's voice from the balcony. "I think you two should get a room."

"Hi," the woman said, breathless with a smile when the man had her upright again. "Come in. I'm Anika and this is my husband, Jack, Dalton's father. Marklynn right?"

"Yes." Markie extended her hand to Anika. "Nice to meet you. Beck speaks fondly of both of you."

Anika pushed her outstretched hand away and hugged her. "We are thrilled to finally meet you."

Beck's stepmother was polished, refined, but not in the country club type of way. She didn't look down on you like the Daniels'. Her smile was warm. It pulled you towards her and embraced you in it.

"Dalton can't stop talking about you," Anika said looking at Markie with a look of intrigue.

"Sweetheart—"

"Okay, moping then. And I can certainly see why. Honey, I think she came to get her man," Anika said looking at Markie again. "It's a good thing you came to your senses or I would—"

"Do you think you should be threatening the woman before she has straightened things out with Dalton?"

Jack smiled and Anika melted. Markie knew how the

woman felt.

"You're right, sweetheart. Dalton is out on the balcony flipping burgers."

"It's not just burgers…"

"I forgot." Anika's hand went to her chest. "It's the Beck's Burger."

"Okay dad, the burgers are almost—"

Beck came in from the balcony. His jeans were ripped at the knees, the apron that covered his white T-shirt said, *"Kiss the cook."*

If his parents weren't standing in front of her, she would have.

Anika looked at Beck then to Marklynn and laughed. "Look who needs a room."

Beck's heart just about stopped when he stepped through the balcony doors and saw Marklynn. In the last week he'd picked up the phone more times than he cared to remember, but put it back down again. She wasn't interested he kept telling himself and forced himself to let her go. The only thing was his heart and head weren't on the same page.

The impromptu barbeque was for his benefit, planned by his father. Just family his father had said to get him out of the funk he had slipped into. He had thought about Marklynn, but never had he dreamt she would show up at his condo.

"Marklynn? What…We…" He couldn't string a sentence together to save his life at that moment. She was wearing the dress that he'd …

"Hi, I should've called first." She started backing up towards the door.

"Nonsense," Anika said. "We were just about to sit down and eat. Join us. Come Jack," she pulled him towards the balcony. "You can show me how to flip the burger with that metal thing with the flat bottom."

"The metal thing with the flat bottom is called a spatula."

"Please, everyone knows you didn't marry me for my

kitchen skills."

With a throaty laugh Anika pulled Jack from the living room to the balcony and Markie doubted they would be flipping burgers.

"They seem really nice."

"They are."

Beck didn't say anything else, just stood there staring at her. All he could think of was the night when he'd taken the dress off her and she stood before him proud and naked. Now she looked like she was ready to bolt.

He should say something to calm her fear, but he pulled back. She came to him and he wanted her to tell him why. He would not give her a way out. Not this time and he sure as hell was not going to let her bolt. Even if he had to nail the door shut.

"Dalton, I…"

"Dalton?"

"That is your name."

"Yes." He had to admit he liked the way it rolled off her tongue, but he still kept his distance as his heart hammered in his chest. "You've never used it."

"I should start using it. I…" She hesitated then swallowed. Anika's laughter drifted from the balcony and she turned her gaze towards the open door then back at Beck. "I realized this past week that I love you."

Beck wanted to pull her in his arms, but something stopped him. There was more she wanted to say and he would let her while his heart exploded with love for this woman.

"The night after the shooting when you left, I wanted to come after you to tell you I was sorry. I never," she shook her head, "meant to call you Jared."

Her voice cracked. She was nervous. He had seem her angry, frustrated and happy but not nervous. He watched the pulse jump at the base of her neck.

"When Jared called off our wedding I was devastated. That's when I came to the conclusion that having a child would define me as a woman. Because I couldn't give Jared what he wanted he left me. I was afraid you would eventually. I guess I didn't want you to think less of me because I can't have…"

"I never thought less of you because of that, Marklynn." He had to say something before they both fell apart.

"I know. I wanted you to think that, but you didn't. And when you didn't I decided to push you away before you pushed me away. If it's not too late I would—"

Beck cut her off with a kiss that left them both breathless. His hand found the zipper of her dress and pulled it down guiding her towards the bedroom.

She pulled away laughing. "Your parents…"

He had forgotten about them. "Come on." He kissed her again on a groan. "Fine." He took her hand pulling her towards the balcony. "Let's go eat then wish them a nice evening."

"Aren't you forgetting something?"

"What?"

"My zipper."

EPILOGUE

Two Months Later

Marklynn was lying on the sofa waiting for Michael Blake's television show to begin. He didn't tell her what it was about but she knew. The only thing his email said was that Jeffrey Booker was no longer employed with Boston PD. That she already knew. O'Malley had already filled her in.

Booker was gone and so was his boss. They'd cleaned house from top to bottom. O'Malley was also one of the casualties. She had offered O'Malley a job at Brooks Investigations. He declined and said he was moving to Florida.

She raised her head when the front door opened and dropped it back down again when a wave of nausea hit her.

The transition moving into Dalton's condo was easier than she had expected. She had decided not to sell her house and had given it to Sydney when she'd returned from Israel to attend their wedding a month ago.

Sydney had enlisted Anika's help to redecorate the house once her assignment in Israel was completed.

Markie loved being Mrs. Dalton Beck and they had a great time on their honeymoon in Belize. However, picking up a bug that she couldn't shake was taking all the fun out of her wedded bliss.

Even the smell of Dalton's cologne made her stomach queasy. The poor man had to shower before he could touch her.

"What did the doctor say?" Dalton asked as he loosened his tie. He dropped his laptop and keys on the dining room table.

Since returning from their honeymoon, he'd been interviewing for a replacement for Malcolm so they could spend more time together.

"Thanks to you I spent the entire afternoon getting poked and prodded like some animal. Oh, and I tried to go into the office today, but Jamie changed the lock on my door. Cate is in on it too. Thanks to you."

Dalton sat on the coffee table in front of her shaking his head in disbelief as if she was some wayward child.

"You need to take better care of yourself and if I have to enlist the help of everyone you know to do it then I will."

"I think you're overreacting."

"Am I? You've been living on crackers and ginger ale for the last three weeks. You don't sleep at nights. It may not bother you, but it sure as hell concerns me." He leaned over, kissed her on the lips then got up, but she held on to his tie extending the kiss.

"Mmm...Mint. Nice."

"I'm going to grab a shower, and then make us dinner or order out. Please think about what you'd like to eat. Crackers are not —"

The ringing of the phone cut him off in mid-sentence. "Saved by the bell." He swatted her on the behind and she laughed reaching for the phone on the glass side table.

"Hello? Yes this Marklynn."

It was Dr. Scott's office and she sat up straight on the sofa swinging her feet to the floor. She reached for the remote muting the television.

Markie stiffened when he told her that one of the tests he'd ordered was a pregnancy test. She and Dalton had discussed adoption, but that was as far as they'd gotten. He had to be joking about ordering a pregnancy test. But she wasn't laughing.

"I don't understand. Why would you? Oh my God!"

A sob tore from her throat. She started fanning herself with her hand. Dalton ran back into the living room. She was speechless.

"Marklynn what's wrong?" He asked, fear in his voice.

She sat there staring at the phone shaking her head. Dalton had to pry her fingers from the cordless.

"This is Dalton Beck. Yes Dr. Scott. Really?" He looked down at Marklynn. "Are you sure? Yes. We can see you tomorrow afternoon."

Markie was in shock. Dalton joined her on the sofa pulling her into his arms. "Are you okay?"

"They said I couldn't. How?"

"Dr. Scott said a woman could get pregnant with one ovary."

"Only if the other ovary is healthy, my odds were not good."

"He also said miracles do happen."

She started to cry and realized he was crying as well.

"I'm going to be a mother. Nan?" She knew. What had she said? *If you stop running long enough to let him catch up to you, you'll be pleasantly surprised.*

"You can call her if you like," Dalton said misunderstanding her cry for her grandmother.

"No. She knows about the baby. She predicted it."

"I don't understand. Is she a psychic or something?"

"Or something," Markie said with a laugh. She would have to tell him about that one day but not now.

"What powers do you have?"

"Let me show you." She snuggled up closer to Dalton unbuttoning his shirt.

"Hey I need to shower. I'm wearing cologne and…" His protest was cut off by a long wet kiss when she pulled him down on the sofa on top of her. Her nausea had suddenly vanished.

"What about dinner?"

"I'm not hungry for…wait there's Michael," Markie

said when she glanced at the television over his shoulder.

Dalton reached for the remote turning up the volume. Markie straightened up on the sofa and Beck pulled her onto his lap.

"…Tonight you will hear a story that mimics the game of Hide and Seek. The players are Jeffery Booker," a picture of Booker red race flashed across the screen. "Cape Cod socialites Roberta and Kennedy Daniels," a picture of the couple flashed across the screen. "And the death of three people, that could have been prevented. Our story begins…"

Markie turned off the television and shifted on the sofa so Beck was on top of her.

"Don't you want to watch the rest of it?"

"That's not what I'm in the mood for," she said against his lips.

"Tell me, Mrs. Beck what are you in the mood for?"

If you enjoyed ***Hide 'N Seek***, follow Samuel O'Malley's adventure in Florida. What happens when a washed up cop meets a rich Daddy's Girl? A heart-stopping romantic suspense in ***Cat 'N Mouse.***

ABOUT THE AUTHOR

With an overactive imagination from an early age, Yvonne created vivid stories in her mind in which she was the lead character. It wasn't long before she decided to take these stories from her mind and pen them to paper.

A romantic at heart, Yvonne loves short stories and romantic suspense. She writes primarily about relationships. At first, she wrote only for herself. Out of her passion for writing evolved a beautiful collection of stories.

Yvonne has published two collections of short stories, *"The Wedding and Other Short Romantic Stories,"* showcasing her romantic collection, *"The Invitation and Other Short Stories,"* a more dramatic collection.

Her debut romantic suspense novel, *Hide 'N Seek* is the first in her suspense series followed by *Cat 'N Mouse*. *Hit 'N Run* is the final novel in the series

Yvonne enjoys hearing from her readers so please email her at info@yvonneharriott.com or visit her website: www.yvonneharriott.com

Oh most generous,
Oh most kind
Oh most merciful
Oh most forgiving God

224 PBS @ 1030 tape Monday program